I0681341

SACRED NIGHT

੭ৡৎ

Valerie Connelly

...weaves a mysterious web of fantasy and terror from the urban jungles of Chicago to the threshold of death on the Amazon...and back.

੭ৡৎ

Nightengale Press
A Nighengale Media LLC Company

SACRED NIGHT

For information about Nightengale Press please
visit our website at www.nightengalemedia.com.
Email: publisher@nightengalepress.com
or send a letter to:
Nightengale Press
10936 N. Port Washington Road,
Mequon, WI 53092
Library of Congress Cataloging-in-Publication Data

Connelly, Valerie, 1947-

Sacred Night / Valerie Connelly.

ISBN: 0-9743348-0-4
ISBN 13: 978-0-9743348-0-6
Fiction, mystery,magic Realism

Copyright Registered : TXu 829-349 1997, 2003
First Published by Nightengale Press in the USA
Second Edition 2009

January 2009

9 8 7 6 5 4 3 2 1

Printed at
Lightning Source, Inc.
LaVergne, TN

Dedication

In memory of my father, Martin Lincoln Green, who taught me to pursue my dreams and to make them come true long before he passed on from Alzheimer's.

$\approx$

Acknowledgements

First, gratitude goes to my husband, Michael Connelly, who encourages me to keep writing when I might do other things; to my readers who laugh, cry and share my books with others; to my friends, family and colleagues who never doubt me for a moment and who have been supportive even when I thought the end was in sight. And to the many Nightengale Press authors, who write their books and come to me for publishing, many with more than one book. Every time I publish another book, I remember I, too, am a writer, and think it is time to write again. You are my inspiration!.

TITLES BY VALERIE CONNELLY

SACRED NIGHT

Once I started reading "Sacred Night," I could not put the book down. Valerie Connelly did an excellent job with writing this debut novel. I look forward to reading other books that she has written since this one. I highly recommend this book to people that enjoy a good mystery with touches of the paranormal thrown in. You will not be disappointed!

—Paige Lovitt, Reviewer for Readerviews

SIDETRACKS

We have all made decisions in our lives that we often wonder about later. What if I had said "Yes" instead of "No"? What if I had turned left instead of right? We drive ourselves crazy wondering about how our lives might have turned out had we taken a different route. "Sidetracks" will interest anyone who has ever asked "what if". Ms. Connelly presents the subject in such a unique way, allowing us to completely follow along with Hannah and Peyton in their "alternate" lives. While I hopefully will never be placed in such a precarious position as they were, reading the book has forced me to consciously look for the sidetracks in my own life and carefully consider all possible choices and consequences before making a decision. I guarantee it will start you thinking as well.

—Cyndy Zoch, Reviewer for Readerviews

ARTHUR, THE CHRISTMAS ELF

In the tale of Arthur, the Christmas Elf by Valerie Connelly, two misguided children are reminded of the joy that Christmas can bring to those with open hearts. Connelly's story is meant to be shared as a family. Part of Arthur's strategy for convincing the children is to provide them with ideas of gifts they can make with their own hands for their loved ones. The tale, along with the craft instructions, contains colorful illustrations to engage the reader. The crafts emphasize the meaning of the story: that one does not have to lack money and possessions to be poor, and Christmas is not about cherishing gifts, but the people behind the gifts.

— Barb Radmore, Editor, Front Street Reviews

CALLING ALL AUTHORS—
How to Publish with Your Eyes Wide Open

This may be the best information that's come out in years for aspiring new authors. It will definitely guide them through the many land mines that exist in today's complex publishing scene.
—Patrika Vaughn,President, A Cappela Publishing

I think the book provides outstanding guidance to authors and should give them helpful information about issues that publishers, editors, etc face and how an author can help simplify those issues. An excellent work! Congratulations!
—Bob Gussin, Oceanview Publishing

Valerie Connelly has written a down-to-earth book that will be of benefit to all authors in their mission to write and sell their books. It will be of value not only to the first-time author but also to the established writer as a constant reminder of the necessity to not only write a book but the requirement to help the publisher market and sell the book. Both the neophyte and the experienced author should keep this book at their fingertips and refer to it frequently.
—John A Henderson MD,Author of: **God.com: A Deity for the New Millennium** and **FEAR FAITH FACT FANTASY and Judging God**

Regardless of your publishing method, Ms. Connelly's CALLING ALL AUTHORS—How To Publish With Your Eyes Wide Open is a must-read for anyone attempting to publish a book. Vital "how-to" information to make the publishing journey easier and more successful!
—Yvonne Perry, Author, Owner and Founder of of Writeers in the Sky Creative Writing Services

"Calling All Authors is a well-organized – and much-needed guide."
—Maryglenn McCombs, Maryglenn McCombs Book Publicity

SACRED NIGHT

PART ONE

1

A black model Z3 BMW made its way along Lake Michigan on Chicago's Outer Drive. Inside, two over-sized young toughs sat crumpling their lanky forms into the bucket seats, staring in stony silence at the gridlock, ignoring the cold winter weather that kept the city dwellers off the pathways along the lake. Moist frost still clung to the back window where the defogger failed to warm the glass. Cursing every stall in the heavy, late Wednesday afternoon traffic from the Field Museum northward, the driver pulled the car west on Congress, and then north again on Michigan Avenue. No one in Rita's Bar a few blocks away suspected the next few minutes might be their last.

As always, a motley crew of has-beens and wanna-be professionals were crowding around the tables in Rita's Bar to indulge in a few hours of easy amnesia, forgetting the pain of the daily grind over an average repast, watered down booze and generally good music. Rita carried herself like the once-upon-a-time dancer she was and still wore the flamboyant theatrical clothing and makeup of her abandoned passion to camouflage her true identity. She wore her adopted alias, Rita Dumas, like a badge of protection from her past and the people who knew her only as Ruthann Mahoney.

"I want you to stay to meet the singer I have coming in tonight," Rita said, as she handed Dan Barton another Irish whiskey with a flourish worthy of a Gilbert and Sullivan character or a vaudeville play. He looked at the intricate designs lacquered onto her artificially long nails. He studied her fiery red-dyed hair and noticed the stars and moons sparkling at the outer corners of her eyes.

Dan spoke with little enthusiasm. "No, I can't stay. I've got to get home to my kids. If I stay here into the night, they'll worry."

"Hungry? I'll get you a sandwich." Rita smiled. She had her own motives to press him into a stall to keep him there. He was, after all, just a male easily made all the more malleable with food and drink. "Running this club isn't easy, but sometimes you've got to bring things together. Thanks for setting up my computer. If only I knew how to work it." Rita constructed a triple-decker deluxe club, flipping salad, tomatoes, bacon, and turkey from the storage bin with the accuracy of a sharp shooter and slathering mayonnaise onto the whole-wheat toast.

"Try the tutorial. Then, I'll show you some computer tricks."

She placed the plate before him and retrieved a couple of napkins from the other end of the bar. "Mangea!"

He wolfed down the meal in a couple of silent minutes, and lit up a cigarette for dessert. Mellowed by the late-afternoon haze of his chain smoking and the warmth of the whiskey he was drinking too much and too often, Dan sat back in his chair and watched Rita work between the brass trimmed bar and the turn of the century mahogany mirrored back bar, where bottles stood like sentinels watching over the ongoing war of life. He knew she felt a generous streak for the men she liked in her bar. She certainly never poured short. She kept her liquor flowing, especially for the itinerant piano players like him, who played with his soul and in turn kept the barflies happy. That he was down and out, or a computer genius seemed to mean nothing to

her. What did matter was his ability to numb the pain of the customers. He figured Rita didn't mind that there were a few songs he didn't
know. If a particular request was unfamiliar to his fingers, he would
play another that could resonate in nearly the same way for the audience. Husky, forty-something with somewhat receding salt and pep-
per hair, a convincing smile and come-to-me blue eyes, she let on that
she liked how Dan's magnetism spoke to the other women, as much
as it spoke to her. He was good for business. His music, slapdash and
unbridled though it was, could make hearts momentarily forget their
pain, a rare talent that brought in the lingering drinkers. So what if
she paid him less from the drawer and poured him a couple of extra
drinks? The patrons kept his tip bowl filled to overflowing every Friday night.

The Z3 reached the Art Institute and stalled again in the chok-
ing gridlock. The occupants rocked the small car in bursts of explosive irritability, slamming fists against the dash and twisting in their
seats to find relief from leg cramps and frustration. Other motorists
were taking notice, honking and shouting at the Z3 to get out of the
way. This only inflamed the already raging tempers trapped inside
the car. The engine roared at the driver's stomping on the accelerator
and jumped forward, only far enough to stop just short of the rear
bumper of the SUV that blocked the view down the immovable line
of traffic.

"Fair enough." Rita picked up his plate. "You've gotta hear this
singer. She needs a piano player for her songs." Rita poured a third
whiskey. "She needs you," she whispered. Dan headed for the pay
phone to call his two sons at the sitter's.

Five rings—six—seven. "Hi, Angelie? This is Dan. Are Ian and
Patrick there?"

"Hi Dan. Yes, they are. Well, no, they're not. They're outside
playing with the other kids. Is there something you want me to tell

10

them for you?" Angelie played on his guilt with coquettish humor. Used to these last minute calls, Angelie could hear in the tone of his voice that he was going to be late again. Dan worked as a part time computer trainer besides playing piano, doing all he could to earn enough to pay childcare expenses and keep life afloat. He used the fact that she wondered how he managed to keep going, out of regular work as he was, and he played on her sympathies to regularly stay out later than most would consider normal for a single father of two.

"Well, just let them know I'll be late. Is it all right with you if I wait till after the rush hour to leave the city? You know I hate the traffic."

"Sure, Dan, I'll feed them dinner. If you're really late, I can—" she paused, knowing he actually wanted not to come back till morning, as he so often did. The pattern was set in stone—call, ask to talk with the boys, complain about traffic, see if he can be late, end up coming back in the morning. She simply played by his rules a game of saving face. "Why not just plan to pick them up in the morning? It'll be easier for both of us that way."

"Okay. You convinced me. But tell them I love them." Dan let his breath escape with a silent puff, releasing himself for the moment from his guilt as an absentee father freed to just be a man on his own for a few more hours. Angelie's cheerful "Sure will. Bye," simply made Dan feel better. Maybe he'd pay a price in the future, but for the present he suppressed his fear of failure as a father into his deep emotional well of regret.

"She's something else," he muttered as he walked to the last booth at the rear of the club to nurse the drink Rita had moved there for him from the bar.

Emily Sanders pulled into the lone parking place in front of the crumbling red brick building and wedged the car between the plowed banks of snow, already gray and dirty like shadows mocking the forgotten pristine white of the previous day's blizzard. Her breath hung like a cloud as she stepped from the car and locked the frosty door with her key. A locally known singer-songwriter, Emily performed at Rita's Bar once a week, trying to get her chops up and perfect her sets. She was not the first to move up the line of aspiring performers moving from one dive club to the next in Chicago's small but loyal cabaret-cum-coffeehouse night life. Rita's Bar paid next to nothing but provided a steady venue, a sense of security and safety. Emily liked that.

"Shit!" Her feet slid on a patch of ice as she squeezed between the snow bank and the car to get to the trunk. She unloaded her guitar case and tape equipment, slammed the lid, and lugged her dreams through the narrow, two-door vestibule front entrance of the bar. "Where is a helping hand when you need one?" She grunted as she bumped her way through the chairs and tables toward the front window stage. Catching Rita's eye she smiled the way a person smiles at the hand that feeds and said, "Hi! Gonna have a good crowd for dinner?" Rita nodded as if she had hardly noticed Emily's arrival.

"I'm staying," called out Marlin, weaving from his barstool as he waved a bit too broadly and nearly falling onto a nearby table. A regular casualty from overwork at an underpaid laborer's job, he routinely drowned his sorrows in beer and sad songs before falling asleep at the bar half an hour before his wife would come to take him home. Other regulars were filling the barstools and tables near the stage earlier than usual. Both Emily and Rita mentally tallied the count against the last week's turnout.

"Great! I'll sing just for you," Emily chuckled as she tweaked Marlin's ear. Quickly setting up her equipment and singing a couple of bars to begin to test the microphone mix, the routine had become nearly automatic over the last couple of months. A plug here, a wire there, and she could play her backup tapes as she played her guitar live to the music she'd written.

12

"Hey, Emily," Rita said, holding up a clipping from the paper. "Look! You got a good review!"

"Really," Emily said, not as a question, but more as the statement of a fact that she hadn't anticipated.

"Listen to this, and I quote, 'As a songwriter, Emily Sanders is talented, among the most refined in her craft. Her personal losses appear in her lyrics, pleasing the crowd of mostly women, who love the visceral pain of the lovelorn and wronged women who populate her lyrics. The men mostly just liked to look at her slender body in action while pretending to listen to her melodies.'" "So true, so true," Marlin warbled to the heavens, clearly eavesdropping on the none too private conversation.

Glaring at him with feigned displeasure, Rita continued her reading. "'The sarcastic humor in some of her songs makes everyone laugh. The universal sorrows make all but the hardest hearts cry. If you are looking for musical risk-taking tinged with talent and a bit of passion, Emily Sanders provides what you want Wednesday nights at Rita's Bar in her not quite country, not quite folk style.' Not bad for a newcomer," Rita said through the clatter of chairs being rearranged by incoming clientele.

Emily strained to smile at the good news while struggling to set the microphone stand at the right height and resuming the ritual of setting the sound levels so she could be heard above the traffic outside and the clatter of dishes inside. She began her opening song, listening for the balance of voice to guitar, when the phone rang, briefly interrupting her concentration. She looked toward the intruding buzz with a mocking half-frown and then began to sing again as Rita picked it up, silencing the noise.

The sports car turned west on Wacker.

A man's voice crackled through the static laden connection. Rita felt her pulse double as she listened. She smiled, acting as if she were still listening to Emily's song, trying to draw no attention to herself. She reached under the bar to find a vial of small white pills. Tapping four into her palm, she dropped two of the tablets into each of two mugs and poured them full with the aromatic Colombian coffee she characteristically served topped with a dollop of sweet whipped cream and nutmeg.

From the back booth, Dan felt himself floating on Emily's voice, unmindful of the trembling of Rita's hand as she brought the coffee mugs to his table.

Emily ducked downstairs to the less than hygienic ladies room stall to change into her slinky royal blue sequined dress. Light-years from the dowdy gray and brown woolens she had worn for so many years as a public school teacher, the royal blue sequins were fast becoming her trademark show rags.

Emily stared at her reflection in the mirror. How long will you be dressing and undressing in basement bathrooms, getting ready for the show, paying your dues to buy your chance at discovery? A strong rush of liberation flushed through her as the sparkling sequins showered her with a burst of optimism. She was a new woman, unbound by convention and unrestricted in her possibilities. She had only to choose which dress to wear, which songs to sing, which heart to break. Her renewal as a free spirit promised each night could bring her success. Emily had begun to live her long ignored dreams to the fullest, throwing all conventional caution to the wind and risking her financial security, her personal sanity and the futures of her two young daughters to invent the new person she knew she had to become if she were to survive her demons.

"You're beautiful. You sing like an angel. You're still in control. You're the best you've got. Go give it all away to them." Repeating aloud her private mantra every night allowed her to believe again and again that she could do her set and mean every word, every note, every tear at least one more time. Then, with a last check of her makeup, she headed up the stairs.

Rita's eyes glanced toward Emily as she reached the top of the stairs. "Dan, I want you to play a few songs at the end of her set. See if you can get her to sing with you," Rita whispered into his ear and kissing it in a teasing manner. "She'd be good for you—you'd be good for her. Try it for me," she said.

"You're kidding, right?" the whiskey slurred his speech. Rita's raised eyebrow and squinted eyes told him she meant it. Dan stared at Emily's sparkling dress the way a child stares at candy offered as a treat. Rita motioned to her to join them in the back booth.

"Emily—this is Dan, the piano man. Dan—Emily, the singer."

Emily sat down across from him. Dan's hand combed through his hair in two quick movements, as he thought about trying to talk with this shimmering person smiling across the table at him.

Rita slipped away leaving them alone. Unnoticed, she took her purse from the desk in the back office, turned off the computer and as silent as a shadow, disappeared out the back door.

The sports car turned north on LaSalle.

An embarrassed silence hung heavy over the booth.

"So, who are you, piano man?" Emily said as she scooped out the whipped cream, licked it from the spoon and blew on the steaming coffee. She took several cautious sips, testing the hot liquid for its intent to burn the tongue.

"Just an out of work corporate vice-president, who lost his fat paycheck and his way up the ladder of success. Just trying to make ends meet in the big city. And, who are you, songbird?" He took a gulp of the coffee forgetting it was hot and sputtered as the liquid burned on the way down. A blob of cream balanced on his mustache. Emily pointed at it.

"Just a once upon a time school teacher turned singer because of some crazy idea she can make it in the music scene. Basically, I'm a dreamer. Are you?"

He wiped the cream away with his hand. "I don't think so. My life in recent years has left me pretty cynical and judgmental. But, I do have two sons, Patrick and Ian," he sipped the coffee again, "fifteen and nine—from my first marriage—they keep me in the game."

Dan's inflection left the impression he had more to say. Speaking rapidly, his defenses reduced by the booze and her voice, he let naked honesty get the best of him. "I—uh, I can tell you that I'm not quite sure what I'm doing here talking with you. And you?"

Emily's response came easily, naïvely, as if she had no fear of being misjudged. "Well, as a dreamer, I believed I could be perfect, twice. The first husband fathered my children, but he turned out to be a sneaky, unfaithful guy. My second was a rich son of a bitch, who couldn't keep his hands in his own financial pockets. When I figured it all out, I got out. For better or for worse, I'm on my own with my two daughters—sixteen and eight. We make for quite a feminist trio on good days." Emily paused to think. "Are you from around here?"

"No," Dan said. "Chicago is my—adopted city. I'm really just a dressed up hillbilly from Tennessee. My mother still lives in the hills with my little sister and her kids. But that's another subject for another time."

"You don't have any southern accent to give you away." She drank a draught of the rapidly cooling java.

The sports car swung back east on Illinois and then south on Clark.

"No, I really never fit the mold. They even used to say somebody must have left me on the porch in a basket." He laughed to lighten the mood, but Emily's quizzical expression made him feel compelled to explain further than her wanted to. "When my Dad left, I was surrounded by females and raised by nothing but women—mostly my grandmother." He looked down, as if ashamed about his upbringing.

"I'm the youngest of three—the accidental baby," Emily said to offer him some comfort. She stopped mid-sentence, distracted by a siren passing in the street. "Now, I'm making my own glory," she said absentmindedly. "I've done all right. I come here on Wednesdays just to help Rita out a little. Are you playing now?" She tried to focus on Dan's face, but instead looked toward the front of the bar.

"Yeah, right here on Fridays," he said lighting another cigarette. "Rita wanted me to hear you. She thinks we could work up a few songs after your set."

Dan gulped the rest of his coffee and reached for his whiskey. Emily tried to ignore his smoking, his alcoholic demeanor, and the curious sadness in his eyes. She finished her coffee in a couple of swallows without passing judgment.

The sports car sped up as it reached a break in the traffic at the corner just north of Rita's Bar.

"Gotta go entertain the paying customers," Emily whispered as she stood up and turned toward the makeshift stage in the front window. "See you when I'm done?" she glanced back at him and smiled.

"Sure."

The sports car smashed through the front window just as the gas tank detonated. The room ignited instantly. White-hot flames incinerated the front half of Rita's Bar, while black smoke choked life from the air. The front super-structure of the building collapsed in seconds, leaving only the back half gaping at the world.

2

*R*ain—wind. Rain—wind. A torrential symphony played against the palm thatch roof sheltering Ahi's tiny cane and palm branch cabin. He listened to the voice of the wind whistling through the leaves and branches, as it rose and fell with the thrust of the storm's hot breath. He knew the water would soon inundate the flooring of the hut, as it had so many times before. Any pathway in the forest was by now a tributary to the great river, pressed into unwilling service by the gushing rivulets caused by this year's first downpour. Within hours, the highwater would double back in flood strength to transform the land into an underwater landscape for the tambaki, the pirrah ku and the giant river turtles, until now confined to the ponds and lakes left by the last high water. Tree-dwelling, three-toed sloths, clumsy on land, could now swim wherever they chose. The rains brought them the freedom to explore the lower realms of the forest.

In this part of the Amazon Basin, abundant marine life lived in symbiotic rhythm with the flora and fauna of the jungle. Only during the high water could the fruit-eating marmoset drop fruit seeds into the floodplain water, which the fish would eat, and in their turn to carry the fruit tree's life force to other regions of the river basin. The often two hundred pound pirrah ku were too large to be caught by hook and line. More often, the Tokablaki fishermen took pirrah ku by harpoon, so the mild white flesh could be sold at market or cooked over glowing embers to a delectable perfection to feed the extended Tokablaki families.

Ahi's education had taught him from childhood that since the beginning of time the red tides have come, occurring every fifteen cycles or so. At the passing of the dry season, and just before the slow, lazy current of the great waters swell to overflowing from the first rain, the red tides bloom. Five times in his lifetime Ahi had seen the fish die in countless numbers and witnessed how the currents of the flood carried them into the reservoir, where they sank to the bottom to dissolve in the muck. Tokablaki medicine men performed secret sacred rituals with their ancient formulas to distill the silty marine fertilizer of the red tides into the life prolonging Algala, to provide for the longevity of the aging chieftains of the tribe. Ahi would soon gather his portion of the river's muck just as his own father had done and his father before him.

Staring from the hut's doorway into the storm, Ahi remembered the sunlight warming his garden, though an eternity had passed since he had last seen it. The highwater came every six moons, and erased any markings of man in favor of the crystal clear waters from the heavens. Tokablaki tribal teachings ingrained in him since his youth still guided Ahi's every decision. The rites of passage into manhood had burned these teachings into every fiber of his being. The sequence of life's events stretched forward as he knew they would, having lived his many seasons by the laws of the ancestors.

He never questioned the coming of the Sacred Night. The final honor was his: to dive into the natural reservoir filled to capacity in the raging flood. His final obligation called him to scoop up the silt from the bottom for his first helping of algala, the ancient and sacred potion of immortality. Every tribal chieftain before him, and all those to follow, would share in this honored blessing of old age, this reward for leadership. Algala brought the promise of wisdom and bought the time to dispense it. But to drink the medicine man's algala induced the Sacred Night, a long and fitful sleep that, if the recipient had led his life purely by the laws, ended with immortalizing rebirth. Ahi had seen his own father awaken from this "sleep of the gods," his energy restored, his smile returned to his face, his eyes bright with knowledge of the otherworld and the future.

Ahi had looked forward to this day all his adult life, when he remembered how the water had time and again teemed with escaping fish, signaling the coming of the red tide. Like rouge on an old woman's face, the red tide blemished the undulating skin of the river. The adult animals in the forest instinctively knew not to drink the waters of the ride tide, though inevitably some of the innocent young strayed to the mud banks to cool their thirst, a fatal choice. Ahi had waited for this moment with patience and dignity, expected of him as chief of the tribe.

He stared at the rain. Gusting winds blew it horizontally. Ahi shivered more from a nameless sense of fear than from anticipation. The distance to the river's natural reservoir was short and his mission, inevitable. He looked back into the dark of the cabin for the last time to see the sacred altar just as the oil lamps flickered and went dark. The water was rising. Ahi's Sacred Night had set the ritual in motion, making this the last moment of his former life. He raised his face toward the sky searching for a single ray of early morning sun. None. The eternally powerful downpour had drowned the sun.

As he made his way to the rim of the reservoir, the rain stung his stooped shoulders the way thorns prick a careless passerby. Without the warming half-light of the oil lamps, his vision grew indistinct and dim. His hands ached, gnarled like an ancient pair of vines. His tough, bare feet cracked and bled from the nettles and sharp stones he crossed to reach his salvation. He grew weary with a crushing fatigue unlike any he had ever known.

Could he endure the swirling of the rising water, so anger filled with the rage of nature? How had his father faced his fear of the coming paralysis, the coming of night, of the chance he might not survive? Could he set the right example of power for his son? Why is the darkness of the storm so terrifying? Is he not meant to seek and receive reward for a long life lived according to the law? He soothed his fears by remembering his strength in the days when he could feel himself nearly fly as he ran. He let the image of his once powerful shoulders cool the heat of sorrow he now felt in his heart for his lost youth. Humid puffs rose from the rainwater almost as soon as it touched the earth. The sound of the foaming water rising beyond him heightened his senses. He stood on a cliff in his mind, preparing to leap outward toward the opposite rim of the ravine, knowing he could do nothing else, yet fearing he would fall instead of fly.

Despair followed him as he stumbled through the deluge toward the reservoir's edge. The water eddied and purled along the flat rocks and cascaded over the edge to fall only three arm lengths to the rising wellspring of the reservoir. Soon the water would reach the rim and pour outward into the forest. Ahi knew his strength was going. He knew it would take every last measure of his manhood to take him to the floor of the reservoir, where he had to pull up the gourdful of bottom silt the medicine man required. So this was the last test, the bravest act ever expected of him: to throw himself on the mercy of the water. He prayed that his leap into the relentless current would find him in the arms of the mythical river goddess, Anmala. She would be the last to see him in his old life, and she would decide whether he would live or die.

SACRED NIGHT

Ahi stepped past the last bush and onto the rocks. Cleansed by the rushing waters that washed them in absolution, his feet stopped bleeding. He felt a holy aura surround him like a cloak of protection against evil. He stepped forward, eyes closed, holding the gourd tightly, feeling the twine tether that kept it lashed to his wrist. Every sensation intensified in the howl of the wind. The rim of the reservoir gave way as his toes reached beyond his foothold throwing him forward into the rheumy depths.

The water held the murky surface light of early dawn for the first few feet. As Ahi swam deeper his ears filled with the silence of the water, the pressure increasing until he thought his head would burst from the pain. Still, he pulled himself deeper, holding every ounce of precious breath he could in his weary lungs. He felt the bottom, cool and silky, broken by scattered lumps of pebble. Tendrils of weeds reached upward toward him, sensuously tangling his legs in their flowing fingers. He put the neck of the gourd in his hand, and with what seemed his last reserve, scooped up enough silt to fill the bell of the gourd to overflowing. Desperately he struggled to put the stopper in the open end of the gourd, while holding in the little air that remained in his lungs to let himself float upward toward the light above.

The softness of the dawn's illumination filtered into the water, revealing to him for the first time Anmala, Goddess of the Amazon. She swam toward him, smiling. Her pure white skin glowed iridescent in the shadowy murkiness of the water. Her long, green hair flowed slowly around her head and body like fingers beckoning him to her. She reached for his hands and carried him upward at the very moment he had spent the last of all that was in him to survive.

When Ahi awoke, the storm had passed. He lay at the water's edge downstream from the reservoir on the peak of a hillock untouched by the high water. Too exhausted to open his eyes, he lay on his back with his head turned slightly. From the intensity of the sun's heat Ahi could guess the day was already maturing toward noon. He became aware of the gourd still lashed to his wrist. It was his, and so was his life. Soon tribal warriors would come to take him back to the village, where for many years he would weave into tales for the young the wisdom of the otherworld he would soon gather in his Sacred Night. He would choose the next chief. Until his final day claimed him, as it had claimed his ancestors, he would live for many more years as before, with eternal honor and strength and the endless freedom to fly.

3

*S*ilence woke her. Emily' eyes blurred from the tears that welled up upon contact with the stinging fumes from acrid sewer gas that seemed to invade every orifice, every pore as she blinked, trying to focus on the window. Soot, heavy on the jagged glass, muted the light so that it seemed to have no life-giving properties, no warmth, casting no shadow and giving no hint to the time of day. Slowly, Emily became aware of her body lying crumpled on its side in the center of a space she had yet to recognize. Stiffness infused her being like a hangover from rotgut wine. Her arms felt numb in the inner upper arm, tingling at the shoulders and down the forearm. Flexing slowly brought minor relief, but the throbbing in her head imposed disorientation. She gazed around the room, looking for something familiar. The speckled linoleum floor slimed with soot and stagnant moisture yawned toward the gutted remains of a lavatory. Both the gas and the slime assaulted her senses. Pushing up on her hands and knees, she crawled toward the filthy commode, nauseated by the stench. Kneeling before the bowl, the disgusting sight of fuzz-laden, gray-orange scum collecting around the inner rim joined the gas and slime to launch the final attack on her unstable stomach. She wretched uncontrollably until there was nothing left. Feeling cold and clammy, huddled with her back against the toilet, she looked back into the room that, she was now certain, had been Rita's Bar.

At the back of the ruins, a moan emerged from the dismembered booth where she had been sitting with Dan Barton. Trembling, Emily awkwardly lifted her hand to reach for the sink. She pulled herself up to a standing crouch like a terrified animal ready to break and run at the slightest hint of danger. Curiosity overcame her fears, as pain and numbness gave way to her unsteady half walk, half lunge through the debris as she stumbled over barstools, pushed aside broken tables and sloshed through puddles of blackened water toward the pathetic sound.

"Hello?"

"Here—I'm here, behind the bench . Just pull it a little— owww—towards you. Emily?"

"Dan?"

"Yeah—oh God—are you all right?" he asked, trying to sit up from the caved-in ruins of the booth wedged precariously under beams fallen from the ceiling.

"I think so—what about you?"

"Nothing broken, nothing detached, I guess—my head is killing me, though. We'd better get out of here." Dan reached up to Emily's hand and she helped him stand. They leaned heavily on each other, stumbling in slow motion out of the ruins and into the strangely unpopulated Chicago streets where, like foreigners in their own city, they gazed at the surreal setting trying to get their bearings.

"I think we'd better walk this way." Dan said projecting the sort of involuntary calm under stress the subconscious mind could design to convince itself and anyone else the situation would turn out right. Taking Emily's hand, he gently led her northward, away from the heart of the city that lay south of the Chicago River.

"Where are you taking me? Why this way?" She tugged at his arm like a child unwilling to go to bed. "Where's my car? Where is everyone?" Her eyes begged him to tell her what she needed to know. "We were in Rita's Bar. I was going to sing. You were going to listen. The club was full of people." Tears brimmed in her eyes, spilling down her cheeks like raindrops on a windowpane. "What happened? Why is it daylight? Who are you?" Emily shouted in anger as she tried to grasp her situation. Disoriented from the blast, Dan blinked at the buildings around them, trying to focus his eyes clearly in hopes of organizing his thinking.

"I'm not sure, but I have a feeling I live in one of these apartment buildings."

"I don't even know you." Emily continued her rant. "I met you only minutes before the explosion. Why weren't we rescued from there? Why were we the only ones remaining? Why were we left behind and no one else?"

"I don't know." Dan barked to stop her tirade. "Maybe the rescue teams didn't see us," he said more gently, trying to stem the flow of her questions.

"It was a snowy night. Now it's a warm day. What day is it? Where are the cars—the buses—the people?" she said, slowing the pace of her words as she came to her senses. The gray and black buildings stood empty, somber and foreboding, staring as if they were spying on the moment. In stark contrast, the intensity of the cobalt blue and cloudless sky nearly laughed at the treeless urban scene.

"Maybe it's very early morning—just a couple of minutes after dawn. Maybe no one is out yet. Keep walking," he said pulling her along with a tone of growing frustration in his voice. "We're almost there." His stern paternal demeanor caused Emily, still unwilling to walk side by side with the irresistible power of this unfamiliar man, to allow him to pull her along like a child.

"I'm not positive, but I think we are close to where I live."

As they passed a small park, an old woman huddled over her shopping bags on one of the old iron benches. A rundown wooden church bordered the back of the park. Several small apartment buildings, some with well-tended front yards, some neglected and abandoned squeezed onto the small parcels of land. Dan stopped abruptly in front of a small, greystone two-flat sandwiched between two bigger six-flats.

"This looks right—I think," he said. "The flowers in that pot up there seem familiar."

The crunch of grit protesting under the leather soles of their shoes, as they negotiated the cracked and partially crumbling stone steps to the slanted floor of the stone front porch that lurched unevenly away from the building, was the only sound. Opening the heavy oak door, Dan stood for a moment at the foot of a long stairwell, as if considering the wisdom of scaling the nearly vertical incline they would have to climb to reach the landing above. Then he led Emily cautiously, one step at a time, up the narrow stairs to the only apartment door on the landing. A streak of sunlight from the skylight danced on the wall, in a cheery mockery of the bizarre circumstance they were both now aware they would not escape. Dan reached for the vaguely familiar brass knob and turned it, slowly, listening to the rasp of the metal and the complaint of the hinges as he pushed open the door.

The apartment yawned before them. On the floor near one wall to the left flopped a lumpy mattress, partially covered by rumpled sheets and a couple of old Army-surplus blankets. Men's clothing lay scattered everywhere. A folding table, near the bay window directly in front of them, staggered under stacks of papers and piles of yellowing newspapers. A small refrigerator crouched in the corner with a short counter, a sink and a couple of cabinets. Two mismatched lawn chairs stood pulled away from the table, the sink overflowed with dirty dishes, and an old typewriter on a rolling typing table squeezed into the space between the upright piano and the angled wall.

"The only thing I recognize is the piano," Dan said in a whisper. "It looks like the one my grandmother had."

The piano pressed against a door. The overhead light fixture dangled from the ceiling, a monstrosity of cracked and chipped globes that partially revealed the naked bulbs inside.

"Look at these!" Dan pushed around some of the papers on the table. "They're poetry and vocal lead sheets. And restaurant receipts, bar napkins and handwritten letters from my sister!"

Emily laughed in a giddy, disbelieving way that betrayed the rapid unraveling of her self-control. Unable to process any more information, she slumped down on the mattress, laughing and crying simultaneously. Ignoring her completely, Dan picked up one of the newspapers.

"Chicago Tribune, Wednesday, May 9th 1973—" his voiced drifted into silence. Emily raised her eyes to his face and pulled herself up, using his arm as a lever.

"1973?" She caught her breath and ran to the bathroom mirror. Looking beyond the dried soap and water spots, smeared fingerprints and traces of spattered toothpaste, she watched as her long ago youthful face gradually replaced the mature visage she had grown to accept, and peered back at her. The long, blond hair she had shorn off when she reached forty again hung straight past her shoulder. She saw no wrinkles and no foundation makeup concealed age spots. Thinner again, she ran her hands down the sides of her body and smiled. The clothes weren't hers, small detail. Rushing back into the main room, Emily looked intently at Dan, wanting to see him more clearly, to take note of any obvious differences in his appearance from the fellow she had met so short a time ago.

"Your mustache is brown, not gray. You're hair is thick, not thinning, and you must have lost forty pounds. Where the hell are we?"

"I haven't a clue. But we are certainly not any worse for wear. I might even get to know you better than I should."

Overcome with an emotion he couldn't name, perhaps like the one a prisoner feels when he gives in to the finality of his sentence, Dan reached out to Emily, pulling her close and hugging her with a reassuring squeeze.

"We're in this together, I guess."

She found his hug a relief from her self-imposed reluctance to welcome his company. Feeling safer in his arms, and feeling stronger with her near, they both started laughing.

"I can reach around you with one arm," she observed. "The old you was a bit rotund—handsome—but round."

"Oh yeah? And, where did you get that long blond hair?" he joked, flipping a lock of her hair up over her forehead and remembering the short cropped style of her bleached blond hair at Rita's. "And, what about your face? Where are all the smile lines and wrinkles you —oops, shouldn't go there." He smiled sheepishly at his faux pas.

"I don't know. Maybe I haven't earned them yet."

Dan's smile evaporated in the grip of uneasiness welling up from the pit of his stomach, as he realized how tenuous was their still indescribable situation.

"Grandma's piano is the only thing I recognize," Dan said, trying to talk about something concrete as a means to gaining control over his environment as best he could. Emily's smile waned into a silence that spread into the room the way fog spreads over the Lake Michigan coastline as a cold front approaches from the northeast. Dan ran his fingers over the keys, then sat down and started to play. The music came easily. He had played parts of several pop songs from the early seventies before he realized he was feeling an ease of accomplished mastery. Surprised, he pulled his hands back from the keys, the way he might if they were suddenly hot to the touch.

"What's going on? I can't play like that. I can only play by ear. If it's really 1973, then I'm twenty-two and you're twenty-six. My kids—aren't—" His voice trailed off under the weight of his words.

"Kids? Yes, what about our kids? Where are our kids?" Emily paced the open space of the room, from wall to wall, touching the sparse furniture and the scattered papers on the table. "I don't see anything referring to kids here—no photos—no toys. Nothing."

"No," Dan said with sadness, "we obviously aren't who or where we were. We are somewhere else." Dan spoke words, but didn't feel like he was talking. He shivered as he realized that he was watching and at the same time living each moment as it happened in a dream-like state of illusion. "This is not right. I don't understand. What's happening here?" Misjudging the distance to its lumpy surface, Dan sat heavily on the mattress. He slumped over, lay on his side and lit a cigarette. Staring into space, flicking ashes onto the floor every so often, suddenly, he got up and walked into the kitchen area. One by one, he opened all the cabinets, looking inside each one but finding nothing. He opened the closet, finding only some flattened cardboard boxes that looked like they had been used for moving things. He slammed the door in anger feeling a flash of rage rising. He sat down again next to Emily. She stared at him hoping he would some-how know the answers to all her questions.

"Don't look at me that way! I can't tell you what's going on!" he shouted at her.

"I didn't say a thing." Emily tried to be very calm as she spoke. "You don't have to yell at me. I am listening."

Not knowing this man, his sudden burst of anger frightened her. It reminded her of the explosive nature of her father, her first husband, many of her boyfriends. She responded with instant calm, so as to not cause more tension. Focusing his eyes on the outline of the door behind the piano, Dan stared at it in silence for a couple of minutes.

"Do you notice anything strange about that door behind the piano?" he asked at last. Emily glanced back and forth from his face to the door several times, trying to see what he was seeing. She visually scoured the image for anything out of place.

"No. It's a door." Then she realized what he was seeing. "Except that the paint looks fresh, and the hinges are shiny, new—" Emily's voice trailed off.

"Help me pull the piano away from the door," Dan said.

Concealed cobwebs tore away and the spiders scurried into the inner sanctum of the soundboard as the piano's old rollers resisted the tug of involuntary motion.

"What do you think's on the other side?"

"Probably just another closet," Emily said hoping she was right.

Dan turned the unresisting knob. As the door opened, a sweet odor poured out, fresh, clean, not musty like the apartment. Music was playing, so softly they had to strain to hear it.

"Prop the door open—I don't want it to close behind us."

Emily hurriedly jammed a folded newspaper under the door to keep it from swinging shut. Curiosity and the opulence of the luxurious living room stretching before them drew them down the stairs from the door and into the room.

"God! This can't be for real," Emily whispered in astonishment as they stepped through the opening. Rich salmon colored walls held impressionist and modern art, hanging at tasteful intervals and set off by track lighting. Silk oriental rugs lay on the highly polished oak floor with furniture placed around them in conversation groupings. Fresh long-stemmed calla lilies graced the low glass tables that serviced the seating clusters on either side of an enormous white-mantled fireplace. From above the mantle, a huge mirror reflected the entire room. The windows to each side of the fireplace invited inhabitants onto a wide lawn that sloped gently to a coastline horizon. Nearly transparent white curtains hung from gleaming brass hardware.

A long wet bar stretched to the other side of the room, well stocked with every imaginable beverage. Crystal glassware hung over the bar and sparkled in the overhead light, breaking prisms onto the bar's polished surface below. Beside the bar, a statuesque, high-tech entertainment center stood waiting to burst into action for viewers who would recline on the overstuffed couches to enjoy whatever diversion they chose. The fourth wall, entirely invisible plate glass, gave out onto a private garden where a granite patio ended at the short retaining wall. On the narrow strip of lawn a wooden sculpture of a voluptuous reclining woman leaned toward a leafy, wooded boundary that infused the soothing calm of nature into the room.

Dan sensed he knew the room and had loved being in it.

"Do you know this place?" he asked, looking closely at Emily's face, trying to be sure of her feelings. "I think I've seen this place," he added to precipitate her reaction.

"Huh, yeah, I feel like I've been here before." Walking away from him, Emily plopped down on one of the couches like a small child. "I think I live here. I sure want to live here. It's so beautiful!" she sighed as she looked past him toward the far end of the room. "Someone's coming!" she said in a forced whisper.

At first, the architecture of the base of the stairs Dan and Emily had descended to enter the room blocked Dan's perspective of the approach of a man and a woman. When they came into his view, he signaled Emily with a silent hand movement to come to him. Emily froze as the couple came into her proximity. They seemed not to notice her. Dan observed that the couple went on about their business as Emily slowly stood and then scurry quickly over to him. The woman mixed two drinks, while the man sat down on the couch Emily had just vacated. The woman came around the bar, crossed the short space to the couch and bent over to kiss the man as she handed him his drink.

"Do you think they know we're here?" Dan whispered in Emily's ear.

"No!" she scoffed, screwing up her face in mockery of his question. "If they did, they certainly would have seen me move over here. This is like a movie. Let's watch." Her fascination with the couple made Dan uneasy.

"No, I want to go back to the apartment and sort all this out."

He took her hand, again having to pull her with him, and started up the stairs and looking up just in time to see the door to the apartment slowly closing. The same creepy feeling Emily had known as a child running up from darkness of the basement caught her full force, sending chills up her spine. Terrified, she pulled away from Dan and ran up the stairs. She grabbed the knob and held the door just long enough for them both to slip through the narrowed opening. Emily's panic gripped him, too, as the door slammed shut on its own. Together they pushed the piano into its original position against the door, trying to block their fear of the unknown.

4

*R*escue workers had found only two people in the rubble, only slightly injured, but unconscious, a man, identified as Dan Barton, and a woman, identified as Emily Sanders. The newspapers were reporting how the building had been a fairly popular after work hangout for the overworked blue collar and underpaid white collar workers who populated the nearby high-rise office buildings. The basement housed the office and kitchen for the first floor restaurant and entertainment lounge, with private storage for supplies on the two floors above. No others, injured or killed had been found in the rubble, even though witnesses confirmed that the establishment had been nearly full of patrons at the time of the first terrorist-style bombing in Chicago since the gangster era of the nineteen twenties. Only the burned out skeleton of the car, twisted by the heat into a pretzel of steel and soot, laying on its side and teetering into the hole in the floor of what had once been the front window stage area, gave testament to the fire storm that had leveled Rita's Bar. No bones. No blood. No tears. Just destruction.

Within a few hours, Emily's college-aged baby sitter had called the police when Emily had failed to return from work that evening.

Angelie had contacted the police in the morning when Dan had failed to come for the boys. The Department of Children and Family Services authorities had been called in to manage the cases of the four children, two girls and two boys, who were waiting for the return of their single parents, gone from home because they were just trying to make a living, albeit in non-conventional ways, and who had not yet been told their mother and their father were lying in a hospital with injuries sustained in a bombing. That this had been a terrorist-style bombing and that these unlucky two people were only two survivors put the children's case in the hands of the DCFS almost immediately. To protect the children from publicity, and the gruesome sensationalizing of the bombing and the mystery of no other bodies or injured, the eminent child psychologist, Dr. Eastman had been offered their case to evaluate how and where it would be best to house the children until their parents had recovered. Shortly before the scheduled arrival of the children, he picked up his phone and called his long-time colleague at DCFS, Ann Johnson.

"Hello, Ann? It's Jim Eastman. Could I take up some of your valuable time? I'm about to meet with the children of the bombing victims."

"Oh yes, Jim! I've been waiting for your call."

"Ann, I want to know what you might suggest we do to give these kids a chance to build a kind of safety net together. I think you'll agree that we should try to keep the unfeeling hand of the court out of their lives as long as we can."

"You know the court would send these kids back to their other biological parents in a heartbeat. Have you tried to contact the other parents?"

"Without much success, I'm afraid. The girls' father, William Pauer, made it quite clear he didn't have the time or the space in his life for his daughters. He told me in no uncertain words to handle the situation for him. The boys' mother keeps her mailing address at a friend's house in Arizona. When I called there, the friend told me their mother had just left on a two month assignment in Africa —she's a photojournalist, you know—and is rarely home enough to raise two kids. Then she thanked me for calling and asked me to handle it for her, since she was about to leave for the airport herself on a vacation to the Bahamas that she had been waiting to take for more than a year. What are parents thinking these days?"

"That they don't have to take on their responsibilities as parents." Ann's voice betrayed her anger, even though she controlled the inflection. "Any other relatives? Aunts, uncles, grandparents?"

"Apparently not. As long as the mother and father are alive, these kids could very well be the best support we could give them for each other, given the peculiar circumstances and unique needs they will have. And I'd like to see them kept together for a while, if I see that to do so is an appropriate decision. Can you make it happen, Ann, if I need you to, can you make it happen?" His insistence betrayed his doubt.

"This is a tall order, Jim. They're not even brothers and sisters." The monotone cadence of her voiced conveyed her reservations.

Dr. Eastman punched his point. "Well, isn't my recommendation enough to start with?" Of course, it is, and you know I know it is.

"Well, it will depend on your evaluation of the children themselves." She paused, allowing herself the time to be sure she could follow through. "I'll start things in motion here, but only because I trust you'll be impartial in your judgment of their true needs as individuals. I agree that on the surface of the situation, it might be better for them to be living together, perhaps in a foster home near the hospital. Lord knows it would be easier from our perspective to protect them in one place." She paused again waiting for any more discussion from

Dr. Eastman. Hearing nothing more, she said simply, "I'll find out what I can."

"Thanks, Ann. These kids need our help, and I know I can count on you, if I can count on anyone." Dr. Eastman hung up the phone and pried the lid off the antacid bottle. The door of his outer office opened, and he heard the bustle of several people sitting in the chairs in concert with the mother hen voice of Ms. Gridley, the DCFS caseworker who so often escorted children to and from his office. He popped two tablets into his mouth and swallowed them without water. She opened his door and peered around the door, smiling her professionally cheery smile. He reached for the glass and the water carafe he kept on the credenza behind his desk.

"Dr. Eastman, would you like to meet the children I've brought along with me?"

"Hello, Ms. Gridley. Yes, I would," he said loudly and clearly as he returned the glass and carafe to their respective places unused. Crossing the room and opening the door wide, he entered his waiting room. Ms. Gridley introduced the children, and in so doing, took the hand of the youngest of the four children. Jennifer Pauer, shy yet willing, entered Dr. Eastman's office.

"Hello, Jennifer, won't you have a seat?" Dr. Eastman tried to make her feel comfortable by leading her to the couch in front of the window. Jennifer's face showed anxiety devoid of fear, but filled with curiosity about why she was there and not with her mother. *She's such a little innocent. How will she ever understand any of this?*

"Do you know where my Mommy is?" Her small voice asked so politely, the words softened Dr. Eastman's strained professional demeanor. Sitting on the couch, so small that her patent-leather shoes dangled inches above the oriental carpet, her twinkling blue eyes and shiny blond hair conjured up Alice in Wonderland in Dr. Eastman's mind's eye. *Gentle now. Be gentle. Tell the truth but softly.*

"Well, yes, I do. She's in the hospital, where the doctors are taking very good care of her."

"Why is she there?" Jennifer asked simply.

"Well, she is sleeping and the doctors are watching her sleep. She'll wake up one day soon," Dr. Eastman tried to reassure her. "How would you like to stay with your sister in a foster home while we wait for your mother to get better?"

"Could we stay at my friend Laura's house? We know her real well."

"I'm not sure yet whose house you'll stay at, but I'm sure the people will be nice." Dr. Eastman decided not to go any further with questions, not wanting to create worries she clearly had not yet developed, being too young to realize what has been going on. "Could you wait in the waiting room now while I talk with your sister, and the boys?"

"Okay," Jennifer said in a musical little voice. They both stood up and walked to the door. "I have a puppy dog. She lives at my Daddy's house," she said.

"You do? You are very lucky. What's her name?" Dr. Eastman said

"Dreena, She's a big puppy dog." Then with the simplicity only a child could have, she extended her hand to shake his. "Thank you for seeing me."

He took her fragile little fingers in his enormous palm and gently pumped her hand a couple of times. "And thank you for spending time with me." Taken aback by her disarming politeness, he relaxed, he smiled and he opened the door, motioning to Miranda Pauer to join him.

Miranda, aged sixteen going on thirty, looked and acted like a street-walker in training. Deep brick red lipstick, carefully drawn eyeliner, and black mascara added years to her face. Cascading deep red hair set off her extremely fair, flawless complexion giving her a striking radiance. The low cut shirt and overtly provocative skin-tight jeans revealed more of her curvaceous silhouette than a young girl would properly show the world.

She dresses this way in an attempt to grow up fast and to gain adult male approval, most likely from her absent father. Early assessment. Textbook.

"Come in—Miranda, isn't it?"

"Yes." She spoke curtly, without feeling. Her left hand fiddled with a tassel hanging from her shoulder purse, which she clutched tightly under her right arm.

Miranda's edgy demeanor made Dr. Eastman feel more on guard than he had expected he would. "You know, we're trying to decide if we should keep the four of you together in one foster home, while we wait for your mother and the boys' father to get better." He waited for a response that did not follow. "It's actually very lucky that they're alive."

"So, why should we stay together? We don't know each other. What difference does it make if their father and my mother are in the same place?" she asked in a matter-of-fact way bordering on hostility.

"Not much of one, although it seems to me you've thought about this possibility," he said, jotting down a couple of notes to keep focused. *Perceptive—tries to guess what I expect her to think, what I want her to say.*

"I've been to psychologists before, you know. Mom took us to someone when she divorced my father. I understand that you have to evaluate us before the DCFS people can place us. If I were older, I'd just go to work and try to support my sister and me till things worked out. But, not being old enough to do that, I'll just try to keep us together."

"Miranda, that's a very mature position you're taking." *Overcompensating.*

"Yes, well, if you knew me, you'd know I've always been this way." Let's see if the hard life story gets him. "As a kid, I had to help Mom a lot with Jennifer, to be responsible for her when Mom was working and we were home alone. I decided to take control of my own life early. I decided to plan, to see options, and to do my best in everything. Watching my mother taught me that life is never easy. You have to go after what you want and be ready for it, just in case you get it." She shifted her position, crossing her legs and releasing the vice grip she had on the purse. "So, instead of talking about my feelings," she tossed her hair back and ran her hand through the unruly front locks, "could you just help me keep me and my sister together?" *Now smile, he'll melt.*

As she stopped talking, the façade slipped away, she smiled more easily a warm smile that softened the harsh edges of her face and changed the extreme makeup into nothing more than the disguise she meant it to be. The shimmer of the child hiding behind the adult mask caused Dr. Eastman to sit back for a moment witness the revelation of an emerging young woman. *Articulate, clearly very intelligent, thinking in ways people many years older might think.*

"Miranda, I'm curious, what would you think about all four of you staying together." A short silence followed his question as she reached into her purse for a stick of gum, which she slowly unwrapped and curled into a roll before putting it in her mouth.

"Well," chewing to soften the gluey mass forming between her teeth, "for now I have to do what's right for Jennifer and me. The boys don't really figure in my plans, but if things turn out okay, then Jennifer and I will just go on as we were."

"And, if not?"

"If not—then we'll be on another road anyway. So it goes."

Again she smiled at him, crossing her legs again and raising her eyebrows, just before looking away to hide the first tears beginning to well up in her eyes.

Seeing her emotion Dr. Eastman wondered why Miranda pretended to be only pre-occupied with the immediate problem of what to do about housing. *There they are, the real tears.*

"You're worried about your mother, aren't you?" he asked, trying to prod her into opening up.

"Of course I am!" Miranda said quickly, anger tingeing her voice and flashing in her eyes. She gulped a very deep breath to control her emotions. "But first things first. Jennifer and I need a place to stay. You're supposed to help us with that. If it has to be with the boys, then that's how it has to be. I'll think about the other things later."

Amazing how fast she pulled back. Don't push her right now. Encourage her and give her some comfort. Dr. Eastman decided to end the conversation.

"Well, I will try to help you, Jennifer and the boys. If they agree, then I'll find a way to make it work out for all of you together."

Miranda tightened her arm around her purse and stood to go. "Well, at least that's better than a sharp stick in the eye," she said.

"What do you mean by that?"

"Oh, it's just something my mother says when things don't work out exactly as planned." They both laughed at the ridiculously sadistic image.

"Could you wait with Jennifer while I talk with Patrick and Ian?"

"Yes, I can." *Hang on girl. You'll be fine.* "And thanks." She smiled almost confidently, as if regaining her place in the outer office returned her to the safety of her composure. She opened the door and pointed to Patrick to go in.

Standing up slowly, Patrick moved with reluctance toward the door like an old man after a long car ride. I'm not saying anything. Not a word. When he finally did enter the room, Dr. Eastman could see immediately he was very distressed. Patrick's silence was long and difficult. Dr. Eastman sat quietly, just observing him. Patrick glanced up at Dr. Eastman every couple of minutes. *What's he waiting for?* He kept his eyes down the rest of the time, taking in every detail of his hands like he had never seen them before. He tried to project a blank stare when he looked up, but Dr. Eastman could see him taking in the details of the office with each glance. Several minutes passed, and finally Patrick spoke. "You gonna wait all day?"

"Are you?" *Curiosity is a strong partner here.*

"I just quit waiting. When are you going to poke and prod and try to get me to tell you how much I hate my life, or something?"

"I'm not." *Rudeness hides fear, and this boy is clearly afraid.*

"Then what good are you?" Patrick raised his voice. "Aren't you guys supposed to be nosy and pick at people?"

"Maybe some are. I'm not. This is your time. I'm just here to figure out if the four of you should stay in the same foster home for a while. Is that okay with you?"

"I don't know." Patrick looked down. *What does he want from me?*

"The girls think it would be okay." Dr. Eastman said, with a tone in his voice that was meant to push Patrick to open up.

My counselor at school told me to take risks with people. Don't like risks.

Silence set in again for a couple of minutes. Patrick had moved every year of his life, bouncing back and forth between schools as regularly as his father had changed jobs trying to escape his own demons. Anything different in his life was very hard for him, and this situation was very different. He wasn't a particularly good student, and his raging hormones sometimes boiled over into fights at school.

He grappled a while with the possibilities, trying to make the idea of staying with the girls okay in his mind.

I don't want to live in someone else's house. Even with Ian there, I'd still be the second oldest. No power. Could I team up with Miranda? She is a babe. Safety could be found in numbers, and she is a babe.

"Okay," Patrick said very quietly. "That would be okay." He curled his right hand into a fist and rubbed it like it hurt with his left.

Dr. Eastman regarded him a moment, remembering how he, too, had been a tough kid like Patrick at about the same age.

"Good. I think you're doing the right thing. Miranda and you could keep track of the littler ones. Is that okay with you?"

"I suppose so." He punched his right hand into his left palm, once, twice.

Dr. Eastman saw the volcano was about to erupt. "Then send in your brother, and we'll be almost done," he said, trying to diffuse the explosion.

Patrick stood up to go, when he turned suddenly, shouting. "I'm going to get the geeks who did this! I'm not just going to sit around waiting!" He slammed his hand against the wall, and looked back over his shoulder with a fire in his eye, a fire lit by rage and tinged with helplessness.

"I believe you. I really do." Pausing to slow his own adrenalin rush, he added, "Do you ever think about writing your feelings down?" Distract him. Dr. Eastman motioned him back to the chair in front of his desk. Patrick's face twisted into a macho expression, chin pushed out, slightly off center, lips pursed to take a hit. Then every muscle relaxed, and he looked down, as if ashamed of his outburst. He dragged his feet into motion and moved to the chair, sitting into it with a heavy plop, every muscle and every bone defeated, his anger deflated and left limp in his heart.

"Yes, my counselor at school makes me do that . . . when I get in trouble."

"And, do you write them down?" Dr. Eastman asked quietly.

"Not very often. She's so stupid. I can write anything and she'll believe it."

Dr. Eastman reached into a drawer and pulled out a cloth-covered book. He held it out to Patrick, who looked at him cautiously.

He took the book and flipped through the pages. "It's blank," he said, looking up at Dr. Eastman.

Dr. Eastman smiled with a joking look in his eye. "Why not write things down for me? I'm not as stupid as I look right now. And, besides, I'll be seeing you even after you get settled in a foster home."

"I'll think about it," Patrick said, his body now completely relaxed, taking on the form of the chair. He flipped the pages once more and looked up at Dr. Eastman who was now standing behind his desk. "Thanks." The simplicity of the remark laid out the terms of the truce, as Patrick rose to go. He held out his hand, which Dr. Eastman shook in that male-bonding way that says, "We're cool."

Patrick left the door open for Ian, who walked in as if his brother had evaporated. *Gee, this guy is rich. Look at all his fancy stuff.* Instead of standing aside, Ian barged through the door, moving quickly all around the room, picking up objects and magazines before sitting down on the couch against the wall to fidget in his seat. Ian could not sit still for more than a couple of minutes. Even while watching a movie or playing a video game, he was on the move. Dr. Eastman knew a hyperactive nature could drive people to distraction and cause them to alienate themselves from those around them. In this case, he more simply saw a terrified nine-year-old boy.

"Ian, I wonder how it feels to know your Dad is in the hospital."

"I'm not stupid, you know. I know my dad is real sick. I know he might even die. I know their mom is real sick too and might die too. I'm going to wait and see. I'm big enough to wait and see." He straightened his back, to seem taller and gave in to the impulse to reach over to the side table and pick up a glass paperweight. He tossed it carelessly back and forth from hand to hand, testing its weight and size before holding it up to the window to look through the ball at the pseudo flowers glimmering hot colors from inside.

"How do they make these?"

"I'm not exactly sure. I know they're made by artists who blow the glass when it is still molten hot."

"You mean like molten lava?"

"Yes, like that, but under control by the artist."

Ian held the ball close to his right eye and kept looking through it, turning it like a kaleidoscope to see how the colors changed. Dr. Eastman took his cue ask his question while Ian pretended to be distracted.

"What would you think about staying with Patrick and the girls in the same foster home?"

"It's okay, I guess. Jennifer told me she'd like to get to know me. Just like a girl. Only I just don't want to stay with people who will look at us with moony eyes, and treat us like babies."

Ian kept fidgeting, finally putting down the paperweight and getting up to walk around the room again.

"So, you want to stay all together, too?"

"Sure. I'll stay with my brother. The girls are okay. It's okay with me. Can I go now?" He jumped up and scooted to the door.

"Wait just a moment." Dr. Eastman crossed the room to open the door. "Kids, would you all come in here for a minute?" The others entered his office. Miranda held Jennifer's hand, and Patrick stood behind Ian, putting his hands on Ian's shoulders to keep him calm. All four stood close, clustering near each other as if taking some comfort from their unity.

SACRED NIGHT

"Ian, and everyone, come on over here and take a seat. I'd like you all to do something for me." As each of the children sat down, Dr. Eastman placed four large pieces of white paper on the table. He took a basket of markers and crayons from a bookshelf and placed it in the center of the table. "Draw me a picture. It can be about anything you'd like. Try to be as detailed as you can be. Make it as wonderful as you can. There's plenty of time. Take as long as you need to draw me the best picture you can."

The young children looked at Miranda, who knew they wanted her to start first. She sat at the end of the table, taking a few bright markers from the basket. *The other guy did this too. He wants to see what we're thinking through our drawings. I'll show him and draw nothing he can understand.* Miranda set about drawing.

This is fun! Jennifer plopped into the chair on one side of the table. Taking crayons from the basket, she began to draw a scene with a river, a tree, some birds flying across the sky, and a smiling sun. She added flowers and some tufts of grass. Then, in the lower left-hand corner she drew in three female figures, one lying on a bed with the two others standing on either side of the bed, each extending an unusually long arm over the bed and clasping the other's hand. In the lower left hand corner, she drew three male figures in the same pose as the females.

Dr. Eastman turned his attention to Patrick. He watched a battle scene evolve. Many beheaded torsos, blood flowing from them, lay strewn over a treeless battlefield. One male figure, larger than life stood in the middle, with his sword held high with enough blood dripping from it to pool on the ground. He was half smiling and half frowning. Dark clouds rained on a house in the background. Airplanes populated the sky, and one red sports car in the lower left-hand corner seemed ready to burst into motion.

Miranda's drawing was entirely abstract, except for a central medallion showing a very detailed jungle image of palm trees and a village of huts. The zigzag lines shot from the medallion like brightly colored lightning. The impact of the design was stunning and very intense. She left no space uncolored.

Ian drew fast and furiously. His images were incomplete and scattered all over the paper. Nothing connected. There were three male figures, one larger than the others, but they were not standing together. The larger of the figures lay in the lower right corner with a pillow under his head. The other two floated randomly in the upper two corners of the drawing. There were several other animals: a snake, a frog, a turtle, a lion and a bear. Each of them was clearly drawn, but they were in strange colors, like purple and blue, pink and orange. There was a realistic dog with brown and black spots and a big tail standing near the smallest of the male figures.

"I'm done!" Ian said loudly as he slammed the marker in his hand down on the table. "That was fun. Thanks." He popped out of his chair like a jack-in-the-box and went to the window to look out.

"Yes, I enjoyed that," Miranda said, quietly picking up the stray crayons on the table and placing them in the basket. *I'm sure he'll think I'm hiding something. Maybe I am. Maybe I can get him to really help us get to the bottom of this thing.*

"Me too!" Jennifer chimed in as she picked up the drawings, which she offered to Dr. Eastman.

Patrick remained aloof. He just looked at Dr. Eastman and shook his head.

"Well, it's time for you all to go with the caseworker. Ms. Gridley will take you back to Harbor House. Thanks for drawing your pictures. I'll keep them a long time," he said, taking them from Jennifer.

"Dr. Eastman?" Miranda asked as the others went into the outer office.

"Yes, Miranda."

"Will we be seeing you again?" *I know we will.*

"I'm sure you will."

"Then, will you tell me what you think of the drawings sometime?"

"Well, yours at least. I'll see you soon," he said as he gently ushered her into the outer office. Dr. Eastman watched from his window as the kids all left together in the company of Ms. Gridley. They're an interesting bunch of kids. He lifted the receiver of his phone and dialed Ann Johnson's office.

"Oh yes, Jim! I've been waiting for your call. Tell me what's up with them?"

"I had them draw, and I think you'd be interested in what I see there."

"I have some time. Go ahead," Ann said with curiosity in her voice.

"Well, little Jennifer is including the boys in the drawing. She's definitely aware of what's happening around her. She shows herself connected to her sister and protective of her mother. She also thinks the boys feel the same way about each other and their father, since she drew them in the same pose as herself and her sister and mother. She's still happy, the sun tells me that. But there's no house. Is she feeling uprooted? Probably. But she includes the other kids, and that's important."

"What about Miranda?" Ann asked.

"Well, I think the lack of people and any reference to her family is very important. She's intellectualizing, avoiding representing her feelings in a realistic manner. There is a central circle with a jungle in it. What that means, I don't know for sure—perhaps she feels like she's in a very foreign territory—lost even. But, the intensity of her zigzag lines simply screams anger and fear. Her choice of clashing colors and sharp edges to the lightning bolts is very interesting. I think she's terrified, and she's shutting it all inside."

"And Patrick?"

"Hmm—His is very interesting. I'm seeing his need to be powerful in an overwhelming situation. He shows himself in a bloody battle, standing victorious over the enemies he's killed with his sword. Clearly, he thinks he will triumph, judging by his victory pose in the center of the drawing. The airplanes and the car probably represent a means of escape to him," Dr. Eastman surmised.

"And trouble for us, " Ann interjected her hunch. "He could be ready to run away."

"Perhaps. He has drawn rain falling on a house."

"Tears?"

"That he can't cry. His actions here—a violent outburst—support me in this."

"Is there any reference to his father or his brother?"

"No, he's clearly very preoccupied with himself."

He paused to look more closely at Ian's drawing. "Ian's picture is very hard to decipher. I'm sure his father is the large reclining figure, but with so many animals in so many colors, and everything so disconnected, I think he's just not at all sure of himself and his predicament."

"Who could be at eight or nine years old?"

"You have that right. So. I recommend they live together. Everything I saw and heard from them pulls me to this decision. You just have to make it happen."

The split-second silence on the line spoke volumes. Ann was not at all sure she had enough strings to pull to satisfy Dr. Eastman's recommendation.

"Use me, abuse me, but don't throw me into that briar patch! Oh, Jim, I hope I can do this."

"You can."

5

*S*ilence permeated the apartment the way the soft music had floated in the air of the luxurious room just beyond the door, now safely barred by the piano Emily and Dan had pushed back into its original position upon their return. The shrill ring of the phone startled them both.

Dan picked up the receiver on the fourth ring. "Hello?"

"Is Emily there please?"

"Yes. It's for you," Dan whispered. Puzzled, Emily shrugged her shoulders as he handed her the phone.

"Hey, Em—How're things?"

"Uh, all right I guess. Who's this?" she said, trying to seem in control.

"Come on Em, it's Jon."

"Jon?"

"Jon Grant. I'm calling to find out if you and Dan could add another weekend to the two coming up. What do you say?"

"Uh, sure." Emily didn't have the slightest idea who she was talking to. "But, just to get it right, tell me what time and where, we're so busy you know."

"You know—Pretty Boy's? Nine PM to one AM, Fridays? Ten to two on Saturdays?" Emily's strange response had piqued his curiosity. "The guys are looking forward to the new material – are you okay?"

"Of course—see you this weekend."

Emily hung up and looked at Dan with wide eyes.

"We have a three weekend gig at a place called Pretty Boy's."

"Where?"

"Pretty Boy's, Friday and Saturday nights. The guy, Jon, on the phone said they want us to do our new material too."

Suddenly agitated, Dan rifled through the papers looking for a phonebook, scattering an envelope and some scraps of paper on the floor. Stuffed between two stacks of newspapers he found it and flipped through the yellow pages, nearly tearing them from the book in his haste.

"Entertainment—no. Dinner clubs—no. Cabarets—here it is! Pretty Boy's Cabaret on Rush Street. 755 North. Sounds like a gay club."

"At least it's something to do. It appears we're working musicians. I wonder what we play." Emily said, laughing at herself, the nervous laugh she couldn't control when everything around her went out of control. "Do you think," she asked, picking up the envelope Dan had knocked to the floor, "that we're supposed to figure out where this Pretty Boy's Cabaret is?" She opened it. Her eyebrows lifted as her jaw dropped in astonishment. "Money!" She flipped through the bills to count them. "Two hundred fifty dollars all in tens and twenties!" Holding the money at arm's length she shook it at him. "They pay fairly well," she said, placing the cash on the table and crumpling the envelope into a wad, which she then threw into the corner.

"Emily, don't you even wonder what is going on here? Doesn't it bother you that we seem to be living some kind of imaginary life?

Isn't it just weird that we have apparently regained our youth and are stuck in this dump? That a phone you've never seen before rings with someone you've never met calling you to work at a job you've never had in a place that you've never heard of?"

"On the surface, the way you describe it, sure, I'd wonder about it. But—"

"Doesn't it concern you even a little bit that your kids don't exist? Doesn't it upset you that you have no idea who you are?" His question hung in the air.

"Yes, of course where my children are—or aren't—concerns me. But look at us. We're different." She let her eyes glide up and down over Dan's body and then slid her hands down her sides, feeling how her own body had changed. "I don't know who you are, or why we're here, or who I am supposed to be now. I didn't know who I was before all this either," Emily said sadly. She looked toward the dirty window as thunder punctuated her words. "Looks like rain." She stopped talking and let the sound of the water pouring on the window calm her nerves. "I love that sound." Then as she looked back at Dan, who had decided to actually listen to her for the first time since they had come to this strange yet familiar place, she said, "I learned a long time ago that we can't always see reasons for things as they happen. Sometimes it takes years—look back and you can see forward."

"Shut up! I hate that stupid psychobabble crap! Don't tell me we've traveled back in time, or we're somebody's guinea pigs in a great cosmic experiment!" He put on a mask of anger that he knew his sarcasm couldn't disguise. Emily read him easily, seeing through his outburst to the helpless feeling it could not hide.

"No, no, I don't mean anything like that." She wasn't sure of how to put her thoughts into words, and the searching gaze from her eyes to his face gave away her own uncertainty. "But Dan, can you even begin to explain what's happened in some logical way? You're not asleep." She twirled around, flinging her arms outward. "This feels real." She put her hand on the cash. "This money is real." She looked at him, pausing to let him respond. When he said nothing, she shouted, "Go ahead, Mr. Cynic! Explain to me where we are. Go on. Tell me this moment isn't happening. Tell me where you plan to go if not here?" Her taunting dug into him, leaving him speechless and without an option. "What choice do we have?" she said softly. "Come on, let's get out of here and find out what's outside this dark little hole."

Emily stuffed the money in her jeans pocket, grabbed Dan's hand and pulled him out the door. At this point, he couldn't argue with her determination. He did not resist her, and for the first time since he was a little boy, he went along with what was happening around him just because it was happening. He cautiously acknowledged that he could not change the situation, and so gave in to the moment.

The storm had passed quickly and left that freshly washed clarity that happens only after a good rain. The sun was shining with a hard-edged brightness that intensified the distinct limits and outlines of every object. As they came to the park, the figure sitting on the bench nearest the corner caught their attention. The old woman sat huddled over, as if looking into the shopping bag between her feet. She wore a black babushka and a dirty dark gray man's overcoat frayed at the sleeves, with patches on the elbows and torn pockets that flopped down as she pulled the coat around her to block the breeze. Oversized red galoshes dwarfed her legs. The bag held other bags, each stacked concentrically inside the first and brimming with all manner of trash more normally found in garbage cans and sidewalk trash bins. The woman's presence invaded Emily and Dan's now comfortable sense of isolation, as they sat down on the second bench.

"Look! It's a bus stop. Let's take a bus back downtown. Let's go find Pretty Boy's Cabaret. What do you say?" Emily encouraged Dan as he glanced sidelong at the strange woman and her bags.

"Hah! Ha ha ha ha!" Her laughter, hysterical and rough, reverberated loud and gravelly from the walls of the surrounding buildings. Then she seemed to speak with an invisible person beside her on the bench, the tone of her voice condemning, almost shouting.

"Who the hell are you to talk to me that way? Put away them dishes! No! Not there! Over here!"

The birds stopped singing.

"What are you doing with that there book? Gimme it! Don't you ever talk at me that way again! You're all wrong. Listen to me. Shut the hell up!"

The whisper of a breeze evaporated into the safety of the shadows.

Then, the old woman smiled as she spoke softly, sweetly. "Listen, honey, I didn't mean it. You're the best kid in the world. I love you."

The distant sound of the water lapping at the beach faded into the only voice that spoke, screaming, "I don't live here. I'm not the one who did it. You are. You are! I can't help you. You need a bath you wormy asshole! Get out of my way!"

The old woman raged at her bags, sweeping her hand over them as if pushing an unseen intruder away from her treasures.

"They took everything I had, those egg sucking bastards! Drop the goddamn bomb on them all! Let me have some peace. Peace all right. Just a cup of coffee will do."

She grasped the handles, pulling them together and lifting the burden to her lap, where she reached around the wrinkled brown paper and hugged the bags as if comforting a frightened child.

"I love you too, honey. I'm sorry you're feeling dead. I'm sorry you never came home. I miss when you hold me. I miss your kisses." Then turned abruptly to her right she swept her hand outward at an imaginary intruder, trying to protect her bags. "Shut up! You're wrong! I'm right! Shut the hell up!" She gently lowered the bags between her legs and crouched over them.

Emily and Dan stood simultaneously in fearful reaction to the strange actions of the bag lady, and moved to the opposite side of the light pole that held the bus stop sign. The hair tingled on their necks as she began the one-way dialogue all over again.

"Who the hell are you to talk to me that way! Put away them dishes! No! Not there! Over here!"

Squinting in the light, Dan peered down the street to locate the source of the only sound to break the silence. He could hear an engine in need of repair, and quickly saw the lumbering waddle of the silver and red painted coach approaching along the curb. "Come on, here comes the bus," Dan said, taking Emily's hand. He pulled her onto the bus, leaving the bag lady ranting on the park bench. There was no time to even laugh in relief when the driver chortled, "Hello! Welcome to the Happy Bus!" Emily handed him a ten dollar bill, and punched Dan in the side with her elbow as the driver made change for them. "Thank you! No one is ever unhappy on the Happy Bus. Good morning to you. Have a seat and enjoy the ride. 'Oh, what a beautiful morning, Oh, what a beautiful day, I got a beautiful feeling, Everything's going my way—' " the driver sang in his full-throated baritone voice.

Emily and Dan looked at each other to acknowledge the oddness of the moment, then found seats at the front of the bus. They silently counted the seven passengers, wondering which one of them might be like the baglady. But they were all smiling, and it was clear that no one minded the cheerfulness of the driver's jovial singing.

Emily leaned toward Dan to whisper in his ear. "Isn't this weird?"

"Yes, but much better than the baglady."

"I've been riding this bus for years," confided a middle-aged woman. "It's just impossible to start the day in a bad mood after hearing Simpson sing a few happy songs on the way to work. I don't care what you do, you can't be unhappy. He's a real gem, a rarity in this God-awful world. I have this boring job, see, and if I couldn't hear Simpson sing every morning, I'd just be heartbroken. I don't think I could go on with the repetition of my life."

Emily looked carefully at the burly form of the driver, taking in his deep chocolate coloring, his paunch and the wrinkles in his uniform, which were so deeply creased that it seemed Simpson never left his driver's seat. His hands were large and powerful, yet he appeared to be nothing but gentle. His unbridled brashness certainly was infectious.

"Goe-thee! Goe-thee's next! You want to get off? Then put one foot in front of the other!" Simpson called out. He opened the door, and four of the seven passengers pulled the stop rope, moved to the doors, and stepped out of the coach to disappear down a side street. The doors clanked shut, and the bus moved along to Chestnut Street, where Emily and Dan had decided to get off so they could walk down Michigan Avenue and window shop on their way to Superior, where they would turn to go to Rush Street and the cabaret. Two tough looking young men wearing black armbands were waiting at the bus stop. As Emily and Dan got off the bus, the toughs stood to the side and watched them with stares of anger that was out of place for the situation. Simpson's voice boomed out, "Hello! Welcome to the Happy Bus—" The door closed. The bus rambled down the deserted street and was gone.

Walking along Michigan Avenue, Emily and Dan stopped frequently to look in the windows of the luxury shops and boutiques. Feeling young and untethered, their circumstances seemed less strange by the moment, even though there were no other shoppers crowding the sidewalks. No street players demanded their attention. No children begged for balloons from the non-existent vendors.

Emily stopped abruptly and pulled on Dan's arm to swing him around to face her. Looking into his eyes and without a smile she said, "Promise, if we ever get any real money, you'll buy me a present from Tiffany's and you'll take me for a weekend at the Ritz."

"Sure, anything you want," Dan said not at all sure of anything she wanted.

"No! I meant it. If we ever get through all this, promise me, you'll still be with me. I need to know that you will."

Dan averted his eyes. He could not make her such a promise, even if, for the moment it seemed simple and harmless to say he could. He gently took her hand and held it in both of his. Speaking conspiratorially, he whispered, "Let's find the cabaret, at least so we know where to go on Friday."

She placed her free hand on his hands, realizing she had gone too far with her demand for luxury and safety from a man she hardly knew. "I'm sorry. I can only imagine how that sounded. I just can't help feeling like we have to hang on to each other."

They endured a long moment of adolescent smiles and the nervous untangling of their hands, before they both laughed at their foolishness.

"I guess we might as well get to know each other, since you— I—we seem to be the only sane people around," Dan said. He took her hand in his and led the way south on Michigan Avenue toward Superior Street. Emily let the strength of his grip flow up her arm to her heart, and hoped she wasn't just settling for the closest man at hand, yet another time.

"If you can't be with the one you love, love the one you're with," she sang.

"'Love the One You're With'—written by Stephen Stills, sung by the Isley Brothers, 1971, Greatest Hits Album." Dan grinned at her.

"You think you're pretty smart don't you."

"I know them all."

They turned west on Superior and quickly found themselves amid decaying three and four flat gray stone buildings. As they wandered back south on Rush Street, they came to a bright magenta awning that seemed out of place among the rundown city dwellings. The art deco lettering on the side was unmistakable, Pretty Boy Cabaret.

"So, here it is." Emily smirked at Dan.

"All right, we'll show up Friday night. But, I still don't see how we know what we're going to play."

"Let's knock on the door and meet this guy, Jon."

"Oh, no you don't. I'm not going in there right now—" Dan backed away.

"Oh, yes you are! We'll find out so much by meeting him. Come on!' she grabbed his hand and pulled him up the stairs under the awning. She tried the handle. It was locked. But the bell rang when she pushed the button. She waited about a minute and rang it again.

"I'm coming! I'm coming!" the high male voice warbled through the heavy door. As the door swung open, a friendly, handsome face greeted them. "Well, hello there, Emily! How are you doing? Dan, it's just been too long—come in, come in. Let's have a midday snort, what do you say?" Jon hustled them from the entrance doorway, through the mirrored lobby, darkened without any lights on during the daytime, and into the next room, where he stepped into the long, polished mahogany rectangle of the enormous and elegant u-shaped bar and started to make the drinks, chattering all the way.

"You're still drinking Jameson, right Dan? And Emily wants a coffee, I'm sure."

"You've a good memory, Jon," Emily giggled. Above the bar was an enormous antique crystal chandelier, that caught the few rays of sunlight coming in through the floor to ceiling window and refracted them into a rainbow on the wall. The decor was elaborate with sculpted plaster moldings at the ceiling and beveled glass windows exquisitely draped with white damask curtains. The dark gray carpeting complimented the black leather bar stools. The rich maroon wallpaper contrasted with the beveled mirrors and glass shelves holding an apparently endless supply of crystal glassware. The room was large, but not cavernous. The intimacy of the flawless decor set off the silver framed etchings of erotic drawings. Looking closely at the feathers of the flying eagle, Emily saw they were actually hundreds of entwined bodies in various states of sexual delight. Several other works echoed the same themes. She looked up when Jon clinked the glasses together.

"Here you are," Jon said, handing them their drinks and walking into a short corridor. "Come into the cabaret room. Let's talk in here."

He led them past a few high tables with tall stools and into an elegant room. Above the fireplace hung an ornate silver medallion, flanked by rococo sconces and mirrors. The grand piano formed an island for close up seating among the other high tables and stools enough to seat forty or fifty people. Jon turned on the stage lighting and to complete the effect. Emily loved the thought of performing here.

"So, this is a piano bar, too," Dan observed aloud.

"Oh, yes. We have many entertainers." Jon looked at him, wondering why Dan had made a comment better suited to a person unfamiliar with Pretty Boy's Cabaret.

"You know, some are strictly piano players who sing a little. Others are singers with their piano players like the two of you." They nodded. "We have comics, small vocal groups, buffoons and divas. They all want to perform here." They nodded again, as if taking in the explanation for the first time.

"So, your clientele is mostly gay men?" Dan felt a squeamish urge rising in his gut.

"The occasional lesbian couple. No cross-dressers or anything bizarre. They go elsewhere for that. Most of our patrons are not even known to be gay. Many are married to women, but have this other secret side."

"Love the one you're with," Emily whispered into Dan's ear. He swatted her away like he would an annoying fly. She blew in his ear to tease him.

"New since you were last here, we've decided to try to attract more straights to the club, that's why we'd like you to do the extra weekend." Jon smiled at them, projecting his best sales face at their confusion.

"Our boys love you, you know. I'm very choosy about our performers. It's really an honor to be booked here, if I do say so myself." Jon giggled at the pretension in his comment. " So." He paused for effect. "Sing me a love song, will you?" he added smiling in a way that made the word "no" impossible.

Emily smiled back, as Dan panicked. "Oh, I don't think so, I don't have my fake book with me," Dan stammered.

"I'd love to hear something." Jon teased and then sat down at the nearest table, crossing his arms over his midsection.

"Well, how about 'Summertime' by George Gershwin?" Emily stared at Dan, sure he could play any song so well known without music. She had heard him play back at the apartment, hadn't she? He could quote songwriters and groups like chapter and verse, recording dates and albums included. Dan stared back at her and reluctantly made his way to the keyboard. The music flowed from his fingers, and

SACRED NIGHT

Emily sang in a warm alto voice, sprinkling the melody with vibrant soprano arpeggios. Jon relaxed his grip and his tightly crossed arms fell to his sides. He smiled with a look of delight.

"Wonderful! Wonderful!" he applauded at the end. "I wish I didn't have work to do. But, I do. Are we settled on three hundred fifty dollars a night?"

"Oh, that will do," Emily said casually, figuring that was a hundred dollar raise over the two-fifty she had found the envelope. "Yes, that will do. Thanks for having us in." She pulled Dan from behind the piano and headed for the front door.

"See you Friday night!" Jon said, waving cheerfully after them as they opened the door.

"Yes, Friday." Dan nodded and pulled the door closed.

They hurried down the steps and half ran, half walked up Rush Street to Superior and turned east toward Michigan Avenue

"See? What did I tell you? Look how much we know now," Emily laughed as Dan took her hand. It felt natural to them both, holding hands, as if they had grown closer in the few moments they spent in the cabaret.

"Just knowing we can earn some money makes me feel much better," he said. "Let's walk over to the Water Tower Park and feed the pigeons."

They made their way back toward Michigan Avenue as the afternoon sun began to drop below the skyscrapers. Crossing over Chicago Avenue and into the park, they hardly noticed it was deserted, except for the popcorn vendor. They bought a bag and made their way into the center where the benches lined the pathway. Traffic noise was muted, so little traffic passed to generate it. Time seemed to move in slow motion. As Dan threw the last bit of popcorn to the multitude of pigeons begging at their feet, a hunched over woman approached them from the far side of the park. Emily put her hand on Dan's arm and squeezed tightly.

"It's her—the baglady. Oh, Dan. She's heading straight for us. I'm afraid of her!"

"What's the big deal? We'll give her a few coins and she'll be gone."

The baglady walked resolutely up to Dan, put down her bags, and stared him in the face.

"Who the hell are you to talk to me that way?" she shouted in his face, the stench of her breath making him step back.

"What way? It's you who's talking rudely here, lady." Dan was unflappable.

"Put away them dishes!" she shouted louder, pointing at her bags. "No! Not there! Over here!" He picked up her bags and moved them near the tree she was pointing at.

"How's that?" he demanded firmly.

"What the hell are you doing with that there book? Gimme!"

"I don't have a book, lady."

"Don't you ever talk at me that way again! You're all wrong!"

"No, you're wrong, lady. And you're crazy as a bat." Dan began to laugh at her. Emily tried to stop him with a disapproving shake of her head.

"Listen to me. Haven't you noticed? You're not real here, I am. All that you see and do is just an illusion, like a rainbow. You've been set up. If you don't change your act, you'll be dead."

Dan was dumbstruck by the sudden lucidity of her words.

"But—"

"Shut the hell up!" she shouted, then softening her tone, "Listen, honey. You're the best kid in the world. I love you. I'm sorry you're feeling dead. But you're not. You have a chance here to work it out. Two days. Get to your kids by Friday. Save the kids. You'll see me again."

"What do you mean?" Dan was desperate to understand, as she launched into her diatribe.

"Drop the goddamn bomb on them all! Let me have some peace. Peace all right. Just a cup of coffee will do. Get out of my way! Go to your room!"

The baglady picked up her bags and started down the street, chanting, "Let me have some peace. Peace all right. Just a cup of coffee will do—just a cup of coffee." She looked back at Dan, repeating into her bags about wanting a cup of coffee till she was out of sight. He looked to Emily, who was watching him.

"Coffee. Coffee. Rita brought us coffee when we met. Do you remember? What do you think she meant about the kids? What's in two days?" Emily analyzed the clues. "She's telling us something."

"She's sorry I'm feeling dead? What does that mean? I feel very much alive!" Dan shivered.

"She said, 'Go to your room!' Remember?" Emily said it in a perfect imitation of the bag lady. "Which room? The apartment or the room behind the piano?"

"If it's not in the apartment, whatever it is, then she means the other room. Aren't you afraid of what we may learn back there?"

"Are you?" she asked.

"Yes."

They walked along the deserted lake front for hours, holding hands, gathering their courage.

6

*D*r. David Blume spoke more quietly than usual as he entered the intensive care unit to see Emily and Dan. Drs. Levin and Goldstein joined him, having come to Chicago at his invitation from Mt. Sinai Trauma Center in New York. A month had gone by since the bombing, and the lack of change in the condition of his patients concerned him. He hoped they would be able to help him sort through the problems he was facing with Dan and Emily's case. The nurse on duty stood up and smiled professionally as she left the room. Dr. Blume whispered when he spoke.

"I'm not quite certain what more we can do for this couple. They're the only survivors of the bombing of Rita's Bar last month. Their vital signs are stable, and they seem to be in no pain. We haven't been able to wake them, yet in the last day or two their rapid eye movements indicate they could be dreaming much of the time. We keep a nurse on duty twenty-four hours a day to monitor changes in metabolism and neurological responses. I wish that comatose patients could show outward signs of what is going on inside. It's a miracle they suffered only superficial cuts and minor burns, given the power of the blast."

"I read that none of the others in the bar survived, and that most of the victims were literally vaporized. I also read that the woman owner of the bar was never found at all," Dr. Levin said.

"Yes, investigators surmise that because these two were at the back of the club, most of the impact was absorbed by the booths and the bar structure itself, which helped them survive the flying debris and the fireball of the bomb. As far as Ruthann Mahoney—also called Rita Dumas—is concerned, it is assumed she was at the point of impact when the car crashed into the bar and exploded," Dr. Blume said. "Even more strange, their other symptoms completely defy the norm. Their blood composition remains the same, with a very slow rate of reduction in content of the foreign substance we found in plentiful quantities. It seems they ingested some form of compound that apparently prevents degeneration. The fluids and nutrients being fed to them intravenously have kept them alive, yet the atrophy process common in motionless muscle tissue hasn't begun at all. Their reflexes remain normal, and the ample fat deposits they both carry have not diminished appreciably," Dr. Blume went on. "This is an intriguing puzzle. The fluid analyses show no foreign organisms, no viruses or bacteria unusual to the healthy human body. They're not sick, just sleeping a very deep sleep, induced, presumably, by the unidentified compound."

"I'd like to read the paperwork and review any full body scans you may have ordered," Dr. Levin said. "I'm curious how that substance shows up, and if there is any interpretation of the data I can contribute, I'll have to see the facts first."

The three doctors stood silently between the beds for a few moments and then left the room. Dr. Blume separated from the others and walked into the visitor's lounge, where Dan's two boys and Emily's two daughters were waiting for him.

"Hello, kids. I'm glad you're all here. I wish I had lots of good news for you today, but not much has changed."

"Oh, yes, it has!" Jennifer piped up. "The nice Family Services people decided not to send us back to our other parents. The Dr. Eastman and the social worker lady teamed up and made it so we get to stay in a foster home, till Mommy and Mr. Barton wake up."

"That's right! The judge is letting us stay together!" Ian couldn't disguise his happiness.

Dr. Blume looked at Miranda and Patrick. "Do you think this is best?"

"Oh, yes! At Harbor House, we've had plenty of time to talk it over and get to know each other better," she glanced at Patrick, who smiled back reassuringly, "and we both think the four of us can do best if we stay together," Miranda said. She stepped closer to Patrick, Jennifer in tow.

"We've lived together anyways since the bombing," Patrick added. "So, we've all decided that until Dad and Mrs. Sanders get better, we'd be happiest staying near them and with each other." He put his arm around Ian, who shrugged it off and punched him playfully in the side.

"Jennifer and I can still visit our dad if he ever wants us to, but he doesn't usually want us to." Miranda's sadness over the distance between her and her father surfaced in her expression, the broad smile drooped to a thin curve, as Jennifer stopped smiling altogether. "I miss my puppy. I miss Dreena."

"Besides, Ian and I hate being in my mother's house. It's not even hers and it's in a desert! Even when we used to just visit on a weekend, we gave her all kinds of grief," Patrick added, to cheer up Miranda and Jennifer. "She's such a bitch!" The kids all snickered at his choice of words.

"Well," said Dr. Blume, somewhat surprised by the boys' comments. "I think it's great you've all been getting to know each other at Harbor House. I'm sure Dr. Eastman will find a good foster family for you soon."

"No, he already did. We've been staying with the Wilkinsons for the last few days. I even have their phone number, " Miranda said as she produced a slip of paper from her purse. Dr. Blume copied it into his pocket-sized day timer notebook, and slipped it back into his front coat pocket.

"Thank you Miranda, for setting me straight on this. However, I want to tell you all, we've noticed your folks are dreaming. We have been monitoring their episodes with many different devices to see if their dream states and their bodily responses can be telling us something. They have a strange set of symptoms, so we need to treat their case very differently than we would a routine medical care situation," Dr. Blume explained as simply as possible.

"You won't hurt them, will you?" Jennifer asked.

"No, we're just going to watch them. They're ready for you to visit them, if you want to. You can stay for an hour or so, if you choose. Try to be sort of quiet, okay? We don't want to disturb the other patients on the floor who might need peace and quiet." Dr. Blume held the door for them as they walked single file into the room. Miranda stopped at the door. She looked up at the doctor with an expression that showed some embarrassment.

"Please, Doctor, do you how to find out about unusual medicinal herbs?" Miranda looked innocent and helpless enough to catch Dr. Blume off guard.

"Well, there might be information on the Web at the web sites of environmental groups and health food manufacturers. Why do you ask?"

"At school, there have been a lot of activities about Earth Day, and saving the rainforest, and things like that. Well, Patrick and I learned that there are lots of plants that produce medicines the tribes have been using for centuries to cure sickness and disease. We were talking about it the other night, and he says he thinks the substance your tests have found in our parents might come from the rainforest."

"What possible connection could there be to the rainforest?" Dr. Blume asked, as he glanced at his watch, stepped to the foot of Emily's bed and flipped back a page on the chart. Miranda followed him into the room, whispering to him.

"Well, I know this is going to sound far fetched, but my grandfather, Landon Pauer, my father's father, has been getting medicine from Brazil for a long time."

"From Brazil?" He studied her facial expressions, looking for a hint of a lie in her eyes. Finding none, he asked, letting go of Emily's chart in favor of Dan's. "How do you know that?"

"Well, when I was a lot younger, he was very absent-minded and he even wandered away from home. Well, then when he started taking these pills, his memory returned and he was just like himself again. Mom explained to me once that granddaddy got better thanks to medicine from the rainforest from some place in Brazil. He and Grandma have been going there on vacations twice a year ever since. I have even seen the pill bottles in their bathroom. I don't know why I feel like there is a chance that the stuff in my mother and Mr. Barton's blood is from Brazil, I just do. And, I'd like to find out more. That's all." Miranda was clearly nervous about asking for help from Dr. Blume. He decided to try to be more patient.

"You might try the local library. I grew up without the Web, and I did learn a few things by reading books. Some libraries even let you surf the Web from their computers." Dr. Blume smiled as Miranda perked up at his suggestions.

"Thanks. We'll try that," Miranda said.

Dr. Blume gave her a little pat on the back as she joined the others in the room. "Kids," he said, as he stepped back into the hallway and walked in the opposite direction from his destination, turning about face and walking the other way down the long hospital corridor, shaking his head and scratching behind his right ear, as if trying to make sense of Miranda's supposition.

Jennifer went immediately to the window and opened the curtains to let the late winter sun stream in. Emily and Dan slept, unmoving and pale as death, with no other sign of life than their slow, regular breathing.

"I hate—I hate all these tubes!" Jennifer stammered, her frustration no longer in check because of the doctor. "They're not sick. Why can't they just wake up and go home? I don't want them to die!" Jennifer said, even though her eight-year-old mind couldn't fully grasp the notion of death. She looked closely at her mother's face, and ran from the room.

"Dr. Blume! Dr. Blume! Come quick! My mother's face is turning pink!"

David Blume looked up from the chart he was holding at the nurse's station and responded to Jennifer's shouts with a hint of amusement. He caught her at a full run and held her at arm's length, trying not to squeeze her arms too tightly.

"Yes, honey, I know. I thought I saw a hint of color today, too. But maybe we're both just hoping too hard. Don't get too excited for now. Go on back and enjoy your visit."

"No! You don't care about them. They're just freaks to you!" Jennifer was shouting to make sure he paid attention. "That's my mommy!" She pointed down the hall toward the room. "That's Ian's daddy! Every change matters. You said it yourself! Every change matters." Her tears began to flow, not from sadness, but from anger. "I know there's a change. Come and look. Please, come and look!"

"All right, all right, but I'm sure it's really not much." Dr. Blume said softly, glancing up at the head nurse who was watching with surprise on her face. Embarrassed in front of the nurses and helpless in the face of the child's rage, he took her hand as started back toward the room. Her tears and her direct and honest anger were the kind that only small children can express, as he, a father of two small children himself, understood.

When Jennifer and Dr. Blume entered the room, the others gathered around the beds, watching with the curious eyes of kids afraid of being orphans. Dr. Blume looked very carefully at his patients, not wanting to see anything that wasn't truly there. He wanted to remain objective. Jennifer stared at his face, searching for any muscle twitch that might give away his thoughts.

"I'm sorry, Jennifer—"

"Look!" Jennifer pointed at Emily's eyes. The lids twitched, and the eyeballs were rolling under them, in quick, jerky movements.

"Look here!" Ian shouted. "Dad's eyes are doing it too!"

"They're both just dreaming," said Dr. Blume, turning his face away to hide the rapid blinking he had to use to force back the tears.

"Wait!" Miranda interrupted. "Look closely. They're smiling, just a little bit."

Everyone huddled closer to see the expressions on the sleeping faces. At the corners of their mouths, a seemingly involuntary twitching settled into a tiny smile.

"I think they're smiling at each other," Jennifer said as she started to cry with happiness.

"Yes, Jennifer, I agree, something is happening here that only they know," Dr. Blume said, thinking again about Miranda's questions.

"What does it mean, doctor?" Miranda asked.

"Only they know," Dr. Blume repeated. "I don't—not yet."

"Mommy—Mommy—" Jennifer whispered as she patted her mother's arm. "You can wake up and we can go to the zoo, or sit on the porch and read a story. Mommy—it's okay. I know you can wake up. Hurry up and wake up." Tears rolled down Jennifer's cheeks. Dr.

SACRED NIGHT

Blume's tears flowed with hers. A few minutes later, the dreams had passed, and Emily and Dan slept deeply without expression. Dr. Blume left the children alone and then called Mr. and Mrs. Wilkinson, the foster parents, asking them to come pick up the children sooner than previously planned. He want to protect them from witnessing anything more, for fear of misleading them, or giving hope where none was likely to exist.

7

*E*mily and Dan finally arrived at their apartment long after night-fall, the intervening hours spent walking up and down the lake front and talking about how to read the bag lady's words, and what they might need to do. They ascended the stairway to the apartment, still holding hands but without speaking. Opening the door, they entered and inspected the room, washed in the dull, harsh light of the cracked, overhead bulbs. Nothing had changed. Dan moved to the piano and slowly pulled it away from the door The non-lubricated wheels creaked under the stress of moving the piano's heavy weight and reflected in sound the depth of Dan's mood, his face expressionless yet tense in a way that could only come from desperation. Emily reached over to him, putting her hand on his arm to stop him.

"Look, we've already gone over this again and again before coming back here. If the bag lady is right, our children are in danger. We're going to have to face the answers to secrets we couldn't otherwise even guess. No one in our other life would ever believe this. Either we'll save our lives, or die trying. Maybe the room holds the answers."

"Maybe." The despondency of his tone, and the brevity of his comment irritated Emily. She needed his support, but she had said too much already. She stepped back, holding her breath and clasping her hands tightly.

"Here goes." Dan opened the door, and the sweet odor wafted over them, the soft music enveloped them. They descended the stairs with caution and moved into the room, unsure of their purpose and even less sure of their resolve.

"No one's here," Emily sighed as she sat down on the couch as she had before.

"Want something to drink?" Dan asked. "I'll bet they only stock the best stuff."

"Sure, but not too strong. Got a margarita on the rocks?"

"Sounds good."

Dan mixed and poured from the array of bottles below the counter. He sat down next to Emily as he handed her the tall, already sweating glass, clinking his to hers and sipping slowly.

"Dan, have you noticed? Since we got here, we haven't eaten anything. What do you make of that?"

"Now that you mention it, I haven't even felt hungry. The last thing was the coffee."

The alcohol was beginning to take effect, but much faster and much more intensely than either had ever experienced before. Emily flushed. Dan began to sweat.

"Cheers!" they said in unison, laughing as they clinked their glasses again.

"I feel giddy," Emily giggled, pushing her hair from where it had fallen across her face. She lowered her eyes as she sipped several more times from her Margarita.

Dan drank a couple of mouthfuls of the sticky sweet and sour liquid before putting down his glass on the table next to the couch.

"Yeah, this is really good booze. Come here, honey, I want to love you," he said in a mock impersonation of a red neck cowboy who had just propositioned a barmaid from one of the old rerun westerns on late night television.

He put his arms around her, kissing her neck. He felt the rush of passion rising through his body.

"No, I don't think this is such a good idea," Emily said as she pushed him away, lying back on the couch, and loosening her blouse, button by button in complete contradiction to her words.

"Neither do I," Dan said watching. He slid her blouse down her arms and let it drop to the floor. He kissed her, moving down her stomach to the intruding waistband of her jeans.

"I don't know you well enough to let you know me this way," Emily said, as he slowly opened the zipper, kissing her with each movement. She pulled him up and made him help her take off his shirt, deciding that removing the remaining garments might be unnecessary to their first attempt at showing affection.

"No, we really shouldn't take time for this now," Emily said, as he lay down next to her. They smiled. Their heartbeats rose as they took turns kissing. They caressed each other's legs and arms, like teenagers who had never been this close to a member of the opposite sex. They lay entwined for a time, until the rush of pleasure had passed. They relaxed into a shallow sleep.

Voices woke them. Emily opened her eyes to see the room filled with people who acted as if they were at a cocktail party.

"Dan! Wake up!" she whispered, shaking him and handing him his shirt. She put on her blouse as fast as she could.

"Oh, God!" he said in disbelief. "We're surrounded by a crowd of strangers. Oh, God. I hope we're still invisible."

The party continued around them without any reference to their presence. The women all wore pale blue sequins and chiffon.

The men were dressed in white tuxedos and white ties. No one's face was familiar, except for the older couple they had seen before. A string quartet played on the lawn. The open windows let the gentle lake breeze blow into the room. Emily and Dan watched the scene as if it were a theatrical production and they were the participating audience seated on the stage.

"You know, David," said one of the men to another, "I think the stock market is going to come back strong in spite of the government's intervention. Thank God for Republicans when the Democrats have the presidency. To cure this problem, we have to determine the cause of the market's wild fluctuations. Maybe taking stronger measures against the Japanese and the Germans can balance the effects of this last event."

"I looked at the charts in the Journal this morning," the man called David said, "and read some of the commentaries coming out of Washington. It doesn't look good. I think our time is running out. It won't be easy to discover whatever is controlling these events. I'd suggest introducing antidotes to the economic poisons we've seen before. Maybe one of them will work on this mess."

"Inflation is rising," another partygoer, this time a woman, said. "Spikes and deep drops in the markets indicate the decay of financial stability. The effects of deficit spending are impossible to interpret. But, I think the international markets are in danger of collapse at any moment."

Emily and Dan listened to the conversation without understanding why the partygoers seemed to circle around them. Emily opened her eyes wide with mischief, as she reached out to touch the man named David, and making a mock surprised expression for Dan's benefit when this person, David, moved away from her. Others returned in new clusters, drifting toward and away from Dan and Emily as they tried without success to touch them. The older couple and David moved into the group directly in front of them. The older man spoke first.

"Now, David, we didn't invite you here to talk politics and economic doom. Emily, why don't you take over here while I go see to the barbecue." Emily and Dan glanced at each other.

"All right, Dan." Speaking in a deliberately coquettish tone, the older woman turned toward her guest. "David? We're here to have a good time and enjoy the lovely summer weather. Come outside with me. We'll play some croquet, or another silly game—like golf on the putting green. No more serious talk."

The older Emily took this David by the arm and led him away. The others dispersed, leaving the young Emily and Dan alone in the room.

"I think they're us," Emily whispered.

"No, really?" Dan's sarcasm underlined the obvious. "This is getting weird. Let's go back to the apartment and talk. Did you hear what they were talking about?"

"Yes, politics and the stock market."

"Not really. What they were saying didn't make any sense financially or politically."

"What were they talking about then?" Emily stared at Dan, searching his face for an answer to her question.

"I don't know, but I'm beginning to think we may have some power to influence what's happening to us. Did you see how they avoided our hands as we tried to touch them?"

"They couldn't even see us, how could they have been avoiding us?"

"Maybe they can see us. Maybe we just think they can't, the same way we thought the bag lady was crazy."

"Yeah, crazy like a genius. She said we had go to our room to find the children. We didn't find them here."

"No, but maybe this isn't the room she meant."

"The apartment?"

"Perhaps."

Dissatisfied and bewildered, Dan led Emily up the stairs, leaving the room, the partygoers and the start of their romance behind. They hadn't even finished their drinks.

8

*A*t two-thirty in the morning, Dr. Blume answered his cellular phone on the first ring. "Hello, this is David Blume."

"Dr. Blume, come to the hospital right away. It's Emily Sanders and Dan Barton. They're—"

Dr. Blume dropped the receiver onto the phone's charger before the nurse could explain. Nothing could be good about this call. He saw no need to wait for an explanation. Speeding on the deserted expressway and silent Chicago streets made getting to the hospital a little easier. Most considered Rush Presbyterian St. Luke Hospital to be the best trauma center and intensive care unit in Chicago, but harder to get to from Dr. Blume's Lake Forest home. David ran into the emergency room and made the trip upward in the elevator in record time.

"Doctor, the seizure started with those smiles. Both their faces then flushed and they began to perspire," the attending nurse said nearly gasping for breath she spoke so quickly.

"His heart rate rose faster than hers, but she showed more rapid neural stimulation. They appeared to be dreaming. The electronic monitors indicated heightened chemical releases of enzymes and hormones in both their brains. Their arousal was graphic, Mr. Barton pulled out his catheters. And Mrs. Sanders tugged at the neckline of her gown."

"It was good you called, Marianne," said Dr. Blume.

"But when I did, in the few seconds I was gone and before the intern entered the room, they pushed their sheets onto the floor, grasping hands across the space between their beds. The railings were down. I'm sorry." Marianne began to cry.

"We picked up the mess from the intravenous bottle that Ms. Sanders knocked over reaching for Mr. Barton. Then I replaced the catheters and the feeding tubes," Dr. Martins explained with strain in her voice. She was a first year intern with only a few months experience on the intensive care unit.

"You both did fine. I'm sure it was frightening."

"Yes, it was pretty tense there for a few minutes."

"I think this means they are past some kind of threshold of paralysis from the compound they ingested. Check the amount of it in their blood." Dr. Blume adjusted the tethers holding their hands and feet to be sure they were not too tight.

"I think they'll be all right for now. Any more findings from the lab today?"

"Yes and no," Dr. Martins said. "I read the reports a little while ago. The substance is not a man-made pharmaceutical. It is probably botanic in origin, but they have not completely ruled out animal origins. The computers have analyzed the samples, and besides the normal blood components and the fact that the caffeine from the coffee has now dissipated, there is nothing more than a hint of light sensitive cells containing something similar to chlorophyll, yet not chlorophyll.

"I want to talk with Detective Cameron. Get him on the phone. There is something I want to run past him." Dr. Blume sat thinking for the few minutes as he waited for the intern to get hold of Detective Cameron. His thoughts turned to Miranda's question about finding herbal medicines and her information about her grandfather's medications.

What if there is something to Miranda's idea about ancient herbal medicines unknown to modern science. Could something like that be the source of the compound that holds Emily and Dan in suspended animation? What if there is one that limits or even reverses degeneration to the extent that injury is minor, or that aging is slowed. What if this substance when taken in overdose can produce a prolonged, coma-like sleep or even kill?

"Dr. Blume?" The intern interrupted David's stream of consciousness. "Detective Cameron wasn't available. I left a voice message to have him call you as soon as he got in."

"Not available at three-thirty in the morning? What's he up to, I wonder?"

PART TWO

9

*A*hi could hear the warrior boatmen coming. The skiffs glided silently on the now glassy smooth high water of the Amazon, but the chant was unmistakable.

"Algala—Anmala—Algala—Anmala."

The male voices rumbled the words in a mantra-like fashion. The calming effect of the sound helped Ahi focus on other sounds emanating from his surroundings. All day long he had been drifting in and out of sleep, dreaming complete stories of his otherlife in the otherworld. The tales of wisdom he would tell to the young would come from these dreams. Each was vivid, and more real to him than the life he once lived. He could feel that he was younger, freer to move without pain. The aching in his joints was nonexistent, where in the days before his sacred night, aching had been a constant irritation.

Knowing he was not to sit or stand on the high ground where the river goddess had left him, Ahi tried to turn his head to gain a view of the approaching boats. He was so weak from the dive that even the slightest movement took much effort. The muscles in his neck seemed disconnected. If his head had not already been rotated slightly to one side, he could not have seen the boats at all. Through the narrow slit between his eyelids he could make out that one of the boats was decorated in flowers, white and purple orchids, and green palm fronds, in the same manner as the dais had been on his coronation day. He remembered his purpose, to become the *Elder of Elders,* and how he was to wait for the ceremony to be held that night in the inner forest, before speaking. It had seemed strange to him that none of the chiefs before him could talk until the first sip of the algala. He wondered at the reasoning, since he felt an overpowering urge to shout to the coming boats. He tried to open his mouth to signal to them that he was there, alive and well. He strained to open his mouth. No sound came from him. He tried to move his arm to wave. He could make no movement. He watched. He let his heart fill with hope instead of the fear of being lost and forgotten that struggled to overtake him.

"Algala—Anmala—Algala—Anmala."

The voices became distinct. He could hear each man separately from the others. He let his hearing scan the voices, until he came to the voice of his own son. He remembered how terrified he had been when he, as a young man, had gone to find his own father. Ahi thought his son's voice betrayed the same doubt, the same fear that his father had not been blessed by the river goddess, that he was going to find his father dead, not a survivor of the flood.

The voices drew closer. The skiffs beached with a whisper in the soft earth of the hillock. The warriors' feet stirred the mud as they leapt from the boats to run up the hill in search of their chief. Ahi was smiling inwardly as he closed his eyes against the glare of the setting sun.

The sleep of the gods took him just as his son's hand touched his. Amahi let his tears flow freely as he looked into his father's face for a sign of life. He made certain Ahi's skin was not blue, and he could see the gentle abdominal rise and fall of his breathing. Amahi looked up at the others and smiled.

The chant grew louder and faster as the warriors lifted Ahi onto the ceremonial cot and carried him carefully back to the boats. They laid him in the center of the flowers on the ceremonial skiff, with a reverence reserved for those of great honor. The lead boat turned and the others followed. Vultures, who had been waiting high in the nearby trees, lowered their heads as they watched their prey being taken from them. A radiant sunset burst over the trees, silhouetting the entire horizon. Stillness silenced the forest creatures. Not even the ceremonial boats bothered the looking-glass surface of the Amazon. Floating in ghostly unison with the fog, the breath of night bore the baritone chant over the water, only to disappear in the undergrowth along the banks of the river.

10

It is five-forty five P. M., Wednesday, June twelfth. Please wait for your messages.

William Pauer noted the current time and date on the message pad as he punched the play button. Two hang-ups. Two beeps.

"Hi, Daddy. It's me, Jennifer. I just wanted to say hi to Dreena. I hope you're happy and that she is too. I love you. Bye."

He bit his lip to manage his irritation at missing his youngest daughter's call. The telephone was his only contact with Miranda and Jennifer, especially now since they lived in a foster home. Where does the time go? They've been there for a couple of months already. Beep. A muffled voice broke into his thoughts.

"They're on their way. You'd better have the rest of the money by midnight. Meet us as planned. Alone. Mess up again, and you'll pay a bitter price."

A slight foreign accent, a cultured vocal inflection spoke to him. William had not heard this voice before, though the message was consistent with the instructions he had received the last time. Troubled, he listened to the fourth message. His mother's voice sounded frantic.

SACRED NIGHT

"*William, darling, your father's gone again. I thought the episode last month might have caused those people at the adult care center to keep closer watch on him. He's been gone all day already—I didn't want to worry you—but after searching all over for him, contacting bus companies, cab companies and car rental agencies, the police had a call from a cab driver who remembered taking an old man to the airport early this afternoon. I checked on it, and I'm sure it's your father. He still remembers his name and is lucid often enough to seem functionally normal to other people. The bank called to say he's taken a substantial sum of money, and the cabby remembered driving him all over town, to buy luggage, clothes, and airplane tickets — first to Chicago, and then to Brazil. We know he got to Chicago several hours ago, and that his flight to Belém, Brazil leaves at eight thirty tomorrow morning. I want you to find him before the police do. I'll call you later. Oh, yes, he left no note.*"
The machine clicked off.

"Fucking old bastard! I wish he'd just be done with it."

Landon Pauer was a tight-fisted millionaire whose fifteen-year mental decline had been mostly gradual. He could function for fairly long periods of time as if he were non-afflicted. Even when detached from reality, he could go on about his business without betraying himself to anyone, except his family. Still, he was becoming a danger. Once he turned the oven to broil, then left the house. Another time he set a fire in the garbage can in the garage, thinking it was a grill. The garage was seriously scorched before anyone knew what he was up to. Frequently, he would take the car and drive till it ran out of gas, usually ending up in Ohio or Indiana, where he would call his wife, Lorraine, to come rescue him.

Anyone who saw Landon Pauer in the throes of a seizure was frightened by the ferocity this otherwise gentle man could unleash. His physical prowess had begun its last descent into that low plain of human agony called old age. The once physically vigorous sixty-five-year-old gentleman, handsome with his snow white hair and warmly engaging smile had been one of the most successful insurance brokers in Chicago, until the seizures robbed him of his dignity. Lorraine convinced him to retire to the horse country near Lexington, Kentucky. Fearing for her own safety, she had been forced to enroll him in an adult day care center as his seizures became more violent and vicious.

He described his seizures as being in a fog, wandering, where people's faces appeared and disappeared unexpectedly. The faces were frightening, distorted in evil smiles and contorted grimaces. Landon would lash out with fists, throwing objects at hand, grabbing nurses and orderlies by their throats, using some inhuman strength to choke them. Only the biggest and strongest male nurse could subdue Landon during a seizure. No one had been injured, but lately several caregivers completely refused to work on his floor in the care center.

This time there had been no call to Lorraine begging for rescue. There had been no note to alleviate her fears. William, in spite of knowing of their secret plans for him to fly to Chicago, was angry at not hearing from his father upon his arrival, and that his mother had tracked him not only to Chicago, but had found out he was heading for Brazil.

Thinking that perhaps he had registered at some hotel near O'Hare instead of follow the plan to call from the airport, William walked into the kitchen to find a phone book. He rummaged through the cookbooks in the closet bookshelf, finding one slightly out of date Yellow Pages.

"Autos—electricians—florists—hotels. Hotels." He flipped the pages of the phonebook looking for the hotels near the airport. William called several, but none had registered a man named Landon Pauer. He put the phone book back into the bookcase with the cookbooks and sat immobile at the kitchen table. The silence in the house closed around him.

"Where is Dreena? She couldn't have been sleeping all this time," he spoke aloud to break the quiet. He flicked on the light switch to the right of the door as he started down the stairs leading to the basement. Silence greeted him. At the bottom of the stairs, he could see Dreena's cage, the door open, with the dog lying half in, half out of the opening. Her tongue protruded grotesquely from her gaping muzzle, already black from strangling. Her heart lay in the center of the pool of blood beginning to dry at the edge. William ran upstairs, two steps at a time to the small powder room just off the kitchen. He missed the toilet on the first heave, finishing the rest on target. He sat back from the mess on the floor, crying and wiping his face with a hand towel.

"They did this." He was still shaking as he said, " How can I ever tell the girls?"

The phone rang.

"Hello?" William tried to control his voice.

"Hello, Son! How's business going?"

"Dad? Where are you? You were supposed to come here straight from the airport."

"Oh, I'm still at the airport. Got in a few hours ago. Called your machine. No one home, no need to come by. But now you're there, I'll pay my dinner and cocktail tab and catch a taxi to your door. Okay?"

"Sure, Dad, sure. Come on over. Is Mother with you?" William said, checking on his father's recollection of their plans.

"No, no. I left her home to take care of the garden, just as we planned. You said I'd come see you. Okay, then? I'll be there in forty-five minutes or so." Landon Pauer hung up. William quickly called his mother.

"Hello?" Lorraine answered on the second ring.

"Hello, Mother. He's here. He's safe. Don't worry and call off the search I'm sure you have pressured the police to continue."

"All right, dear. I'm glad he's with you. Send him home soon, won't you?"

"Sure, Mother. I'll keep him a few days and then send him back to you. Bye now."

He hung up abruptly, not wanting to talk with her. William was irritated by the inconvenience his father had already caused by letting his mother get involved. He fumbled with the briefcase filled with money. His nerves stretched thinner by the moment. He had to get rid of the dog's carcass, but it was still daylight. He had to keep tonight's activities secret, even from his father. Somehow, he would manage it all. He'd do anything to please his father, especially now. It was a small price to pay for his own future sanity.

In retirement, Landon and Lorraine had traveled on every inhabited continent. But over all, they spent most of the travel time in Brazil, where Lorraine's family had laid down two generations of religious and medical history as missionaries. Their home was filled with ancient artifacts and museum quality art treasures from all over the world. On one visit to a remote village, they learned of the possibility that tribal medicine men used an ages old concoction from the muck at the bottom of the Amazon River that ensures long life and could prevent the degeneration of the mind and body.

From then on, Landon's fascination with the jungle dwelling tribes of the Amazon River in Brazil developed into an obsession with discovering a substance that would prevent the excruciating indignity of his inevitable demise as a victim of Alzheimer's. Diagnosed at the age of fifty, he spared no expense, refused no opportunity to find his way to the inner reaches of the Brazilian jungles in search of his salvation. Lorraine knew her husband's supply line to the jungle concoctions was precarious. In recent years, younger men did most of the traveling, and then charged her husband ten times the cost of the compound and all it took to smuggle it out. They treated him rudely and threatened his safety. Landon didn't care. He needed the potions to keep himself as lucid as possible for as long as possible. Nothing else mattered to Landon.

Lorraine and William did care. They cared more than they should and not about Landon. Lorraine saw his decline and felt deeply threatened by the inevitability of being widowed too soon for her tastes. William felt sure his mind would also precede his body, when the time came for him to follow in his father's genetic footsteps. He feared becoming nothing more than a decrepit bag of bones waiting to die. Senile dementia, Alzheimer's disease, whatever the diagnosis, the result is the same. William wanted to avoid it himself. To help his father meant ultimately helping himself. The father's strengths translated into the son's weaknesses, in this moment just as they had all of William's life.

Landon Pauer left the terminal and hailed a taxi, more at ease thinking he had come this far undiscovered. No one suspected what he and William were up to. That was all he needed to know. The ride to William's house was short. William opened the front door and went to the taxi to help Landon bring his things into the house.

"I'm glad you had dinner at the airport," he said slamming the door with a more than generous push. "I haven't got much in the fridge. Besides, you'll need to rest up for your flight tomorrow," William took control of the circumstances immediately, hoping to keep Landon in the house and out of the way.

"Are you upset about something, Son?"

'No, just want to make sure you're comfortable before we hit the sack," he lied with conviction.

"Well, now that you mention it, I am feeling a little tuckered out from the flight. I had to drive all over Lexington in a cab to get the things I need for the trip. Lorraine would have known I was up to something if I had taken my things from the house. I forgot my compound, though. Do you have any here?"

"No, we sent it to you last month when your supply ran short, remember?"

"No, but, if you don't have any, you don't have any, and that is that. I'll be all right till I get to Belém tomorrow. It'll only be a few hours till I have the new supply. Not to worry, Son, not to worry." Landon was being uncharacteristically cooperative, and pleasant about it to boot, which added pressure to William's already aggravated and jangled nerves. He hoped this wasn't just the calm before another of Landon's storms.

The two men sat in the living room, reviewing their plans, checking and rechecking the timetable and Landon's flight schedule, mostly because Landon couldn't keep it straight two times in a row. William grew impatient as his deadline from the dealers drew near.

"Dad, I have some business to attend to, and it just might be the best thing for you to go to bed a little early. Catch up on some sleep. I'll wake you in the morning in plenty of time to get to the airport. What do you say?'

"I'm so revved up, I wonder if I can sleep. You're right. I should at least get some rest. Good night. I'll see you tomorrow." With no further discussion, Landon stood up and went upstairs to the guest room.

William sat in the living room until he heard his father get into bed. The ten minutes' wait meant ten minutes of wasted time, and made him even more agitated. He finally felt he could slip out to the garage to get a shovel. He made his way through the darkness to the back corner of the garden. Even in the soft, well-worked soil behind the tallest flowers, it took him more time than he had wanted to spend to dig a hole deep enough to bury the dog. He left the shovel and went back into the house, stopping in the kitchen to get a large garbage bag.

SACRED NIGHT

He went down to the basement, his nerves already hardened against the carnage he knew he'd see there again. He looked for a dry place on the fur to pick up the dog while getting as little blood on his hands as he could manage. He placed the stiffening body in the garbage bag, tying the flaps tightly as he pushed out as much air as he could around the dog's form, the way he did to lock in the freshness of food in a zip-lock bag. Then he went into the laundry room, took the mop, wetted it with hot water and returned to clean the floor. William scrubbed hardest at the drying edge of the pool of blood. Leaving no residue meant leaving no sign of the dog's death. His girls would never suspect that Dreena had been a victim of their father's ineptitude, killed in his own basement as a warning to him to follow orders exactly, or someone close to him would be next. He had no doubt that that someone would not be canine. He could explain to the girls that she had run away, perhaps to look for them. He groaned involuntarily as he lifted the bag, surprised at the weight of it. He could even place an ad in the paper advertising for a lost dog, to make sure they believed his excuse. He lugged the carcass to the garden, dropping it roughly into the hole. He had to keep Dreena alive in Miranda and Jennifer's mind, especially in Jennifer's mind. She was so young and vulnerable, and had been through so much loss as a child. He felt he should make at least some effort to protect her from this.

Time was short. He had to get to the boat launch in Wilmette Harbor with the money for the dealers. He threw dirt into the hole, filling it just to the level of the garden, not wanting to leave a mound. He rushed to shovel the last bit of earth over the garden to disperse it. He returned the shovel to the garage and ran back into the house to get the package from its hiding place in the basement. Rushing back up the stairs, he left the basement door ajar and ran to the car. He backed out and drove toward the harbor.

There were no other cars on the road—no stars—no wind. Isolation invaded William's awareness with every turn in the road. Foreboding thoughts teased apart his mind the way a comb teases apart snarled and ratted hair. William hated his father's schemes. All his life he'd been afraid to go against his father's demands. Now he was heading into the most dangerous and precarious moments of the last ten years, and only he knew to what extent the dealers would go. The car phone jolted him from the silence. He hesitated as he reached for the receiver, then slowly put the phone to his ear.

"If we don't get our money tonight, then the next name on our list will be sacrificed. You have fifteen minutes." The phone went dead.

It had been up to him to keep the hush money flowing to his underworld connections. The secret drain on his father's wealth was becoming serious. Only William knew Landon's millions were dwindling away with every extorted payment. He had no choice in the matter, and it tore at him. If his father ever knew to what extent the drug runners had infiltrated the business, he would hate William forever. With every secret payment, with every negotiated increase, with every 'elimination' of unwilling participants in the trade, he felt another shred of his integrity fall away.

He parked the car at the end of the empty lot and walked to the boat launch nearest the end of the pier, frequently glancing around to be certain no one was watching. As planned, he picked up the battered suitcase at the end of the short walk leading from the boathouse to the pier. Then he dropped his package into the nearest waste bin containing loose papers to better camouflage the simple newspaper wrapping on the package. He didn't want some passer by or rummaging homeless person to find it before the dealers did.

The distortion of the overhead lamp's dull illumination increased William's uneasiness. He imagined faceless assassins, hiding behind the nearest pylon, haunting his every step. He couldn't follow through with the plans he had made with the dealers, but he was still unsure at what point he would deviate from the long imposed routine. Ever since he had been forced to step into Landon's role in building the black market network for the compound, he had felt something beginning to rot at his own inner core. The players in the network, the ones who stood to lose the most if he didn't allow them more control, were ruthless. He could no longer ignore the stench of his own immorality, as he looked the other way, never acknowledging the kinds of control these unscrupulous thugs exercised against even their own members. Dreena was his warning. He knew that to be undeniable. Satisfied he had done as he was told, William quickly made his way back to the car.

He drove to the end of the parking lot, turned right onto Sheridan Road to head north along the lake. Turns and twists in the road kept him alert, though a heavy fatigue was settling on his mind like a cloud. The intensity of constant pressure had worn him down. Lines in his forehead deepened as he squinted into the rolling lake fog rising like a ghost from the nearby lakefront. He lowered his headlight beams, until he reached Clavey Road where he turned them off completely. The fog momentarily swallowed his fears and cloaked his guilt as he crept along the side streets like a blind man in a new place.

As Detective Cameron drove North along the Edens Expressway, the police radio squawked in the relative silence of his unmarked squad car, "Domestic disturbance, suspicious goings on in the neighborhood near Ravinia Park. Someone digging in the back yard. A noisy dog gone silent. It's the home of William Pauer. The neighbor who called does not want to be identified, but thinks the activity was strange. Like someone was burying a body."

He pulled the squad to the side of the road.

"Got an address, honey?" he said to Carla Gibbons, the late-night dispatcher on the graveyard shift, "I can take this one, I'm in the area anyway."

"Oh, you can, can you? I thought you were going home—tired and worn out, I think you said." He could hear Carla cracking her gum as she spoke, and he pictured her athletically fit silhouette relaxing against the chair back in the dispatch room as she rummaged through the papers and scattered pencils he knew she had strewn across the desk.

"I've got my second—no—twentieth wind. So, common honey, let me entertain myself another couple of hours. I'll hit the hay at dawn."

"Okay, Cameron, you old codger. You go to Clavey, head east to Green Bay Road. Turn right, east again, on Roger Williams and go to the first house on right of the last residential block before you get to Sheridan. You be careful you old goat."

He noted down the directions on the computer the department had recently given to him to try to push him into the twenty-first century technology. "Sure, like I can't take care of myself," he said, as he punched in the name William Pauer to see what popped up on the screen. "Huh. This guy is a deadbeat dad. Doesn't pay his child support. DCFS is on him like rot on garbage. Rich S.O.B. Sure lives in a posh neck of the woods. Huh. His ex-wife is Emily Sanders. Now if that doesn't take the cake." He read the rest of the computerized information and pulled the squad onto the nearly deserted highway, speeding north to the Clavey Road exit, and turned off the police radio to give himself the quiet to think.

A retired, twenty-five-year veteran undercover cop in Chicago, he currently sold his services as a private detective to the wealthy North Shore suburbs. Before his years in police work, and since his tour of duty in Vietnam, Detective Cameron had been a bomb expert. Renowned as the best in bomb disarmament in the entire Midwest region, he retired after losing two fingers and taking shrapnel to his chest from a small package. The risks had begun to go beyond the rewards in active duty. As a well-paid consultant, a safety factor he liked both for his financial stability and his personal longevity, Detective Cameron routinely turned down many more jobs than he took. His friends on the Chicago bomb squad had contracted him to oversee the investigation of the bombing of Rita's Bar, partly to keep local control of the investigation, and mostly to keep him busy. As he drove eastward toward the lake, he decided he liked the serendipity of these late night adventures. He felt useful, just as he had felt as a younger cop ready to do a good turn for society.

The silence of this exclusive bedroom community remained undisturbed by his arrival at the home of William Pauer. Detective Cameron's mood wasn't particularly friendly. He bordered on exhaustion from days of sleep deprivation, and the late evening spicy Mexican dinner that hadn't been sitting right for hours was still burning in his gut in spite of extra doses of antacids. He doused his headlights as he pulled up in front of the house.

William Pauer, hearing a car in front of this house, looked through the peephole to see an obviously unmarked squad car. Adrenalin flushed through his body as he bolted into action. He opened the front door and turned on the porch light, thinking he might avoid any problems with the police by seeming extremely helpful and forthcoming. He didn't know what could possibly have brought a cop to his door at this hour, but he decided ignorance was his ally for the time being at least. Walking with difficulty up the front steps, Detective Cameron began immediately to explain why he was there, not allowing William a moment to speak.

"Good evening—or good morning, I'm Detective Cameron," he said, showing his badge and giving a little nod, as making it clear that he was a legitimate cop. "Pardon me for coming at this awful hour. I haven't the slightest idea why anyone would call the cops on a neighbor at this hour of the night. Robberies by kids burglarizing homes for loot to sell for drug money are up in this neighborhood. So, I guess the folks next door just thought it was strange to see someone digging in the garden so late at night."

William acted surprised, but still didn't speak.

"I'll need to ask you a few quick questions—for the report, you know. May I come in?" Detective Cameron took one step toward the door.

William opened the door to its fullest extent, stepped back and gestured with a wide sweep of the hand for Detective Cameron to enter. As they moved into the living room he glanced toward the stairs, half expecting to see his father coming down to see what was going on. Relieved to see no one, he turned toward Detective Cameron and again with a broad hand gesture indicated the couch. "Please have a seat Detective," William said, his voice cracking. "Detective Cameron, was it?"

"Yes. I suppose you should tell me where you were earlier this evening?" Detective Cameron asked, not sitting down.

"I've been busy with my senile father all evening. He, uh, arrived here behind schedule, and actually, I had quite a little scare, thinking he had wandered away or some such, as he is wont to do on occasion. After a bit of hasty searching he did turn up, unharmed and happy to be here. Luckily, all's well that ends well, and we returned home a little while ago. I settled him in bed and came downstairs for a nightcap. And then, Detective, you rang the doorbell." William's fabricated alibi was close enough to the truth, so that even if his father did come up with some wild variation, his would be the more believable to any rational listener. He considered that there actually were times when his father's senility came in handy.

"Do you have a dog?"

"No. Why would you ask?" The unflinching look of compliance he had carefully molded to his face betrayed nothing of his lie.

"Your neighbor said you have a big dog that barks all the time, but for some reason tonight, it hasn't made a sound. He also said that he saw you, or someone who looks like you, digging a deep hole in the garden. Can you explain that?"

"No, sir, I can't. As I told you, I was out with my father this evening. He may have seen me take out the garbage, and actually, yes, I did step into the garden to pick up a bag of yard waste, weeds and the like, that I had left there. Again, to collect the garbage for the pickup tomorrow," he said, pleased with himself for keeping the lie close enough to the truth so that no one can actually refute it.

"Do you know any of the victims of the bombing of Rita's Bar last month?" Detective Cameron figured it was worth a shot out of the blue to test his hunches.

"No, I don't even know of a place called Rita's Bar." This time his face began to show the strain of keeping his expression bland and unreadable.

"Isn't your ex-wife named Emily Sanders?"

"Yes, she goes by her second ex-husband's name. How did you know that?"

"You knew she was a singer at Rita's Bar, didn't you?"

"No, I don't keep track of her. I stopped caring about her and what she does years ago. I only contact her when I have to, usually once or twice a month to make arrangements spend time with my daughters, whom I never get to see enough. How she got custody, I'll never understand." His reserve was crumbling, and as the pearls of perspiration beaded his hairline, he felt a clammy sweat rise on his palms and nausea forming in his stomach. He took a couple of slow deep breaths, hoping to control his nerves before they took complete control of him.

Detective Cameron mentally registered William's discomfort with the observation that he harbored a condescending dislike for his ex-wife and chose to tell an obvious lie about his relationship with his children, Miranda and Jennifer Pauer.

"I'm curious about that comment. The Department of Children and Family Services has it on record that you don't keep up with your child support." Detective Cameron waited for a rebuttal. Getting none he continued, "And, they notified you about your ex-wife's predicament almost immediately after the bombing. You indicated you didn't have the time or space for your children here—in this nice, big house," he said with sarcasm as he gazed around the living room, "You did not contest the decision when the court sent your daughters to live in a foster home rather than with you."

"Well, that doesn't mean I don't miss them. Recently, my lifestyle has not been particularly conducive to the secure and steady upbringing children need, but more than that, the courts nearly always place the children with the mother, whether that's all for the best or not," he said, trying hard to twist the direction of the conversation away from his responsibility not taken and push it onto Emily and the courts, to deflect it from the guilt he felt joining with the nausea on the assault of his composure. "As for the child support thing, I have done my duty, and she's trying to squeeze me for more. So I stopped paying while the issue gets settled in court. That's not unusual, is it?"

"Only if the amount of money you pay reflects the amount of love and concern you have for your children."

"Now listen here—"

Detective Cameron cut him off. "You know that your ex-wife and a man named Dan Barton were the only two survivors of that terrorist-style car bombing, don't you?"

"Uh, well, okay, yes I do," William stammered, his face now glistening with sweat and his hands beginning to shake. Detective Cameron pushed him further.

"Did you know this Barton fellow?"

"No, I didn't. What does this have to do with the neighbors? I am beginning to think you have come here under pretense, Detective." He felt the upper hand turning his way in the conversation. "My ex-wife and her circumstances are no business of mine."

"No suspects have even been named as yet, but you are not to leave the state for any reason without notifying me. Any attempt to disobey this order will result in your immediate arrest. The consequences can be quite severe, and as her ex-husband you should know you are high on the list of suspects." The bluff was not entirely unfounded.

"Threats will get you nowhere, Detective. I have no reason to harm my ex-wife, no matter how much I detest her."

"And, we will need to search your house," Detective Cameron said casually, knowing he was getting to William, "especially in the light of your neighbor's assertions that suspicious events occurred here tonight. I trust you will allow such a search."

"Search my house? Looking for a dog I don't have? Limit my freedoms because my ex-wife is mixed up in something I know nothing about? I think I'd better not say anything more till I can meet with my attorney."

"Does this travel limitation extend to me, sir?" asked Landon, who had come down the stairs like a voyeur wanting to go unnoticed until he spoke. "I have a flight to catch in the morning. I'm going for a short vacation in Brazil."

William startled at the sound of his father's voice, realizing the old man's intrusion provided him the only convenient ploy he could use to end the conversation abruptly. Turning toward Detective Cameron with a renewed sense of composure, he said in a firm voice and with a plastered on smile that masked any trace of insecurity, "Detective, this is my father, Landon Pauer, whom I need to return to his home as soon as possible, owing to the confused mental condition he suffers. My mother is waiting for him to come back tomorrow. His flight is for Lexington, Kentucky, not Brazil." William stared hard at his father hoping the old man would catch the ruse and play along with him.

Detective Cameron sensed the disingenuous tone in William's voice and pushed again, upping the stakes to see if they would comply, or not.

"As for you, Mr. Pauer, you will be allowed to return to Kentucky, but the police will handle your arrangements. Going to Brazil is out of the question for the time being. You would be well advised to cancel your flight and try to get your money back."

"No one talks to me that way! No one tells Landon Pauer where he can go, and I warn you—"

Detective Cameron kept his tone cool and professional, seeing through both men's the deceit as if looking through the bubbled and wavy glass in an ancient windowpane.

"I'm sorry, Mr. Pauer. You have no choice in this matter. If you choose to disregard my orders, you will be arrested and restrained. You don't really want that, do you?"

Landon Pauer and Detective Cameron locked gazes in a visual test of wills.

"I'll call my wife and have her come for me, as I have before. Is that agreeable?" Landon conceded, looking to the side, disappointed in himself for giving in.

"Agreeable, yes. But, I want to talk with her myself, make sure she's on the up and up, you know," Detective Cameron said to make Landon Pauer feel he had no way out. William took Detective Cameron by the arm, leading him into the kitchen and out of earshot of his father.

"Listen, my father is a mentally unstable old man. What can he really do, or where could he go that would jeopardize your investigation of this bombing?"

"I'm not so sure he's as unstable as you would have me believe. I'm going back to the station to fill out my report and to obtain a warrant to search the premises. I will call you in about an hour with the arrangements for Mr. Pauer's return to Kentucky. You both will be expected to appear at the local police station first thing in the morning. Just to be a nice guy, I'll let you sleep an hour or two and meet you there at six-thirty. Or, you can come with me now."

"My father needs his rest. I promise we'll be there by six-thirty."

Detective Cameron noted the obvious discomfort of both men. He understood that not taking them in immediately might create a flight risk, but that possibility did not over-ride his strong suspicion that the trip to Brazil might somehow be connected to his investigation. He stepped toward the door.

"I think you both can appreciate that your activities and whereabouts are under scrutiny, and if you do anything unusual to heighten the suspicions that already surround you and this case, you will have more trouble on your plate than you could possibly imagine. Do yourselves a favor, and stay home." He watched their faces for any change of expression that would betray their true intent.

"Yes, sir. We'll certainly do as you say." William responded with the obeisance of a compliant child, who wanted to undo the wrong of his impertinent behavior. Nodding his head and regarding his father's glazed look, William was inwardly fraught with concern. He intended to garner Landon's compliance, but saw that his father had gone to that other place his mind took him as a seizure approached. "Come on, Dad, let's get some rest." He took Landon by the arm and closed door on Detective Cameron.

As he left the house, Detective Cameron took a short walk around the backyard. The garden had been strewn with dirt, possibly from the uprooting of weeds, as William had suggested. But even in the half-light of the coming dawn, it was clear someone had been digging there. The mound of loose dirt in the bare spot toward the back of the garden lay naked in the overgrown flowers and ground-covers. The side door to the garage was slightly open and three, smeared, muddy footprints crossed the little walk leading back to the house from the garage. Still wet prints stepped onto the lawn where smudges of moist soil still clung to the dewy grass. Watching for the lights go out in the Pauer house, Detective Cameron returned to his car, jotted down a few notes and then drove toward the city, hoping his interference would worry William and Landon for at least the next few hours.

Inside the darkened house, William lay awake staring out the bedroom window. The phone rang. Annoyed, he picked up his bedside phone on the fourth ring. The muffled voice sounded like the one on the answering machine.

"Finally, you left the money just as we told you to. Good boy. Now, make sure your father gets out of the country tomorrow morning, or we'll have to eliminate him, too. He's becoming a problem to us, and will end up just like that stupid dog of yours. And, tell him it's his last vacation. We'll take care of the singer and that bozo who survived with her in the next couple of days."

"Why them?" William asked, terrified of the answer.

"Let's just say they got in the way."

The line disconnected before William could respond.

11

*M*iranda and Patrick entered the computer lab at the library. He put his book-bag on the floor as she slipped the strap of her purse over the back of the chair in front of the computer they had chosen to use. They sat staring at the screen for several minutes trying to build up the courage to begin. Surfing the Net was not new to either of them, thanks to the computer classes at school, but the obscurity of what they were looking for was daunting. Miranda sat in the driver's seat in front of the terminal at the local library where they had rented time on the Net by pre-paying a half hour use time. With the money they had pooled, Miranda and Patrick figured they had enough to spend several hours researching their hunches. They weren't due back to the foster care home until five o'clock, which gave them at least an hour to start researching what they could in that short time.

"Let's look up herbal medicines and see what we get," Patrick suggested at last.

It took only seconds to find over sixty thousand possibilities for herbal medicines worldwide.

"Wow! Maybe we can bring it down some with rainforest references." Miranda filled in the search keywords, rainforest herbal medicines. Within seconds, they had over nine thousand sites to explore. She chose one to see what it was. "Herbal tonics, teas and supplements for increased energy, better food absorption, and how to order. Not exactly what we're looking for." She sat back for a moment and considered the possibilities. "Well, like I said to Dr. Blume, the pills Granddaddy took were from Brazil. Should we try Brazil in the keyword string?"

"Okay. That will get the Chinese sites off the list. Let's try weird plants—like, uh, algae and plankton," Patrick suggested. Miranda looked at him like he was nuts.

'Okay, Algae in Brazil." She typed in the keywords and activated the search button.

Up came over eleven thousand sites offering information about the hydra green algae, phytonurtient and phytochemicals derived from fresh water algae. Miranda clicked on the first few sites. Some algae were used in teas and as food additives. Many were toxic, incredibly poisonous. She found long histories of what happens to the weather, the water supplies, as well as to animals and humans when the red tides occur worldwide. After another fifteen minutes of clicking and scrolling, the two teenagers sat back and stared at each other, shaking their heads in disbelief.

"I wonder if we'll ever find what we're looking for," sighed Miranda, "I'm almost ready to give up, and we've hardly begun." She pushed her hair back, shook her head and sighed again.

"There's too much to go through. We'll never find anything we can use. I wish I could remember the name of the stuff my grandfather used," she said drifting into thought, staring at her hands and pushing her mind through memories of her childhood to see if she could recall the name of the pills.

Patrick slammed the palms of his hands down on the desktop. "Wait! Let's try one more thing—try the word 'secret' in front of 'herbal medicines from Brazil' and see if that does anything." Patrick liked to thinking of odd combinations of things.

"Bingo! Only eight references," Miranda said, as she clicked on one site about spiritual medicines. The commentary read like a confession. *"Not long after that I read that in the rainforests of South America the medicine people believe that unless a plant has come into your dreams, waking or sleeping, you are not empowered to heal with it. A plant can be an ally on many levels, both physical and spiritual."*

"I don't think that's what we're looking for," Patrick said, distracted by the stares from one of the librarians.

Miranda tried three more, finding only sites selling secret herbal substances that were not at all secret: Glucosamine based products for arthritis, St. John's Wort for depression and Ginseng for energy, Kelp and other seaweed concoctions and one that claimed to have the herbal secret to masculine vitality. Two more came up 'Page cannot be displayed.'

"Hmmm—'Live With No Fear of Aging.'" Miranda pushed the submit button on the last site in the list. An icon of a skeleton appeared and then vanished. The screen went dark. The browser returned to the start page and only offered the option to disconnect.

"Whoa! What was that?" Miranda gasped.

"What we're looking for? Let's use a different computer. That librarian is watching us." Patrick glanced at the main desk. The librarian saw him and turned abruptly away to conceal her stare.

"Let's try that one more time to see if we can avoid the shutdown," Miranda said, trying to get Patrick to ignore his paranoia as she sat down at another computer the next row of terminals over.

"The librarian probably just wants to be sure we're not looking up pornographic sites or something like that."

SACRED NIGHT

Signing on again, they typed in the same keywords: 'secret herbal medicines from Brazil' and arrived at the same list of web sites. She clicked on the last listing, and this time the skeleton icon appeared, slowly faded, as a child's face materialized, smiling happily. The head rotated to look at a glowing orange icon button on the black background. Miranda clicked on the button. A photographic quality, virtual reality depiction of a sunrise over a forest canopy appeared. The viewer might be standing on a high cliff, looking into a valley where luxuriant trees and flowering plants flourished. Multi-colored parrots flew in the early morning air. The daylight increased and the view descended into the forest, stopping on a path in the heart of the jungle.

"Wow!" Both Patrick and Miranda gasped at the beauty of the vision. The image moved down the path, stopping at several different plants, automatically listing the common and the botanical names, if there were names at all. Then another glowing icon appeared in the center of a purple orchid- like flower. Miranda clicked on it, and a laboratory replaced the forest. Cages arranged like a honeycomb lined one wall. Each cage housed a monkey.

While most of the animals were agitated and jumping, some were just sitting and staring into space. The view zoomed in on the cage of one of the staring monkeys. The caption under the now still image said: *"This rhesus monkey is afflicted with symptoms like those of Alzheimer's disease. Although he is the equivalent in human years to a sixty year old person, his future is not as bleak as it seems."*

The image of the forlorn monkey faded out as the active image of another monkey faded in. This monkey was robust, jumping from rope to rope in a large, room-like cage. He ran up and down the cubic modules stacked around the cage as nimbly as a youth. The image froze into a still photograph as the caption appeared, *"This is the same rhesus monkey seen in the previous segment. He has been treated for his mental disorder with the power of the rainforest. The product is derived from an ancient tribal compound that is found only in remote, secret reservoirs, sacred to local tribesmen, and located in jungle areas now restricted from deforestation. Access to these areas and the compound is available only to our agents."*

The last icon button, a sun shaped ball, appeared in the lower right hand corner of the screen. Miranda clicked on it, and the screen went blank.

"Time's up!" The librarian spoke in a hushed librarian's voice. Her forced smile couldn't hide her suspicious curiosity, as she looked over their shoulders to see what they were reading. The darkened screen troubled Patrick.

"We want to buy another half hour!" he said too loudly.

"No, the library is closing in just a few minutes, so we have shut down the computers. You'll have to leave now."

The librarian's overly solicitous smile successfully underscored her undeniable superiority of position. Which meant Miranda and Patrick could not refuse to go, if only to avoid calling attention to what they had been doing. Without hesitation, they stood up. Miranda put her purse over her shoulder and flipped her hair back, as Patrick grabbed his backpack and stepped on his untied shoelace, nearly tripping himself. He bent down to tie his shoe, as quickly as possible, and straightening up to his fullest height, he led Miranda out the revolving door to the street as calmly as he could.

"Can you believe that?" Miranda asked. "It seemed too good to be true. I only wish we had been able to get to the last page to find out who to contact."

The frown on Patrick's face greeted her comments in sullen silence. "I'm not waiting another day!" he said, knowing their options were few. "We're going to find another computer before today is over. Let me think. Let me think."

SACRED NIGHT

"There isn't a computer at the Wilkinson's."

"Yeah, and they have only one phone," Patrick said thinking faster than he was talking. "Think of someone who might have access to the Web. Lots of kids have computers and their own modems. We've got to get back to that web site."

His mood quickly spread to Miranda. "Yeah, but do we really want to let any of them in on this?"

"Naw, they'll blab it all over school."

"Let's see if Dr. Blume has one. He was the person who gave us the idea in the first place. If not, maybe he knows someone who does." She reached for her purse, opened the side zipper and pulled out her address book. "I have his address and number right here."

જ્જ

But Dr. Blume was not thinking about websites at the moment. He was looking at the complex tangle of information from the last set of tests administered to Emily and Dan. The results showed their metabolic stability, so important to their future survival, had begun to deteriorate. Unpredictable episodes of wildly spastic movement, more frequent periods of radical irregular heartbeat and respiration indicated a desperate countdown had begun. The mysterious compound appeared to be eroding the normal functions of the entire metabolic process. Increased brain activity, dramatic body temperature fluctuations, broad peaks and valleys in blood sugars and enzymes, pointed to a general malfunctioning of interrelated anatomical systems. The compound seemed to be systematically testing each anatomical system and then leaving that part of the body to function on its own, minutely changed yet functioning. That their episodes happened simultaneously was even more confusing. Dr. Blume could not avoid the notion that death was threatening his patients. The hopeful possibility that Emily and Dan would one day just simply wake up was clearly becoming much more remote.

Dr. Blume sat down near the window in the staff lounge to watch the wind blowing through the trees in the courtyard. The gentle waving of the branches produced a powerful sadness. Feeling emotion for patients had always proved too painful, too difficult for doctors to endure over the course of a career, and so medical training included strategies for remaining detached. Keeping some distance from a patient's personal story usually helped a doctor maintain a clinical perspective when interpreting test results. But this time, the people he was treating had become the condition he was seeking to cure. He didn't know them, but he knew their children, and he couldn't keep his professional distance from them the way he could with adults. He hoped that his friend and colleague, Dr. Eastman might be able to help him.

Sitting in his office, rubbing the sore muscles of his neck with one hand, and massaging the tension in this scalp with the other, Dr. Eastman was feeling the strain of four new patients he had added to his already overbooked schedule. He was thinking about how he worked best with kids. Although he maintained a family practice, adults were usually too unwilling to change their habits. Kids, even some of the most rigid or manipulative teenagers, could usually be turned around. In search of relief for the oncoming migraine, he was focusing his aching brain on the fact that, unlike most other kids in trouble Patrick and Miranda, and to a lesser extent Jennifer and Ian responded with creative thought and a willingness to become in-volved in seeking answers to the questions they had about the condi-tion of their parents.

Breathing deeply and exhaling slowly, Dr. Eastman turned his mind to the mystery of their circumstances, which was as intriguing as it was frustrating. How could anyone explain to kids that their parents were victims of some diabolical plot, when no one could know for certain that was true? He moved his hands from his head and neck to his upper shoulder muscles. Pinching them and rubbing them, the pain his actions created felt therapeutic, as if his fingers were untying the knots in the muscles, one by one. How could anyone tell these children that their parents would eventually be just fine, when no one could know that was true? How does even the best child psychologist keep hope alive for kids like these? At least they resisted the more common response of, at worst, emotional breakdown or at best, depression. Their constant curiosity was perhaps the ingredient that would bring them through this experience all the stronger for it. Therapeutic rubbing or not, the pain in his shoulders was not abating.

Dr. Eastman picked up the police report of the bombing, read it again, and methodically compared it again to the latest medical report on Emily Sanders and Dan Barton. Where was the connection? How could he make enough sense of this before he saw the kids again?

The phone rang. It was Dr. Blume.

"Hello, Jim?"

"Hey, David! How're you doing? I was just re-reading the info I have on the bombing of Rita's Bar, and your medical report, as you asked me to. I can't see any missing elements. In fact, I can't really make much sense of it at all." His cheerful tone did little to alter his mood.

"That's okay. I'm actually more interested in your evaluations of the kids, in particular Miranda and Patrick, the older two."

"What are you looking for?" Dr. Eastman picked up the Tylenol Migraine bottle, poured three tabs into his palm, and washed them down with a gulp of water from the glass he always kept full from the thermos pitcher his wife had given him for his birthday last year.

"I know this is going to sound crazy, but has either of them mentioned a theory about herbal medicines or the rainforest holding the secret to a cure to aging? They wanted me to consider such an idea, so I sent them on a cyber-wild goose chase to find out that there was no such thing. You know, I like the pharmaceutical companies to come up with cures and the FDA to approve them. But our lab reports keep finding this strange, light sensitive compound that we can't identify as either purely botanical or purely animal. It has properties of both. The effects don't appear to be permanent. A growing instability in this baffling medical situation makes me think they did ingest something just before the bombing, something that may have protected them. But, the coma-like state of suspended animation is beginning to change, and I want to—I have to figure out how to turn off this substance before they're dead."

Dr. Eastman considered the client–physician confidentiality code he followed with extreme vigor.

"David, you know I can't reveal anything about the kids. I can tell you my professional opinion about their state of mind, but I can't really divulge the content of the conversations I've had with them. I can say that over the course of several meetings, Miranda and Patrick have grown increasingly more out spoken about helping their parents in some way."

"Jim, we're not talking about revealing anything that would injure them, or endanger them in any way. I just need to know if they've shared their theories with you. If so, then I need to know more details than I have from them directly. Even though I usually dismiss such ideas as foolishness, I can't ignore that they may be on to something. This time a gut feeling tells me to follow up."

"Let's put it this way, David. They have a clear sense of purpose and a goal to achieve. They are motivated by love for their parents and by the mystery of the hunt, so to speak. Psychologically speaking, a healthy dose of adolescent imagination and the powerful motive to save their parents keeps them going."

"So, what you're saying in the most convoluted way you can, is yes, they have revealed their theory to you, but you won't tell me what it is."

"You might ask them again yourself. I think that would be the best thing. I am not playing cat and mouse with you. I just have this aversion to telling what my clients are talking about. I've given you the most information I can from my professional point of view. I think they'll respond to your interest and be very forthcoming. Catch you later?"

"Catch you later, and thanks," Dr. Blume said.

Dr. Eastman, wondering if he had done right by his old friend, stood up from his desk, turned off the lights and left his office to go home for what he hoped would be a good dinner and a long night's sleep. Dr. Blume hung up the phone and twisted his swivel office chair away from the desk, picked up the controller and flipped on the desktop television he kept on top of the bookshelf. Almost instantly his phone rang. He flipped the television off as he picked up the phone.

"Hello, Dr. Blume? This is Miranda Pauer. I'm with Patrick Barton, and we took your suggestion about looking for information on the Worldwide Web. And, I think we've found something. But we need another computer other than the one at the library. Do you know where we can use one?"

"Well, I have one, but I won't be home till late this evening."

"That's all right. We'll sneak out of the house if we have to. You've got to see what we found. It's incredible."

"No, no. You can't be out after curfew. Let's plan on meeting tomorrow at the hospital. We'll make arrangements then, okay?"

"We'll be there first thing in the morning," Miranda replied.

She hung up the phone, even more anxious to get back on the Web. Miranda's idea of an herbal compound intrigued Dr. Blume more than any possibility had for a long time, if only because he feared that Emily Sanders and Dan Barton lay helpless and on the brink of death, and he had no clue as to what he could do about it.

12

*A*bove the submerged riverbank, the village women were
waiting at the makeshift landing site for the skiffs. The village stilt
houses hovered just at the surface of the water. The women received
the lead skiff, wailing a mournful sound. The landing site was in
actuality the midway point of the highest hill in the area. The top,
where the ceremonial rebirth dances would occur, had never been
taken in the high water. The medicine men waited for the gourd to
arrive, standing shoulder to shoulder, not moving a muscle, not even
seeming to breathe in keeping with their serene patience. The women
stopped wailing, one by one as Amahi removed the gourd from his
father's wrist and placed it in the ancient basket of reeds and sticks
held out to him by the chief of the medicine men. Silently turning
away from Amahi, the medicine men entered the hut of the sacred
altar to prepare the algala, leaving Ahi to the care of the women who
knew how to prepare his body for the coming Sacred Night.

The women took Ahi, still immobile and unable to speak, into
the second hut and anointed his body with oils and herbs. It was a
ritual of death to birth that would begin with the act of wrapping

the chief's living body as if preparing it for embalming. The women soaked the layered strips of cloth in the mint aroma herbs and warm coconut oils as they wrapped them around Ahi's entire form. They left just enough opening for his nose to breathe and inserted a cane in his mouth for him to drink the algala when it was ready.

For just a moment before the women weighted his eyes shut with gold coins and wrapped them tightly in the mint and oil soaked cloths, Ahi caught a glance at Amahi, who stood watching in the shadows. His son seemed terrified by the scene, but Ahi remembered his own fears, as he had watched is own father swathed for the Sacred Night. That last glance gave him the last picture of the last moments of his aged life. Then the women sealed his ears with soft grass-like fibers dipped in wax, so he could hear no sound, as they wrapped his head in more of the cloths. Silence and blindness, imposed upon him to purify his vision and his ability to hear only truth, terrified him more than the pain inducing heat of the aromatic oil entering every pore of his skin. The intensity of aromatic herbs filled his head through the opening to his nose, and their mind-altering effects lifted his spirit until he floated above his surroundings. The heady herbal pungency drew him higher and higher toward a light shining above him.

Though blind, he could see visions of his children playing in the yard in front of his house during the dry season. Though deaf, he could hear the melodies of their laughter ringing in his ears. The sensations in his limbs alternated in rapid succession between burning and cooling. In the heat he wanted to cry out, as if burning in a fire, and in the cold he wanted to pant for air, as if immersed in icy water. But his mouth was immobile. He could not move under the weight of the wrappings, the effects of the herbs and the fatigue from the strain of the dive the night before.

Fear of death enveloped Ahi's soul just as death's cloak and oils embalmed his body. He could see death approaching him in the light. The heat of the oils and herbs intensified. A black figure floated toward him. He could not scream. He could not run. To face this fear of dying in the loneliness of rebirth, Ahi let all that had gone before in his life pass away.

A loud crack resembling thunder exploded in his head. A strong, electrical vibration, as if lightning had struck very nearby, shook him. The vision of death floated above him as he ran on a spinning path. He ran for his life. He passed through his own moment of birth, his own childhood, his own youth, his own marriage, his own day-to-day memories. His heart was pounding, and in the silence he could hear only his blood rushing through his brain. Ahi was about to burst from the exertion, when in an instant he was shivering in the chill of the spices.

Icy spikes ran through every nerve. The pain wrenched him from the spinning path and threw him into a fog. There he floated helplessly before grotesque faces of agony conjured up by the heavy herbal atmosphere he took in with every breath. He tried to strike out at the faces. They terrified him. He could not understand the significance of their expressions. He could only fear them.

The women watched as Ahi's wrapped form contorted in the agony brought on by the oils and herbs. They held his feet and head. They placed heavy stones on his chest to stop his writhing. In the darkness of the hut, they watched the old life of the chief symbolically waft away in the smoke from the fire. At the same moment, Ahi's agony subsided and he lay in the half life of unconsciousness. But the women knew his salvation was near. They removed the stones. They released their grip on his feet and head. They unwrapped his body and left him naked in the dark. The cloths still encased his head to hold his eyes closed, keep his ears deaf and support the cane upright in his mouth.

SACRED NIGHT

Outside, the drums pulsed the rhythms for the dance of rebirth. The tribal drummers sat on the ground encircling the bonfire, their faces distorted by the shadows cast by the flickering of the flames of the fire The villagers stood in uneven lines behind the drummers, eyes wide and white in the firelight, as the warrior dancers entered the space between the drummers and the fire. They wore only loincloths, their bodies caked with dried mud. Each mask of bark, small animal bones and feathers was more terrifying than the last. Their mildly rhythmic movements, more like a swaying to the drums than a dance, moved in slow rotation around the fire, casting their shadows upward toward the treetops and the night sky.

All at once, the drummers smacked the skins of their instruments in a loud, explosion of sound, like a gunshot. The drums then fell silent. One drummer beat a lighter rhythm, and the head medicine man made his way through the crowd, which parted so he could pass. In his hands, which he held high above his head, he carried a vase with purple and white orchids tied around it. As he reached the inner circle, voices began to chant.

"Algala—Algala—Anmala, Anmala—Algala—Algala ..."

The women lifted the cot that held the limp body of Ahi, the chief. They carried him from the hut, through the crowd and the line of dancers to the fire. They set his cot on the raised platform beside the fire and showered him with orchid petals. Aware of himself again, Ahi's pain was gone. His head remained heavy, and he still could not see or hear, but he could be sure that he was alive. His body felt light and cool. The villagers' voices rose to a screaming pitch as the medicine man came forward carrying the vase toward Ahi's supine form.

The medicine man lifted the vase high for all to see. Silence fell on the lips of the villagers. The moment of rebirth had come. Lowering the vase slowly to the widened, open tip of the cane protruding from Ahi's mouth, the medicine man poured the first golden drops of algala into the opening.

SACRED NIGHT

Ahi tasted the warm milkiness of the potion as it poured past his tongue. The cane bypassed his tongue and opened his throat to allow the algala to enter directly into his stomach. He could not swallow. The overflow of the algala filled his mouth and rose up the back of his nasal passages. In one quick motion, the medicine man yanked the cane from the wrappings, causing Ahi to sputter and spit, cough and choke. In a unified action that appeared to be nearly one movement, the women turned him on his side to remove the wrappings. The overflow from his mouth and nose spilled rudely onto the ground. Removing the waxed fibers from his ears the women unwound the last layer of cloth, and the gold coins fell from his eyes into the mixture of dust and algala.

Taking the first burning breath of his new life, Ahi cried out. He could hear the villagers cheering, raising a loud vibrato of high-pitched wailing to the heavens. Ahi's entire being tingled, every nerve tight with the sensations of new life. He opened his eyes for the first time to see Amahi, who was watching his father's rebirth from his place among the privileged few who would come into power in the next generation, and wept with joy.

13

*L*andon Pauer was waiting more patiently than most of the passengers in the crowded departure lounge at O'Hare Airport. He was reading the back of his ticket while waiting to get on the plane, seemingly completely unaware of being followed. Detective Cameron had allowed the older man to feel vindicated and empowered by rescinding Landon's travel restrictions, to be able to see exactly where he went, whom he met, and what he did without a chance of missing any details, knowing that the only way to be sure of the accuracy of any information that turned up would be to tail Landon Pauer.

"Boarding for the Air Inter flight to Belém, Brazil will begin at this time. First class, please line up at the entrance to the loading walkway to your right," said the flight attendant in her best intercom voice. "Economy class, please use the left entrance."

The intrigue of the unknown had always been irresistible to the veteran police officer, and as he stood concealed by a pillar in the airport terminal, he could not ignore the voice of something in his beat cop soul that told him that this old man was involved in something more than a vacation trip to Brazil. Detective Cameron checked his seat number, making sure one more time it was the first one in the economy cabin, closest to the entrance to first class, as he had requested. He waited until all the other economy passengers had boarded from the rear of the aircraft before entering the plane. He waited for the others to load their carryon luggage, and squeeze into their seats before he made his way up the aisle and took his seat at the bulkhead. He could see Landon Pauer through the slit where the curtain separated to allow access into the first class cabin.

"Perfect," he said softly to the air.

Landon patted an envelope of money inside his coat just to be sure that it was still where he thought he had put it, as he sat comfortably in his first class seat. He noticed in the seat next to him, a young woman in her early twenties sat reading the exit instructions she had taken from the storage pouch on the back of the seat in front of her. More a girl than a woman, her long blond hair and flawless fair skin suggested Scandinavian heritage. She looked over at Landon and smiled the way a stranger smiles at a stranger.

"Hello. I suppose we're going to spend a few hours sitting next to each other. So, I'd like to introduce myself. I'm—"

"No, no," Landon said chuckling. "Don't tell me your name. If I know your name I'd have to tell you mine, and I couldn't remain anonymous to you."

"Well, at least let's shake hands to greet each other. I hate to sit silently next to strangers on long flights."

Landon smiled, raising his right index finger to his lips as if to silence her. The engines revved, and the plane taxied to the runway. As the roar drowned out all possibility of talk, he tried to focus his thoughts on his upcoming meeting with Mickey Straader, the man he had hired years before to go into the jungle to get his compound for him. Straader had been a successful agent, if not truly loyal to anything or anyone other than the dollar.

"Please, let's chat for a little while. I'm traveling to South America to study for two years: post graduate preparation for a career in the diplomatic corps. How about you?" Landon glanced at her with a mock frown and a shake of his head, pursing his lips tightly, zipping them shut and throwing away the key the way he might have had he been playing a game with a child.

"Come on," she whined in a girlish tone. "Why not tell me the reason you're going to South America?" She spoke in an innocently seductive way, weakening Landon's resolve to remain aloof.

"Well, all right, I'm going to Belém, Brazil to visit my brother-in-law. He owns a particularly quiet restaurant–hotel called La Casa del Norte," Landon answered, smiling in a grandfatherly way at the young woman.

Detective Cameron strained to hear what Landon was saying, although he couldn't see to whom it was he was talking. It seemed logical that he was conversing with someone across the aisle. So, the investigator leaned over to the edge of the doorway and positioned his small carryon under his seat. Then he ran the wire of an amplifying tape recorder microphone across the few inches of carpet on the floor to the base of the bulkhead, where he ran it up the edge and fastened its Velcro patch to the carpeting on the wall. It aimed directly into the first class cabin, but was not obvious to anyone in either cabin. He put the headset on, and listened, certain he would hear something of interest from Landon during the flight, while seeming to listen to music to anyone else.

Landon's mind drifted on his recollections that not all of his wife Lorraine's family had felt the old-fashioned altruistic passion and missionary zeal of their forbearers to save the natives. Her brother, Harry Smithers, personified the antithesis of his family's religious fervor. In fact, had it not been for Harry's greedy, selfish nature, Landon could not have gathered his compound all these years. Harry had all the right contacts and knew all the right people to help Landon transact his black market business from Brazil, and Landon had the money and willingness to spend it that Harry looked for in any man he would come to call his friend, family or not.

But, Mickey Straader had been indispensable to Landon's quest because he spoke several tribal languages and knew the way into the most remote parts of the jungle, where the tribes had retreated to escape the cutting and burning of their forest for cattle ranchers, loggers and farmers. During the twenty-five years of his life that he had spent becoming a liaison between the Amazon tribes, Mickey had earned their trust. More recently, he had concentrated on connecting the tribes with the modern world. Landon's need for the algala compound coincided neatly with Mickey's need to get rich, any way he could. Harry and Mickey had the same goals, and Landon had always been content to contribute to their success as long as he got what he wanted.

Over time, Mickey Straader developed an underground network for the algala compound, which the Tokablaki had harvested for centuries for their own use. His friendship with the native populations allowed him to slowly take monopolistic control over the growth of production in the world outside Amazonia.

"Is that all? Aren't you going to take in the sights?" The girl's interest in Landon's plans jolted him back to the airplane and her smile flattered him into conversation.

"Well, as a matter of fact, I am traveling to the interior of the Amazon River jungles in search of the cure for old age." He was boasting with the bravado of a foolish old man, and loving the wide-eyed gaze of the blond beauty next to him. Lowering his voice in a tone of conspiracy, he leaned toward her to whisper in her ear. "Of course, the risks involved are great, since the secret compound is derived from an algae that creates the red tides in the inland waterways of Brazil."

Detective Cameron closed his eyes, as if sleeping, and listened to the one-sided conversation coming in through his earphones.

"What are red tides?" she asked, her eyes wide and willing as she devoured the dinner on the tray before her. Landon waved away the food and indicated he wanted only drinks offered by the flight attendant. Continuing to huddle toward the girl, he regaled her with every detail he could remember.

"Well, red tides are incredibly dangerous. Any bodily contact with the algae during the red tide cycle means a cruelly painful demise within twenty-four hours. It poisons the fish and in turn, the humans who eat them," he said, acting as scientific wise man to this woman, this gorgeous, smiling angel, who seemed to care about his knowledge. Landon drank his second glass of champagne in three gulps, a dribble of which rolled down his chin a dripped onto his tie, without his awareness that he had spilled.

Detective Cameron tapped the headset, wondering why he only heard Landon's voice and no one else's.

"How can this compound be the cure for old age?" she asked, wiping her lips and then his chin with her linen napkin and drinking deeply of the complimentary champagne poured for a second time into her glass. "I thought old age was just plain old unavoidable."

Landon drank all of the third glass of champagne in one swig. "No, no, no. Not at all. Because, once the red tides dissipate, the rest of the life cycle of the algae is harmless. After it dies, the decay of these primitive plants and the fish that die in the red tide releases residues that seep into the bottom silt of the estuaries and tributaries of the Amazon River. The plant and fish-carcass mass builds up in underwater deposits, which become safe harbor to minute, plankton-like creatures called Planalgazon. Increasing to astronomical numbers, the microscopic, red, single-celled dinoflagellate plankton gymnodinium breve expels a paralyzing toxic waste into the waters of the river."

"How disgusting," she said, squirming in her seat and leaning away from him.

"Then, upon completing their life cycle, planalgazon die on the river bottom, building up a crystalline deposit atop the mud and muck. The catalytic interaction between all these natural elements causes the curative compound to form."

"The natives eat the muck?" she asked, her face wrinkled like someone had released the odor of rotten eggs into the cabin.

It was clear to Detective Cameron that Landon Pauer was talking to himself.

"No, not exactly. Eons of repetition of this cycle have left vast deposits of this *algala*, the natives call it, spread over certain deeper reservoirs in the Amazon River area like a layer of age-defying silt. The natives have mastered the collection, filtering and concentration of the carcasses of astronomical numbers of these minute photosensitive creatures, allowing them to harvest once a year the raw materials for their life preserving compound. And, that's why I go there about this time on a yearly basis."

Landon looked around him, trying to stop the airplane cabin from spinning. His vision blurred as he stared at the young women, trying to focus and suddenly becoming aware that he'd never see her again. His mind was wandering. He saw Mickey Straader's face. He saw a rich, old man with Alzheimer's paying Mickey a king's ransom for the algala compound. He blinked to focus on the girl's face as his mind cleared and the swirling stopped.

"I believe the challenge to stop the inevitable execution of human beings by age and senility is the next technological frontier," his speech slurred as the fourth glass of champagne took effect. "Harry Smithers, my own brother-in-law had no concern for anyone else's well-being, and intended only to cash in on the bonanza the discovery of this compound would elicit from all mankind."

"You'd think the big city drug companies would want to develop it," she said.

"So, there is much more to this trip, and Landon in the eye of the hurricane," he thought to himself. Detective Cameron glanced down into parted lips of the unzipped bag to check the tape recorder. "Much more." He wouldn't sleep again tonight, he was certain of that.

"Yes, you'd think so, but not so far," Landon answered. "The legitimate medical community had looked very far askance at the compound Harry had once presented to them for consideration. Over a short period of time one by one, the large pharmaceutical firms had discredited the medicinal properties in the substance and embarrassed Harry, leaving him no legitimate marketing strategy but to turn to alternate markets for the compound. In the black market underworld of drug trafficking, Harry Smithers discovered Mickey Straader and brought him to me, in my first time of need. The fledgling business grew successful with help from my business management and practical operations knowledge."

"How long have you been taking these trips? You don't look old enough to have been doing this for very long," she was bating him now, and the tease made him think back to the other women he had known.

For fifteen years, Harry's discretion and careful planning had been essential to Landon. Harry had kept the secrets for Landon that would have broken Lorraine's heart. For years without fail, Harry made sure that his sister couldn't know much about the side trips he and Landon took to enjoy the attentions of a steady stream of Brazilian women. The South American women that Harry provided were beautiful and willing playmates for the wealthy gentlemen from North America.

"Oh, for many years, I'm not as young as I look," he said drowsily. "This time, I won't actually be going inland. Physical troubles prevent me from enjoying the 'great explore.' I hire younger men to find what I need for me and bring it to me."

Closing his eyes, he pondered how even on his vacations with Lorraine, Harry had provided him a harem. He returned to the moment about fifteen years ago when Harry had introduced him to then thirty-five year old Marguerite Maria Juanita Kohl. As he drifted into sleep, Landon saw her as she had been then, the beautiful daughter of a Nazi SS officer who had resettled in Brazil after World War II and a Brazilian beauty. When her father was at last caught and returned to Germany for trial, Marguerite had stayed in the village where her mother raised her in extreme poverty. At the age of fifteen she fled to Belém to learn how to be a hairdresser and call girl. From there, she traveled to Rio to become a hairdresser and call girl to the rich on vacation and famous film stars on location. By the time Mickey brought Landon to Marguerite for a coiffure, she had become a very successful independent businesswoman.

Landon had fallen in love with her at first sight and would have no one else. Because she had been lonely for too long, the vulnerable Marguerite had given in to him as to no one else from the beginning of their relationship. When Landon returned a year later, he found Marguerite the mother of his physically handicapped, but mentally normal child and accepted his responsibility by offering to keep her and the baby in a style she had never known. She would be his permanent mistress and devote herself to raising the child. She had agreed, and for one short time in every year of the last fifteen, Landon and Marguerite had shared a passionate love affair when he arrived to vacation, less and less often with Lorraine, and more frequently on his own.

The flight was long. Detective Cameron turned off the tape recorder when he saw that Landon had fallen asleep for good. Snoring softly and dreaming of Marguerite, Landon slept soundly. When he awoke, dawn was creeping onto the horizon and the young woman was no longer in her seat. He pushed the call button.

"I'm sorry to bother you. Where is the young woman who sat with me during the flight?"

"Sir?" the flight attendant said with a puzzled look. "There was no one sitting there. You've had the row to yourself all flight long. You slept most of the trip. Can I get you some coffee before we serve breakfast?"

"Uh—yes—you may. Are you sure there was no young woman?"

"Yes, sir. You did mumble in your sleep, but there was no one. How about a croissant and some fruit for breakfast? I'll bring it to you before we begin the regular service, if you'd like."

"Well, all right. I am rather hungry," Landon replied. He rummaged through the pouch in front of him, his coat pockets, and under the seat, looking for something he couldn't find.

"May I help you find something?" the attendant asked as she placed the tray of food on the pull-down table in front of the seat next to him.

"No, no, that's all right, I'll find it myself." His face felt cold, and his hands were clammy and stiffening in the chill that crept through his body. He knew the chill and the apparition were signaling the onset of another episode. Knowing that Belém was less than an hour away only increased his sense of anxiety. His foot tapped on the floor, his fingers drummed on the armrest, and when his shoulders twitched in agitation he couldn't disguise the action with some other action. By touchdown, Landon was shaking all over in small spasms that he knew would soon become forceful and violent. He left the airplane, holding onto the railing for balance and support. Detective Cameron stayed a comfortable distance behind Landon, but followed him to the pick up area in front of the airport entrance.

It was a very small airport, similar to the ones in rural areas, and not much more architecturally sound than a corrugated barn. The private car Harry had arranged to pick up Landon had been waiting at the exit from the airport, and drove Landon directly to the hotel-restaurant. So, by noon, he pulled up to in La Casa del Norte, Harry's establishment. Marguerite ran to him, hugging and kissing him, and taking his hand to lead him into the restaurant. By ten after, he was and drinking a cup of coffee and talking incessantly with Marguerite and Harry to try to delay his loss of control over himself, as they all waited for Mickey to show up.

Detective Cameron picked up the rental car he had had the foresight to pre-arrange at the last minute in the airport back in Chicago, only a minute or two after Landon had stepped into his limo. He followed the limo through the dusty streets, parking his beater under a pathetically scrawny tree across the street from La Casa del Norte only a couple of minutes after Landon's arrival there. The sun baked through the sparse leaves of the tree, bringing the temperature inside the car to an uncomfortable enough level, that Detective Cameron was sweating from every pore as he set up his surveillance camera. It whirred softly from inside the specially designed camouflage duffel sports bag he had carefully placed on top of his pile of luggage in the back seat, just as a breeze wafted through the window, cooling his sweat slicked face. His slovenly clothes and unkempt appearance reflected the hard night he had spent listening to Landon and not sleeping in the torturous economy coach seat. He would avoid direct contact with the suspects at all cost, simply watching and recording their comings and goings for later study. His short conversation with the flight attendants as he left the plane had provided little more information. They had only recounted that Landon had been drinking champagne and mumbling incoherently, before sleeping fitfully most of the rest of the flight.

Just as Detective Cameron stepped into the jet way the last flight attendant stopped him and said, "You know, sir, the gentleman you referred to did ask about some young woman he had been talking to on the plane last night."

"Yes, well, I'm not surprised. He always tries to pick up someone on the longer flights," he said, playing along.

"Perhaps, sir, but there had been no young woman with him," the flight attendant added.

"Yes, well thank you," Detective Cameron said. "I'll remember that."

As he settled into the front seat behind the wheel, swung his feet onto the seat and sat with his back against the door, he was pleased to understand that his tape recorder had caught much more than a one-sided conversation with an imaginary girl. It had caught vital information that could lead him to the solution of the crime back in Chicago. His hunches rarely let him down. He couldn't use his microphone here, and had to rely only on his eyes and camera for the next part of his surveillance.

Inside the restaurant, Landon was talking. "I guess this could be my last trip," he said. "I'll need Mickey to come to Chicago next time. Lorraine and a bunch of doctors have decided I'm not clear-headed enough to travel alone. She told me in no uncertain terms, this would be my last trip. Why she let me go alone after that comment, I don't know, but it must be the mess with William and his ex-wife that kept her home." His hands were trembling as he tried to steady one of them enough to drink his coffee without spilling. Marguerite rested her hand on his, to help him.

The young woman on the plane crossed his mind. He shrugged off the memory as he smiled nervously, trying to seem normal and in control of his faculties. He started to explain the recent events in Chicago, but found it hard to connect his thoughts.

"There was a bombing in the city, and William's ex-wife was in it. She's in a coma. The man she was with is in the hospital too. Someone murdered the dog in the basement, but William doesn't know that I know. A Detective Cameron came to the house asking about a barking dog that wasn't barking anymore, and William said he didn't have a dog —"

"Landon, dear, wouldn't you like to take me and Paulo to a cinema tonight? I'd really love to get him out of the apartment, if we could," Marguerite tried to sidetrack him.

"Oh, that's nice. But it was a real adventure getting here. There was a beautiful young woman who sat with me on the plane, but in the morning, the flight attendant insisted there was no one in my row. Isn't that funny?"

"I don't know what's keeping Mickey," Harry tried to interrupt.

"She was so beautiful, and friendly. I'm glad I met her, even if she jumped out of the plane or something while I was sleeping."

Marguerite turned to Harry and whispered in his ear, "I think he's having trouble. If Mickey doesn't get here soon with some of the algala, he's going to lose touch with reality entirely."

"Yeah, sure seems that way." Harry shook his head slowly as if to say he felt sorry for her. "Uh, Landon, how about a sandwich and another cup of coffee?" Harry asked.

"It wasn't too long before we got to the airport," Landon rambled on, looking out the door for something or someone.

"Landon, dear, you need to eat something. Perhaps some flan, or some fruit?" Marguerite said, hoping to divert his attention to the act of eating to bring him into the here and now.

He shook his head. "I really don't know what to think about it all, William and his girls. They never see each other—" Harry and Marguerite sat in stony silence as Landon strung random ideas into sentences, no context, no sense to what he was saying, and let him talk. He never noticed they were staring out the window, not listening.

"Hello, amigos!" Mickey shouted, bursting through the door and slapping Harry on the back and grabbing Landon's hand to shake it, a bit too vigorously and with too broad a smile, the kind that projects 'no sincerity intended.'

"You're two hours late," Harry seethed at him through his teeth. "Any reason for it?"

"The natives were restless, and the traffic was hell. I just couldn't tear myself away from a sweet young thing at the last stop on my trip here. Hope you kept a seat warm for me."

"We did," Harry said, "but now I have a roomful of hungry customers, which I didn't have two hours ago, and I can't sit here talking with you about your love life and let them starve."

Marguerite tapped Landon on the shoulder, "Honey, I have to go home to Paulo. I'll wait up for you." She kissed him on the cheek and left. Harry gave a few orders to the kitchen about that evening's menu and returned to sit with Mickey and Landon.

Detective Cameron's camera caught Mickey's arrival and Marguerite's departure, and then he trained the telephoto lens through the front window and focused it on the three men as they sat around the table.

"Too bad I couldn't wire the place," he muttered into the cup of warm water he had poured from his handy travel canteen.

"Well, Mick, have you got my compound? I ran short a little sooner than I thought I would. I must have miscalculated. Anyway, let me see what you've got." For the moment, Landon was back in control.

"Sure, old man, I didn't let you down. But, the price has gone up again. I had some trouble with the middlemen and their bosses. The natives are moving further up river, because of all the real estate development going on, and the word is, their medicine chests are getting scarce, if you know what I mean. I got you a year's supply. But it'll take three years worth of money to get it."

The smile on Landon's face soured into a sneer. "No one does that to me. I won't pay you a cent more than a year and a half's price. Take it or leave it."

Mickey stood up, knocking over his chair for emphasis. "No, that's no deal. Two and a half year's worth, maybe."

"Two." The tone of Landon's voice fell to the floor like a rock hitting the bottom of a deep ravine.

"Okay, old man, but don't come back for more without figuring four year's worth next time." He sat in the next chair, leaving his turned over on its side.

"You'll be coming to Chicago, next time, punk. The cost will be negotiated then," Landon said, reaching for Mickey's shirt, then thinking better of his actions. "I've got more business for you, too. One of the rich old coots in the place I spend the day said he'd come in on the next deal. He's got millions." Landon paused to read Mickey's face, which showed the slightest hint of a smirk at the left corner of his mouth. "Money's no object. But you've got to come up there. I won't be able to get out of the house considering the way Lorraine's controlling my life. Without my business smarts all these years, you'd be nowhere, and if I withdraw my services, you'll be back in jail for small-timing theft, just like before you met me. This is my last trip, so don't threaten me again with price increases, you old asshole."

Mickey slapped him on the back and broke down laughing. "I hate to hear a grain of truth from anyone, and least of all you. But it is fun to watch you get all worked up."

Landon handed Mickey the envelope with fifty thousand dollars in it. He had figured the double rate very accurately. Mickey smiled as he counted the bills.

"You old fox! You knew what I'd settle for, didn't you?" he said as he handed over the compound.

"How long have I been bargaining for my freedom, Mickey?"

Landon said, as he popped two pills into his mouth and washed them down with the now tepid coffee. "Ten, maybe fifteen years? When I started, everything was cheap. So, take your money, pay off your middle men, and tell me you'll see me in Chicago next year."

"Sure. Next year. No problem." Mickey finished Marguerite's drink in one swallow, burped and slapped Harry on the back again. "Adios, amigos. See you next year!" he said, and was gone.

Landon turned to Harry and frowned.

"Your man's a thief, Harry. What does that make you?" Landon studied his brother-in-law's face.

"Not much better. But, that's the way of the world, and you won't live to see it get any better. Neither will I. So, I'm taking my cut before I drop dead. Marguerite is waiting for you at the apartment, if you're interested. I've got hungry people to satisfy, so, I'm getting back to work, okay?"

Landon hailed a taxi and set off across town to the high-class apartments where Marguerite and Paulo, her son, lived. Detective Cameron followed the taxi in the cloud of dust it produced on the unpaved streets. When they hit the high-class part of town, Detective Cameron dropped back a few cars in the sparse traffic. He pulled into an alley and set his camera in a direct line of sight to the front door of the apartment high rise. He settled in to wait for whatever would happen.

Back at La Casa del Norte, Harry went to his office. He sat down at his desk and looked over the papers scattered by the breeze from the open window. He roughly shuffled them together, leaving the phone message from a Rita Dumas on top.

"Another rich mixed blood bitch," he thought cynically. "But blending races can make beautiful women out of any blood line." Harry sneered lustfully as his mind's eye drew a picture of a thirty-something dark-haired beauty, wearing simple clothes and one two or three carat emerald surrounded by diamonds on her left hand. Noticing the number was in Rio, he picked up the phone, and let the phone ring more than the usual six rings.

"Hello?"

"Is this Rita Dumas?"

"Yes? Who is this?" Rita said, disguising her normally edgy voice, with a clear, cultured quality that softened it to a whispery contralto, not at all like her usual urban bark.

"Harry Smithers returning your call, Miss Dumas. How did you get my name and number?"

"That doesn't matter, Mr. Smithers. What does matter is that I need to buy the medicinal compound my contact tells me you are able to procure from the Tokablaki tribesmen. I have an ailing, elderly father who could benefit from the compound, at least, that's what I understand." She increased the trembling in her voice, to increase the effect of sadness she was attempting to project over the crackling connection of the ancient phone line. "He's been in the assisted care hospital for a couple of months with a degenerative mental condition the doctors can't or won't do anything to treat." She took a deep breath as if trying to control a rising sob. "I learned of the compound you have access to, how scarce it is and how difficult to get. Money is no object, Mr. Smithers. I have control of my father's estate. He never trusted lawyers, so he simply gave it all to me, on the one condition that I would take care of him. I'm a good enough daughter to keep that part of the bargain."

Her tears were audible. Harry was not moved by her apparent emotion, although her supposed unlimited wealth tantalized him into testing her conviction.

"Listen, Miss Dumas. I must caution you. The compound doesn't affect everyone the same way. It helps some of my clients. In fact, it helps most of them. But, on occasion, the physical makeup of the client prevents the compound from having the desired effects. In extreme cases, the patient falls into a coma-like state. In that case, more often than not, he dies from the effects the compound has on the entire metabolism. Improperly administered, the hallucinogenic makeup of the compound also causes severe disorientation in the waking state, and violent dreaming in the coma-like state it induces."

"Is there an antidote?" Rita led him to her purpose with an innocent tone in her voice.

"Yes, but the antidote is rarely available outside Brazil. Even here, it is scarce. The tribesmen refine the compound from the organic state and keep the residual antidote. There is so much less of the antidote, they simply refuse to provide it. Oh, I've tried to purchase it. But as of now, only a vigorous constitution can save the person who does not take well to the compound. The elderly simply don't have a chance. Let me warn you, dosages are tricky. A healthy, fit person under fifty will usually be all right with the right dosage, but a bit too much? So long. Not quite enough? Nightmares and insanity. It is best if the client can come to Brazil for the native experts to administer the first dosage. I have the means to introduce the tribal medicine men to the new client. So, if you could bring your father here?" Harry took a breath. He hated giving this long explanation every time there was a new prospect to sell.

"I know all that. And, you can't scare me off, Mr. Smithers." Her voice revealed an edge that put Harry on notice. "I must get some of the compound, and some of the antidote, and get it soon." She realized the crisp tonality was creeping back into her voice. She took a breath to pause and to adjust her impersonation, getting her vocal control back. "I know an old Brazilian doctor in the States who insists he used it here years ago. He's a friend of my father. He's my contact. He told me to come here, to call you. How do I get it? I'll do and pay anything." Her voice ran like honey through the phone line. She waited for him to respond, knowing that when dealing with a man whose greed and corruptibility knew no limit, she had to play her role just right. Her act as a helpless, long-suffering yet loving daughter was her only cover. She had to make sure that all he could see was another direct line into some rich guy's estate.

Rita picked up the newspaper clipping with the photo of the destruction of her bar. Anger rose in her throat. The lust for money and power had destroyed her life. She had agreed to take laundered money to allow Landon Pauer to use her club as a drop point for the smuggled algala for his burgeoning black market. But no one can trust a smuggler. As insurance she had routinely kept a few samples from each delivery. Only because she had known one unpublicized aide effect of algala provided immunity to injury to the body, had she dropped the last sample from the last delivery into Emily and Dan's coffee, hoping to protect them from the bomb blast that had been imminent. They would, by now, be suffering the negative effects of algala because the dose was not regulated to their systems. Was she really any different from Harry? Would she go to any length to get what she wanted?

The headline answered her: Local Bar Owner Presumed Dead in Bombing. She read the words that freed her to do all she could to get the algala compound and its antidote. She held the photo closer to the light. She ground her teeth in frustration. All the innocent victims. She steeled her nerves against the urge to cry. All she wanted now was to get even. Harry might be telling the truth about the scarcity of the antidote. No matter, she would have it and her revenge.

"So, how can we make arrangements, Mr. Smithers? My circumstances here in Rio will only allow me to come to Belém a day or two from now. I can fly there tomorrow night and meet you the day after tomorrow. Name the time and place. I will pay double the current price for a year's supply. That's fifty thousand dollars, right?"

"Miss Dumas. This year's supply has been scarce. The price has been increased to one hundred thousand, but it includes the antidote. Your figures reflect the price without the antidote."

Rita spoke without missing a beat.

"All right. I won't insult you by dickering. Let's just make arrangements to meet."

"The day after tomorrow, eleven-thirty in the morning at my restaurant in Belém, La Casa del Norte. I'll bring my supplier, Mickey Straader along too."

Rita wrote down both names, scribbling a note next to Mickey's name: 'smuggler.' "I'll be there at the appointed hour," she said, abruptly hanging up the receiver on the old rotary phone in her hotel room. She didn't like Rio. Too similar to every other big city, international bland even infected its famous beaches. But her phone call from Rio had served to make Harry Smithers think she was a rich somebody, and she felt confident that he had no idea she was Ruthann Mahoney, the bar owner he had once known back in Chicago. Her cover was in place and it made her aggressive juices flow.

As she drove to the airport and booked a flight to Belém before midnight, her mind was racing with ideas for planning how to find out who threw the bomb into her bar that evening. Now that she had Emily and Dan's compound and antidote within reach, she had some time to find out which little landing strip Mickey used to fly in and out of the rainforest. Maybe she could even find his log. Rita wanted her way. Mickey Straader had to be the first link in the chain she was going to break to get it.

14

*E*mily and Dan entered their disheveled apartment bewildered and frustrated. The visit to the room had produced no answers to their questions, which only increased their fears of the bag lady's warning that their time was running out, and stymied their hopes of finding their children in time to save them.

"We can't just look up a phone number in the yellow pages and call a missing children's bureau. Maybe we should start by contacting Maggie, your sister. We did see a letter from her on the table remember? Wasn't her phone number on it?" Emily rustled through the pile of papers on the table and brought out the letter, handing it to Dan.

He stared at the page without really reading for a minute or two, caught by the wrinkles in the paper and curving artfully around three of the four corners, the cartoon border in pastel colors of children playing hopscotch in a park, others swinging on swings and still others running, their balloons flying carefree behind them. Looking for more detail, he saw that each section of the border depicted the same four children, two boys and two girls, dressed differently, yet recognizably the same children. That the fourth corner was torn off seemed strange. He glanced at Emily, deciding not to point out his observation to her, feeling sure that he was making more of it in his mind than it deserved.

"Well, I suppose there's no harm in calling. At worst she won't be home. At best, we'll find out something." He picked up the receiver and dialed.

"The number you have reached has been disconnected." The voice cut off after the recorded message, leaving him with three options, to dial again, to pretend he was talking to someone, or to tell Emily the number is disconnected. Taking a deep breath, Dan dialed again.

"The number you have reached has been disconnected." The voice cut off again. He frowned at this, lowering his head and turning away from Emily to blink away the burning mist rising in his eyes.

"What's wrong?" Emily asked, staring at him.

Dan turned toward her, having regained his composure, and said, with a tone of optimism contrived to keep Emily calm, "The number has been disconnected. Maybe information has another one." Dan trapped the handset between his left ear and shoulder, dialing information in Detroit, Michigan, as he cracked his knuckles to relieve some of the tension his nerves were exerting on his all his joints and muscles.

"I'm sorry, there is no listing for that name in Detroit or its suburbs."

"Do you have a forwarding number for the disconnected one?"

"No, sir, I'm sorry. Nothing at all. Have a nice day." The operator hung up. Dan listened to the hiss on the line until the dial tone returned. Slowly hanging up the receiver, he turned toward Emily, unable to mask his agitation any longer. He paced the floor in a circle, saying nothing, lighting a cigarette and taking four deep drags on it.

"Something's not right," he said, exhaling a cloud of smoke that rose to the ceiling to deposit its molecules of nicotine on the already grime streaked surface. "Maggie wouldn't move without telling me. Maybe Mom knows where Maggie is."

Dan picked up the phone again, but immediately began punching the receiver button, trying to get it to connect. He continued for a minute, pausing for a second or two to see if the line would come to life, each time punching the button faster and harder than the time before. He threw the handset onto the cradle, and whirled around toward the window, moving like a bull enraged by the toreador's cloak and shouting, "No dial tone. Nothing. The line's dead. I don't get it. I was just using it. What's going on here?" He picked up the phone and threw it against the wall.

"Jeez, Dan. What did you do that for? Come on. Let's go for a walk. Maybe we'll think of something." Emily went to the door of the apartment. She turned the knob. It fell off in her hand.

"Dan? Can you fix this?"

He tried to fit the knob into the mechanism, but the rest of it had fallen into the hallway.

"No, not without opening the door," he groaned as he jabbed at the hole with the broken knob, trying to force the door to unlock. Emily went to the window that gave out onto the fire escape and pulled upward to open it.

"Dan?" Her voice rose slowly on his name, wanting to call him but not alarm him. "The window won't open either." She gave a couple more tugs on the handles, exhaling a groan as she winched all her strength into her hands and back. "Uuaaggh!"

"Stand back!" Dan lunged toward the table, grabbing a chair, hoisting it over his head and launching it at the window with all his strength to shatter one large pane of glass that stood between them and the out of doors. The chair bounced back into the room and broke apart as it landed like a game of pick up sticks on the worn tiles of the floor, digging yet one more series of gouges into the soft and cracking linoleum.

"Dan, we're trapped! We're trapped!" Emily panicked. She ran back and forth from door to window, kicking the door and pounding her fists on the window, screaming at the rigid and unrelenting barriers, "Let us out, goddam it, let us out!" Dan grabbed her and shook her hard.

"Stop it, Emily! Stop!" He pulled her into his chest, binding his arms around her to contain her frantic movements. "We've got to think clearly." He felt her body relax against him as she connected to his words and felt his protection encircling her. "We've got to think clearly to get out of here." He pulled her with him toward the mattress, not releasing her from his grasp until he felt she would follow his example. "We have to sit down for a moment and think," he said, lowering his voice and slowing his speech to keep control himself, as much as to calm her fear. But he was frightened by the imposed limitations of forced confinement, just as he had been when his father had made him stand for hours in the front hall closet to pay penance for his childish indiscretions. He let go of Emily and pulled her down to the mattress where they both sat shaking, trying to breathe deeply, waiting for the adrenalin to subside and clarity of thought to return.

❧

The night nurse sat sleepily in the chair between the beds where Emily and Dan lay tied down. From time to time, one or the other of them would struggle spastically against the tethers, pulling pathetically at them, but to no avail. The nurse watched, feeling sorry for them. She was young and only a part time replacement nurse at the hospital. Her job was to check their monitors every half hour and adjust the tethers hourly, since the pulling tended to cause the tethers to rub as they tightened. Blisters and raw patches were developing under the straps. The nurse marked her observations on the charts and decided to bandage their sores.

She brought a cart with tape, bandages and ointments between the beds. She removed Emily's tethers one at a time, bandaging her wrists and ankles thickly with gauze and adhesive tape to protect the sores. She then placed ace bandages over the dressing to keep it in place. Emily lay still as the nurse worked to ease the chaffing, loosening the tethers to be less restricting. Dan remained immobile as she gave him the same treatment. Forty-five minutes passed. The monitors ticked rhythmically, like metronomes keeping time for a silent orchestra. The couple was sleeping soundly, unresponsive to her ministrations. According to her instructions, the nurse removed the intravenous feeding needles to move them to an unbruised vein. Bruising all up and down the arms and legs of the patients from repeated use of the needles made the order nearly impossible to carry out. She searched carefully, at last finding a spot that could accept the needle, which she inserted, taped and checked for flow before sitting down in her chair to watch over her charges. The quiet in the room and her own fatigue began to overtake her, until she fell asleep in her chair, snoring softly in time with the rhythm of the monitors.

⁂

"The only way out may be through the room. I think we ought to go back there and find a way out." Dan said, already standing at the door. He turned the handle. The door opened, allowing the sweet odor to pour out toward them. Emily followed him down the stairs and into the room, walking on the balls of her feet like a ballerina to eliminate any sound from walking on the high-gloss hard wood floors. They sat on the same couch where they had made love, not saying anything for a few minutes. The piano version of 'Gymnopédie' by Saint-Saens played in the background, setting a melodic, slow, and dirge-like mood that calmed their nerves.

"Doesn't it bother you that no one can see or hear us?" Emily said, unable to keep silent for very long. "Don't you think that's strange?" she asked, like a child who wanted affirmation of the obvious to feel safer and more secure.

"Yes, and I want to talk with that older couple living here . . . to see if they know how we might get out of here."

"How are you going to do that when we know they don't see or hear us?"

"Just open my mouth and talk." Dan shook his head at Emily's apparent lack of ability to reason beyond the obvious.

As if on cue, the couple entered from the hallway to the left, busily conversing, and entirely unaware of Emily and Dan's presence in the room, just as before. They paused near the bar, where the older Emily went around behind it to make some drinks. She took two glasses and some ice, poured vodka, Clamato and Tabasco sauce over the ice, stirring the two Bloody Marys with a stalk of celery as she spoke.

"I still think we need to let the children know our intentions. Setting up a living trust is one thing. Making sure they all feel provided for is another. They're all so different. Let's get them all to come here for a family meeting—like we used to have when they were kids. Then we could explain to them why we're dividing the estate as we are, don't you think?" she asked, as she handed the now adequately stirred and highly spiced Bloody Mary to the older Dan as he sat down on another of the overstuffed couches in the room.

"Honey, you and I have argued about this a thousand times —that Miranda doesn't need a dime, but she deserves the most reward, having worked so hard for her success. Jennifer needs money the most to support her twins, but that deadbeat ex-husband—well, at least he's an ex-husband and has not rights to anything she gets. Ian and Patrick dangling so precariously in that little business of theirs could consume an inheritance in just a few months. What they really need a substantial infusion of venture capital, if they're going to make it. Why won't you listen to me on this? Different needs, different amounts. That is the only fair thing to do."

"No, my dear. We can't give them different amounts in spite of their different financial needs. They'll just accuse us of playing favorites. They all should get the same percentages and under the same conditions. The bulk of our money goes to the Longevity Institute. After all, if it hadn't been for the compound we'd—"

"I don't need to hear it all again," the older Emily interrupted. "We survived. The medicines were developed. We have all benefited from the near tragedy, including the children and the world's population of elderly. We've made our contribution, paid our debt, and the Institute is solid. I'm going into the other room to call them. We'll have them all over for dinner tonight, since they're all in town this weekend anyway." She turned on her heels and hastily disappeared down the hallway to the right, taking her drink with her.

The older Dan sighed, standing up out of politeness as she left. Then moving stiffly to the bar to lean against it, he pursed his lips and released little puffs of breath through his nose, as if laughing inside. He shook his head at his wife's logic. "She knows she's going to win," he said under his breath.

The younger Emily and Dan saw their opportunity. Dan stood up and slowly sauntered over to the bar, leaning against it in the same manner as the older version of himself.

"I think she's right, actually. We could never treat them all the same way." To the younger Dan's surprise, the older Dan turned to him.

"Listen, young man, I've aged. The kids will always be my kids to me, with their petty jealousies and their manipulative sibling rivalries intact. I want my remaining years to be as simple as I can make them. Give the kids all the same amount, and they can't bicker."

"Are you willing to talk with them all tonight anyway?"

"Sure. They'll all be here in just a few hours. I see your woman friend there is interested in our conversation. She reminds me of my dear Emily when she was younger and more—no, she has never been more beautiful to me than she is today."

The older Dan raised his hand, motioning to Emily to join them. With a certain air of timidity, she crossed to the bar and stood, smiling, in front of them for a minute looking from one to the other, trying to make sense of the picture.

"I'm seeing the future and the past all rolled into one. My young Dan and my old Dan chatting in this strange place."

"That's right, young lady. We're the same man, aware of each other now only because the time bubble controlled by the amount of drug in your bodies is changing."

"Time bubble? What are you saying?" Emily's skepticism peaked as she considered the implausibility of the moment.

"I'm only here, we're only here, my wife and I, because of the fact that your conscious minds are aware of your deep subconscious minds. All your life experiences, wishes, hopes, fears and dreams mix with your awareness of the danger you are in at all times."

"What do you mean?" she asked, not following his logic.

"You know, when you get a gut feeling, or you hear that 'little voice' that tells you to do something you hadn't actually thought about doing?"

"Intuition? Is that what you mean?"

"Yes, exactly. My wife and I represent your possible future, your hopes. You imagine us the way you imagine another option when your intuition kicks in. If you listen, you'll understand your only way back to your true reality is through that door."

He pointed to the apartment. Emily and Dan glanced at each other.

"We tried to get out of the apartment, but the lock and knob to only door to the outside have fallen apart and the window is unbreakable."

"Not actually. If this is not a true reality, where do think you are in your true reality?" He let the question hang in the air.

"In a hospital." Dan surmised. "So, if we're in a hospital, what's wrong with us?"

"Think about why you feel so compelled to escape. What could your condition be?"

"We could be unconscious," Emily suggested her eyes widening as she began to see the direction of his hints.

"Or in a coma?" Dan stumbled on the words, disbelieving this possibility. "Close to death?"

"Well, perhaps."

"How do you know all this?" Dan asked, still not believing.

"I am your subconscious, aware of your true reality, because you are, even though to the doctors, you are out of touch. They cannot see or hear us, but we are aware of them."

"I read somewhere once that when patients in a coma they can hear what someone says to them, and that it's important to say only encouraging things to them," Emily said.

"That's it. Now and again your conscious world invades this one, but without the awareness of those 'out there.'" He pointed toward the apartment. "The partygoers were actually the medical teams tending you during your last episode."

"So, if I catch your drift, you're saying that the doctors have tied us down to keep us from hurting ourselves when we flail about."

"That's right. And, as soon as you're physically freed, you'll be able to exit your apartment to whatever place you imagine. You may or may not recall us. They don't realize they're inhibiting your progress by tying you down. They don't realize you may become permanently trapped here. If you do, we all will die. If they find an antidote, you'll become conscious, and this realm will evaporate. Can you accept what I'm saying?" The older Dan peered at them both intently, as if trying to will them to understand their situation. The younger Dan stepped toward the couch, pulling Emily with him, as if trying to place distance between himself and an enemy.

"Who is the bag lady?"

"You've seen her?"

"Yes."

"Have you spoken to her?"

"Yes."

The older Dan's face grew slack, his eyes clouded over with the haze of deep thought. When ready to speak, he stared into their eyes from across the space that now separated them, and spoke with a voice filled with longing.

"When the kids arrive here tonight, I'll send them all into the space outside your apartment door. Imagine a park and look for children there. When you find them, at that exact same moment, your children will be gathering around your beds in the conscious world. You must cross over to contact them. And—you must destroy your apartment as you leave it. This room will cease to exist. Without this realm, you must go toward the conscious world beyond your apartment. If you meet the bag lady again, you must escape her. She is Death. She is omnipotent. She is not to be trifled with."

"But, she warned us, saying we had to save our children."

"Then you must. To fail will mean death, swift and forever. Tonight is all the time you have. Remember, in the conscious world time passes differently. Days, weeks, even months can go by out there. Here, we experience only seconds, minutes, and hours. Lifetimes can pass out there, but we feel only a short time go by. Now, go to your apartment and don't turn back. Good-bye and good luck."

The older Dan smiled, shook Dan's hand, hugged Emily, and then left the room through the same door as the older Emily. Emily and Dan walked slowly up the stairs to the apartment. The door closed. They pushed the piano back in place for the last time. They sat down on the mattress. Emily looked back at the door.

"Look at the door—" she gasped. The fresh painted color was fading, and the shine was tarnishing before their eyes. Dan understood the room beyond was gone.

"We must remain calm until they take off the tethers. We'll just have to wait to meet the children after old Dan sends them outside." He put his arms around Emily and cuddled her on the mattress. They slept. They did not dream.

❧

The night nurse awoke with a start. She checked her watch to see how long she had been asleep.

"Three hours! Oh, my God! Oh, my God!" She panicked. The slow heart rates set off the monitors. Depressed and shallow breathing and falling body temperatures had set off the warning buzzers. The flattening lines on the brainwave monitor showed distinct irregularities. She did not notice the parallel rates of change. She simply panicked and ran from the room to find help.

The intern on duty rushed to Emily and Dan's room. He unhooked the intravenous lines and removed the tethers as two orderlies worked fast transferring Emily and Dan to the two flat-bed gurneys.

"Move them to the ICU... stat!"

SACRED NIGHT

Emily and Dan woke with a start. They jumped up and ran to the door. It opened easily.

"He said destroy the apartment," Emily reminded Dan, grabbing his shoulder and digging her nails into him. "How?"

"Fire."

Dan ran to the table, grabbing a pile of newspapers and scattering them all around the room. He fumbled through the remaining papers on the table and grabbed some matches. But as he crumpled some of the paper to make it light more easily, a scrap of paper on the floor caught his eye. His heart pounding, he picked it up and stuffed it in his pocket. He then moved quickly around the room, igniting newspaper fires all around the perimeter.

Emily and Dan paused at the threshold of the door to the outside, looking back into the apartment through the rising gray smoke that billowed from the smoldering newspaper as the draft from the hallway gave breath to the flames. One after another, the fires ignited, licking the walls and catching on the wastepaper strewn across the floor. They watched, hearing the roar of the fire increase as it spread to the mattress, feeding on the dry stuffing like sharks devouring a helpless victim, until the entire room burst into flame. Fear pumped in their veins, as they ran into the sunlight outside the apartment building. They looked back to see smoke and flames billowing from the windows. They watched, overcome by a sense of loss and infused with a sense of hope as flames engulfed the entire building. Then, without a word, they set off at a jog.

SACRED NIGHT

The monitors went berserk. The heartbeats jumped from sixty-five beats a minute to one hundred fifty beats. The brainwaves showed high activity, much like a fight or flight response. The body temperatures rose to ninety-nine point eight. Emily and Dan began to perspire and then sweat, their breathing labored and heavy. They flailed about in running movements with their legs and powerful arm thrusts. Only the sidebars of the beds kept them from falling. The intern grabbed Dan's arm, forcing it to the bed, while the nurse injected a mild tranquilizer. They did the same to Emily. Both patients responded quickly to the drugs.

๛

"Dan, I've got to rest. I can't keep running."

"Okay, let's stop here for a few minutes and catch our breath." Dan flopped down under a tree, pretending to spread a blanket for Emily to lie on.

"I don't know why I feel so tired. I can't be that much out of shape." Emily felt herself falling asleep. "I feel drunk—like I drank too much—"

She passed out. Dan looked at her and reached over to shake her. Suddenly dizzy, nauseated, the last image he saw before blacking out was the swirling park, people, trees, benches, sky, clouds, grass and pathways swimming in circles. Then nothing.

15

*L*andon and Marguerite spent several days enjoying the privacy of the luxurious apartment they had shared for so many years each time he came to Brazil. Marguerite always treated Landon like the sexiest man in the world, sparing no delight for his enjoyment. In return, he loved her with his life. A warm, compassionate, caring woman, she only regretted that she could never provide him another child.

Paulo's physical handicaps had resulted from a particularly difficult breach delivery. Marguerite had always been a small woman, not more than a hundred and ten pounds and only five feet tall. He had been a large baby, over eleven pounds, the pregnancy had been hard for her. She had gained nearly fifty pounds, and the strain on her system in the ninth month had sent her to bed to wait for delivery. Deep in her heart she blamed her body for not delivering her son as a healthy, normal child, even thought the delivery had nearly taken her life. The doctors had tried everything short of a Cesarean to bring Paulo into the world. To be born alive at all, nerve damage at birth had been unavoidable. The process had left the baby with legs unable to walk and a left hand unable to grasp. Yet, that day, a saving grace had spared his mind and his right hand.

Paulo could talk and write, and talk and write he did. A playful child, verbally and intellectually precocious, by the age of fifteen he had already graduated high school, and was planning to enter the University of Chicago on special scholarship with special arrangements for his physical needs. He was a talented writer, particularly interested in biochemical neuro-regeneration. The future promised much for Paulo, and Landon was able to feel great pride for his Brazilian son.

The stark contrast of Landon's life lay in the hard, cold realities of his home life back in the States. Lorraine Pauer had raised her only child, William, to become an exact replica of his father. She had lived a bitter, calculating life, making every effort to induce William to live up to her expectations. He had floundered in the cold sea of a loveless home. In childhood, neither of his parents had considered the obvious sensitivities that drew him toward the arts via his talent for drawing and painting when making choices for his future. His young life had evolved along the lines of their design for him, not his own. He might have been a great artist, but his parents had wanted a lawyer in the family, so even though he proved to be only academically average, they bought his way into the halls of the most prestigious prep schools, universities and law schools.

Lorraine and Landon had ignored the signs and the pain of William's struggle to become everything he could never be. They couldn't see his heart grow hard. They didn't hear the simmering anger in his words. For their own sense of comfort as parents, they had made sure that from childhood to middle age his fundamental insecurities kept him vulnerable and controllable. The result lay in the manner in which William still related to others only in reference to how he, himself, was feeling at the moment, trapped in a childlike view of world, forced upon him at hands of his own parents.

Landon carried little regret about William, having always chosen instead to remain more concerned for Marguerite and Paulo. He cleared his throat, as if clearing fear from his heart as he was searching for the right words to use that night as he and Marguerite undressed for bed. He fumbled with the pillbox, took out his usual dose of two tablets, and washed them down with some water from the carafe that stood on the night stand next to his side of the bed. Turning toward her, and sitting on the edge of the bed, he took a deep breath

"Marguerite, these last few days have been, well, very meaningful to me. I'm an old man, and you're a fine woman—"

"Landon, you don't have to say anything. Remember, you're married. You come down here for only one reason. You are unbelievably generous to Paulo and me. It is enough," she said, walking toward him.

"No, Marguerite, it is not enough. My American wife and I have been living in numb resignation to each other for so long, I can't remember the last time I felt anything for her. She's been running roughshod over me in her own way for thirty years." He paused to cough and drink some more water, stalling to face the fear that Marguerite would reject the plan he was about to propose.

"You mean much more to me than a few nights a year of sex and entertainment. You are my Brazilian wife."

"Landon, dear, you don't have to say these words. I know you love me," she said, placing her hands on either side of his face and holding it up to her lips. "And, I love you."

"Hear me out, Marguerite," he said, wrapping his arms gently around her waist. "I've changed my will to include you and Paulo. You must continue to live in comfort when I'm gone. I called my attorney to set the changes to my will in motion just before I came here. There is nothing Lorraine or anyone else can do to stop them. It's a done deal."

Marguerite tried to hush him, gently placing her fingers on his lips. He took her hand, gently kissing it.

"If you reject the money, it goes directly into a trust for Paulo to make sure he gets the education he deserves. His needs will be cared for the rest of his life. If I died tonight, no one could change a thing. I have nothing else to give you. My life is nearly over anyway, and I need to make things right for you and Paulo to rest in peace."

Marguerite blinked away her tears. "No, Landon. I can't accept this. I don't need more money. I have saved a sizable nest egg. If I have to, I can go back to work as a hairdresser to make ends meet. At least I won't have to be a call girl. Besides, you're going to live a long time. Why are we talking about this?"

"Because of twenty million dollars. Nothing will change my mind. I want you to have it." His eyes flashed with the passion of his convictions. "Please, I beg you not to reject my offer," he said, the tears brimming in his eyes, pouring down his cheeks and falling onto the lapel of his silk pajamas. "I have to go home tomorrow, and the Lorraine and my doctors won't let me come back," he said, his voice quavering as he tried to contain the sobs welling up from his soul. "I will be unable to see you and Paulo ever again," Landon said, wrapping her in his arms and kissing her. She pulled away and turned toward the window, her own tears welling up and overflowing.

"Just let me make my own way. Don't be like this. I can't help you be remembered. I can only go on as I have, caring for Paulo, being available for you."

"Come here, Marguerite."

As she turned around, Landon approached her. With nervously fumbling fingers, he slowly unzipped her dress. He kissed her until she did what pleased him most, removing each article of clothing sensuously, kissing him all over. He pulled her to the bed, and lay back, reaching up to caress her breasts. Her perspiration ran sparkling down her belly to his until she shimmered like a beautiful otherworldly creature. In the silver light pouring through the half-closed

Venetian blinds drew perfect midnight zebra-striped shadows in the moon glow that spilled across her breasts.

Landon watched the shadows spread, undulating with Marguerite's rhythmic movements. Landon looked beyond his beautiful Marguerite to see vaguely human-shaped, shadowy figures floating in the room. One, larger than the rest, stood behind Marguerite, spreading its arms wide. Landon heard a wail, horrible and terrifying, which Marguerite did not acknowledge. Terror, unlike any he had ever known, gripped him as felt the claws of the creature's hands pulling him away from his Marguerite, away from his life. He trembled uncontrollably. Horror rose into Marguerite from her lover's body, as his skin turned white and clammy, and he gasped for breath. Writhing in pain, he clutched his chest to wrench the hands of the phantom from his body. His pain, increasing with every movement, overcame his resolve to survive. Landon's body fell limp and lifeless as the phantom pulled him upward, drifting away with him into the shadows.

Marguerite leaped to her feet and grabbing the phone, she called Smithers' office. He picked up the phone on the third ring.

"Oh Harry! Harry! Call the ambulance! Landon is having a seizure. I don't know what's wrong! It's awful! Hurry! Hurry!"

Only a few minutes passed before Harry entered the bedroom, out of breath and sweating. Marguerite sat on the couch wearing only her slip, crying inconsolably.

"Too late, Harry. He's dead. He just died, like that, no warning. I didn't do anything unusual. We were making love and suddenly he was dead. Oh, Harry, I can't help feeling sick to my stomach."

She ran to the bathroom holding one hand over her mouth to hold back her revulsion. When she came back a few minutes later, Harry was on the phone to his sister.

"Lorraine, I don't know how to say this to you." The line crackled in response to thunderstorms somewhere between Belém and Lexington that threatened to cut communications.

"Harry, what's wrong? Is it Landon?" More static on the line sent Lorraine into shivers.

"Yes—he—uh, just died. It was—a heart attack. One minute, we were sitting at the table talking, and the next, he was dead. It was fast, Lorraine. I don't think he even knew what hit him." He gazed and Marguerite, shaking his head and trying to quiet her verbal protest with the look in his eyes. She didn't utter the words that rose from her heart.

"Send him to Chicago," Lorraine whispered softly, clearing her throat. The line cut out and in again.

"What was that?" Harry shouted into the phone willing the line to stay connected.

"I said, 'Send him to Chicago.' I'll contact the Hauser-Croft Funeral Home and tell them to wait for your phone call with the particulars about flight arrivals, when you get it all arranged. Can you do that?"

"Yes, yes, I will," Harry said, still holding Marguerite's eyes with his.

"I'm sorry. I can't be there now to help you." The line crackled again. "Harry? Do you hear me? Can you take care of him for me?" Like a little girl talking to her big brother, Lorraine was no longer the self-assured wife of a wealthy man.

"Sure, honey. I'll take care of everything down here. Why don't you go up to William's house to make arrangements for burial services and all that. He'll help you up there. I'll take care of things down here." The line sizzled and sputtered into silence.

"All right. I'll go tonight," she agreed, realizing the line was dead. "Good-bye," she said to emptiness in the phone.

Smithers hung up the phone and looked coldly at Marguerite.

"I'm sorry—don't take it so hard. He was getting old. He wanted it this way. I'm sure he did. He died with everything going his way.

So, what more could anyone ask?" He crossed the room, lighting up a cigarette, and watching the smoke curl up from the upturned end of the unfiltered Camel.

"For Pete's sake, Harry! I was making love to him when died. He had just told me he had set up a trust in his will for Paulo and me." She stared at his casual posture with the wide eyes of a doe helpless in the headlights of the oncoming truck. "I know this is going to become a big problem for me. Can you imagine it? And now he's dead while I was with him. Does this look awful or not?" She began to tremble with fear.

"Who knew? Who knows? You and I do. You heard what I told Lorraine. We can make it be any way we want it to be. No one ever needs to know the truth about how he died. And, you know I will take care of you—that I care for you. Just leave things to me."

Harry reached out to take her hand. She pulled it away.

"No, Harry. This is different from all those years ago. Landon wasn't a bad john who got out of line. He was the only man ever I loved and who ever loved me." Marguerite began to cry again but without changing her expression. "Now, he's left Paulo and me a lot of money." A hard-edged resignation appeared on her face, as the last of her tears slowly poured down her cheeks. "Don't think for a moment there isn't going to be trouble over it. The minute Lorraine learns about the change in the will, nothing we say will be heard. The tabloids will have a field day. 'Dead American Millionaire Leaves Fortune to Longtime Call Girl Mistress.' I can see the headline, Harry. It will reach out to you too." Her tears had stopped. Her eyes, red with crying, tore into him with the precision of lasers. She saw recognition of her words flicker and die in his eyes. Another emotion replaced it. Guilt. She saw his guilt.

Harry looked away. "Listen, Marguerite, I'll handle it." He knew that Landon's death wasn't from natural causes. Harry raised his eyes to her face again, as a rush of lust flushed across his own face.

157

"Landon will be on a plane back to the States in less than twenty-four hours. Lorraine has never known what he's been up to here, except to get his compound. She'll be indignant for a few days or weeks, but there's so much to go around, she'll get over it." Harry's compassionate tone of voice transformed into the flippant arrogance he used to disguise his own emotions as he spoke.

"You take her for a fool, don't you Harry?" she pressed him, looking to push the right button that would reveal his charade.

"No. She's no fool. She knows he left millions to that jerk of a kid of his, William, and some to me. Can you believe it? He left money to me. She knows money is all he had to give, Marguerite. If she gets hers, she'll back away."

"You underestimate the jealous rage of a woman who thinks she's been wronged. Money coming to me will not be invisible. She will know everything then. But I think she knows everything now, and has for a long time."

"Just enjoy the fruits of your labors, Marguerite. I'll take care of you. What more could you ask?"

Marguerite felt a restless discomfort about his indifference to the circumstances surrounding Landon's death and her predicament. She pulled the curtain aside to find that morning had arrived without fanfare. She picked up her clothes and headed for the bathroom.

"Nothing, Harry. I'm leaving. I'm taking Paulo with me to make sure he gets to go on with his life." She dressed quickly, and returned to the bedroom to throw a few articles of clothing into a travel bag, and to collect her purse and her shoes. She slipped her right foot into the simple white sandal she had tossed near the door. "I won't be back—not for you or anyone else." She slipped her left foot into her other sandal and turned the knob leading into the hallway between her room and Paulo's high-tech care facility bedroom. "When the Will is read, give mine to the Church. You know which one. Do what you want to with this apartment. So long, Harry." She slammed the door and left.

Harry sat stunned and angry for a few minutes. "Bitch. She'll pay for this," the words seething from his clenched teeth like the hiss of a snake. "She can't turn me down like that and get away with it." He picked up the phone and made arrangements to fly Landon's body back to the States the following evening. Then he called someone else to tell them the good news: Landon was dead, and Marguerite would be leaving town, permanently.

Detective Cameron spent the slow time listening to the recording from the airplane. It had caught everything he had heard in the earphones. Then he had watched all the comings and goings, sensing that something had gone wrong when he saw one of the men from the restaurant go in alone in the darkness of the wee hours and the same woman from the restaurant leave pushing someone in his wheelchair, shortly after dawn, obviously in a hurry and carrying a couple of travel bags. After she disappeared around the corner, he was tempted to sneak into the apartment building for a closer look, but decided to wait just a little longer, confident that the camera was taking it all in. Detective Cameron poured himself the last of the tepid water from his thermos. The man hadn't come out yet, but an ambulance arrived, sirens blaring, and two husky paramedics wrestled a gurney into the building. Minutes later, one of the paramedics wheeled a draped body to the back of the waiting vehicle. He tried to open the ambulance doors, but finding them locked, he scurried back into the building in search of the other paramedic. Detective Cameron stepped out of his car and walked quickly to the gurney holding the body, looking around him to make sure no one noticed him. Cautiously but quickly, he lifted the sheet at the head end.

"Landon Pauer." Detective Cameron nodded slightly to himself as he dropped the sheet and walked into the lobby of the building.

"Excuse me," he said politely to the concierge, a wizened old man with spectacles perched on the end of his nose to read his morning paper. He looked up at the sound of a voice.

"Could you tell me who that woman was who left here pushing the wheel chair?"

"Who wants to know?" the old man replied with a British pronunciation infused with a Portuguese accent, and squinting over his glasses with distrust written on his face.

"Let's just say I need her name for a police matter up in the States," he said producing his badge. The old man took the badge to look at it more closely, and handed it back, clearly unimpressed.

"American police have no power here." He smiled, and looked back to his paper. Detective Cameron reached over the counter and placed a fifty dollar bill in the fold of the newspaper so that it stood up, showing the numbers. The old man quickly slipped it from the paper and into his shirt pocket.

"Her name is Marguerite Kohl. She was that guy's mistress," he said glancing at the gurney.

"And the man who went up to her apartment earlier this morning, before dawn?"

The concierge smiled again. Detective Cameron held out another fifty, which the old man grabbed quickly from his hand.

"Harry Smithers, the dead guy's brother-in-law."

"Gracias," Detective Cameron said, with his very American accent. The old man returned his attention to the newspaper as Detective Cameron quickly returned to his car and rolled down the window to listen to whatever the paramedics might say. A minute later, Harry Smithers came out of the apartment building in the company of both paramedics.

"Take the body to the Air Inter loading dock at the airport," Harry said, loud enough that Detective Cameron overheard the instruction. "They'll package it for shipping back to the States on the next flight to Miami."

"Yes, sir." The driver said as the other man shoved the gurney roughly to the now open doors of the ambulance. As the gurney legs collapsed into the back end of the vehicle, they both shoved it hard, slamming the head end into the far wall of the truck.

"No respect for the dead," muttered Detective Cameron. "Dead less than an hour, and you're nothing but somebody else's job." He shook his head, as if trying to dislodge that idea from his mind as the ambulance drove away. Adjusting the setting and exposure on the camera for daylight, Detective Cameron decided to remain at Marguerite's apartment to find a way to get in to search it, hopefully without paying another hundred dollars to do so. Without warning, a taxi careened erratically through the light traffic and stopped in front of the apartment building. Marguerite stepped out.

"Wait here. I'll be right back," she said, as Detective Cameron leapt from his car and ran across the street. She turned toward the lobby door just as he caught up with her.

"Excuse me—Ms. Kohl, isn't it?"

"Who are you? What do you want?" she replied in a clipped, hostile tone.

"I'm Detective Cameron. Mrs. Landon Pauer, hired me to follow her husband while he's here," he lied convincingly. "She didn't expect him to die, though, I, uh, well, I'm sorry about Mr. Pauer."

"I don't want to talk to you. I have other things I must do," she pushed past him to go inside.

"Well, I have to ask you some questions on American police business," he answered, walking with her. "Wasn't Mr. Pauer involved in the procurement of drugs?"

"I don't have to tell you anything. You're in my country, and have no power to question me. I don't have to say a thing. Now, you're in my way. Get away from me!" she shouted. Pushing her way inside, she ran for the elevators.

"Ms. Kohl—Ms. Kohl—I have reason to believe Mr. Pauer was murdered—that he didn't die of natural causes."

She looked at him, her eyes filling with tears of anger. "Outrageous!"

"Harry is mixed up in this, he may be a ringleader—" At last he had her attention. "I even think he may have ordered a drug overdose —do you have access to any medications Mr. Pauer was taking?" He knew he was guessing, but she didn't.

Marguerite looked at him long and hard. She was in no emotional condition to think clearly, but Harry's behavior toward her and this odd little man's assertions fit together.

"Yes—I do," she said cautiously.

"Could I take a sample for analysis?

"By whom?"

"By the police lab in Chicago. There may be a connection to a bombing that happened up there. Mr. Pauer may have been involved. You could help me clear his name," he added, hoping to influence her by weighting the possibility of guilt with a gentle tone of voice.

Marguerite added up the circumstances of the last couple of hours and the last fifteen years, deciding that to give him what he wanted would get him to go away.

"Well, yes, I could give you a sample. Wait here," she said firmly. A few minutes later she handed one of the purple caplets she had seen Landon take earlier in the evening to Detective Cameron. "Now, leave me alone."

"Thank you, Ms. Kohl. This may just be the evidence we need," he said with professional candor as she disappeared inside the elevator to escape his questions and the temptation to respond. "I hope this is the real thing," he said inside the safety of his car.

SACRED NIGHT

Detective Cameron drove the short distance back to La Casa del Norte. He pulled the car alongside the road opposite the restaurant and dozed on and off for a few hours in the car while the camera took in whatever events would occur at the restaurant. The plane taking Landon back to Chicago wouldn't leave until the next day, after midday. From beneath the mental sedative of sleep deprivation, his instincts told him tonight would be his last chance to rest.

16

When Lorraine Pauer hung up from Harry's call, she went directly to the garage and her pale yellow Mercedes convertible. Night driving was not her favorite endeavor, but tonight she had to overcome her reluctance and risk driving the dark back roads. She backed carefully out of the garage, driving slowly down the long drive to the main road as if she were about to lose control of the car. Turning toward Lexington, she kept to the back roads as long as possible for fear of encountering other cars. Then, for the last couple of miles, she had to take the expressway to the airport. Relieved to be off the high-speed thoroughfare, she parked in a remote lot, not wanting to draw any attention to herself. She simply walked into the terminal, purchased a ticket to Chicago, and went to the ladies room to stay out of sight until just before her flight.

She passed the half hour wait slowly pacing in the drab depression of grime-laden tiles and dripping faucets. In just a matter of hours the news of Landon's death would hit the papers.

"Harry's good at camouflaging almost any situation, but shipping dead bodies is a conspicuous task. Loading a casket into the luggage compartment on a passenger plane potentially could cause a stir, if only among the airport personnel," Lorraine thought aloud as she looked at her reflection in the cracked mirror above the washbasin. "I have to get to William's place before Landon's body arrives in Chicago. I need to be shocked and bereaved in front of witnesses. The next few weeks are going to be very public and probably very messy. The Will must be read. Landon's fortune must pass to me. William will contest his penniless status. Harry will raise hell over getting nothing. None of Landon's favored charities will receive their expected donations. No one will get a cent. No one but me," she smiled greedily, stifling the wicked laugh that erupted from her soul.

Landon's death passed control and power to Lorraine. For so long she had played the helpless, fragile wife. Now she could hardly wait to take ownership of Landon's fortune. During the past ten years, Landon never knew how Lorraine had quietly built her own relationships with his brokers, financiers, attorneys, and accountants. The paperwork Landon had thought was in his control was effectively just a house of cards. Over the years, she had laid the inroads of her influence on the foundation of Landon's mental degeneration. She had convinced all of the professionals involved that Landon was mentally incompetent. She had instructed them to let him think they were doing his bidding, no matter how ridiculous his requests became. She had known all along about Marguerite and her son. She had known when Landon changed the Will to include them. But it didn't even matter. She was in fact the executrix of the estate. All of it would come to her and she would do as she pleased.

She snuggled comfortably into the first class seat to enjoy her first sips of champagne and a momentary rush of exhilaration as the plane took off. It was only a forty-minute flight to Chicago. She would step out of a taxi at William's house by two in the morning. Arriving at that hour to tell William of his father's demise face to face and to validate her grief with bizarre behavior would serve to make him easier to control in the days to come.

17

*R*ita arrived in Belém from Rio just before midnight in an adrenalin-induced state of alert. She drove the rented car straight to the hotel to attempt a couple of hours of rest before setting out to find out who was responsible for the bombing of her bar. She had a hunch both Harry Smithers and Mickey Straader had been part of the plot to bomb her out of existence, even though Harry had been the one to recruit her to bring the compound to Chicago for him. Once she had provided him and Mickey with the connections, she suspected they wanted to eliminate her from the inner circle even though she knew the two men were incapable of direct conflict. The money, which Harry had promised to pay for her services, was certainly enough to be his motive to hire her executioners. As simply as that, greed dipped its hand into every raw deal.

To Harry and Mickey, she had long been dead. The police investigation and the newspapers concluded she had been at the point of impact and therefore was simply vaporized by the power of the bomb itself. Confident that her conversation with him on the phone hadn't tipped Harry off either, she checked in using her alias, Rita

Dumas. She remembered how the patrons of her bar had often called her Rita, instead of Ruthann, but that was just a result of their confusion of her name with the name of the bar. She added the Dumas on a bet from a customer. The name stuck. Ruthann Mahoney, the only name known to Harry Smithers and Mickey Straader, had died in the bombing. Rita Dumas was alive and well.

As the hotel room door swung open, Rita caught a glimpse of her reflection in the mirror across the room. Her disguise would be enough to fool anyone. She didn't even recognize herself. Her once fiery red hair was now blond and pulled back in a tight bun. Her flashing green eyes were now azure blue. A well-tailored, conservative suit replaced her flamboyantly trendy mode of dress. The look of the rich and beautiful oozed from every pore. Her makeup removed some time from her features and intensified the seductive aura of power she projected. The shoes she wore and the bag she carried were the best money could buy. Harry and Mickey would succumb to the aura of wealth exuding from her every pore and would not recognize her, unless she let them know who she was.

Setting her baggage next to the armoire, she slipped into a black jumpsuit and cap. Placing the hand-drawn map to Mickey's airport hangar on the bedside table next to the car keys and setting her travel alarm for three-thirty in the morning, she laid down on the bed, and instantly fell asleep.

The alarm jolted her from a dream. She stood up as she slapped the clock into silence. Refreshed from the nap, Rita shook off her fatigue, grabbed her fanny pack, left the hotel and hurriedly started up the rental car. Once she turned onto the back roads, she doused the headlights, driving the rest of the way by moonlight. She could see her way as easily along the road as if driving on a lighted city street. The two-way road diminished to a one-car path through the trees as it neared the airport. She parked in the bushes. The airport was nothing more than a landing strip with a few rickety corrugated tin hangars housing the few light planes used for forays into the interior. Wholesale tour operators, offering their clientele the wild and remote vacation destinations, rented the spaces for the slick Piper cubs they used to ferry their exclusive customers on high priced, once in a life time excursions to the "remotest parts" of the Amazon River jungles.

Rita slipped through the half open door into the hangar where Mickey Straader kept his plane. The dilapidated sign read: *Mickey's Transport Company, Inc.* That he ran a small package transport service to cover his drug runs into the interior with a legitimate business purpose made Rita chuckle at the name.

"Maybe Disney is taking over the world," she whispered to herself. "What a name for an airline."

Toward the back, a soft light glowed in the blackness. A computer! Lucky break. Rita silently negotiated the dark, feeling her way along. I'll see if I can get the log of contacts from a database and maybe a list of all his clients too. Why doesn't he just keep a handwritten register, instead of the computer? It's too high tech for such a small operation as this.

She sat in his chair and at the first movement of the mouse the screen saver disappeared, revealing a skeleton icon that looked like a web page. No password protection on the system. She easily bypassed the icon to enter the control panel of the system.

Child's play. He must be the only guy around here who even knows what a computer is. She took a single floppy from the box and inserted it into the A:\ drive on the computer to download the files. Error code. Unformatted disk. Of course, simple old computer, simple old diskettes. She clicked on the format button and waited. Minutes passed, nothing completed. She ejected the disk and pulled out another. This one she formatted first, and then dragged and dropped the files on the computer. *Not enough space, insert another diskette. Damn, and I have to format it first. Another wait. Her hands were clammy. She tapped her foot on the floor. Ready. Set. Go.* She dragged and dropped the remaining files. They copied. She opened one file list to see the contents. There were all the shippers, warehousing and client lists, and the native formulae for the compound and its antidote. She popped the diskette out of the drive and slipped them into the fanny pack on her belt.

As Rita turned to leave, the coughing of a rough running engine broke the silence. The hangar door squealed unwillingly as two men forced it open to accommodate their truck. Rita slipped behind the filing cabinet, just as a third man drove the rusted flatbed pickup into the space between Mickey's plane and the door. One of the first two men opened the engine compartment and tinkered with the mechanism for just a couple of minutes as the other headed toward the computer. Rita froze, not daring to breathe as the intruder passed near her hiding place. Taking a diskette from his pocket and inserting it into the computer, he keyed a few commands, waited a few seconds, removed the diskette and slipped back to the plane. Neither man spoke. One man then returned to the truck and took a small package from the front seat. He loosened the wires as they returned to the plane, handing the mechanism to the other man. Both worked to quickly finish what they were there to do. Rita waited with the adrenaline-heightened sensitivity to sight and sound of prey hiding from the predator until the men left as they came.

Like storm clouds lifting from a mountain peak, Rita's suspicions rose and swirled in her mind. *These are ruthless killers determined to gain control of the compound and kill everyone connected with it. They copied the ETERNAL HAPPINESS data files from the compute, too. They didn't see me.* Her ears throbbed from the pulse of the blood rushing to her head, as she strained to hear them to go.

Rumbling in protest, the truck backed out from the hangar. Rita waited, immobile, until the sounds of the engine faded into the jungle and then slithered to the front of the plane, looking up at the engine. She pulled a chair to the side where they had opened the compartment. She flipped the latch and raised the door just enough to peer inside the engine. The illuminated dome of the lime green on-light beamed back at her. She decided that the wires from the mechanism were attached to the ignition, if her time working under the hood of her father's car as a kid had taught her anything at all. She couldn't remove the mechanism without risking setting it off. Rita panicked. Her breathing raced as she stumbled into the bushes to her car. She had to get hold of herself.

Almost without the glow of dawn, the sun was rising. So close to the equator, the sun rose at six every morning and set at six every evening with only a few minutes of variance all year long. Daylight and heat would soon betray the coolness of the cover of darkness. She would then run the risk of discovery by an airport overseer who might arrive any minute.

Rita's car careened down the road to Belém, as if she were escaping from the fear she had met at the airstrip, but not knowing she was driving to her inevitable date with destiny.

18

*M*iranda couldn't sleep. The magazine perfect rooms, undisturbed even when in use, the aroma of coffee at dawn, the sound of the insects buzzing on the screens in search of the light every night of the summer, the smell of forgotten waste in the bathrooms and the medicine cabinets filled to capacity with pill bottles when all she wanted was a tooth brush and some toothpaste and countless other disjointed details from her childhood visits to her grandparents' home stirred her mind, and pushed her to get up, get dressed and tiptoe to Patrick and Ian's room. She knocked as softly as she could.

"Patrick!" she whispered in a stage whisper. "Wake up! I have to talk to you! Patrick! It's Miranda! Open the door!"

Ian heard her and went to the door, opening it just a crack.

"Ian, wake up Patrick! I have to talk to him," she whispered.

"Okay—wait a minute," Ian yawned as he crossed the dark room to his brother's bed. He shook it just enough to cause Patrick to stir.

"Hey, Patrick. Miranda wants to talk to you. Wake up!" Ian shook the bed as he whispered.

"What? Miranda? What does she want?" Patrick sat up, rubbing his face to bring some circulation to his skin.

"I don't know. She's standing at the door. Go talk to her!" he said, crawling into his own bed.

Patrick stumbled across the room and opened the door to the hallway. "What do you want?"

"Listen, we have to go to Dr. Blume's house tonight. I've just figured out how my grandfather's medicine is connected to the bombing of Rita's Bar. We can't wait till morning to meet with him. We have to get on the Web tonight and convince him to believe me."

"How can you do that?" Patrick's mind had not yet cleared enough to follow her reasoning.

"I remember, when I was a little girl, taking the pill bottle to my grandfather during summer long visits to him and my grandmother. So many times, over and over, I took the pills from the medicine cabinet for him. I remember the label was printed in Spanish or Portuguese, one or the other. But I remember the label read Belém, Brazil. I've spent hours thinking about it and picturing those bottles. I'm positive the label had Belém, Brazil printed on it. The website we found was also in Belém, Brazil, remember? We just have to go to Dr. Blume tonight. He'll listen to us, I know he will."

Her tone insisted on action. Now fully awake, Patrick acquiesced to her pressure, and set his thoughts on the adventure he saw in his mind's eye as he pulled on his baggy jeans.

"Stuff your bed with your pillow and a blanket, make it look like you're in it. I'll do the same thing," Miranda said. "We don't want the foster parents to notice any sooner than necessary."

"Yeah, and we can get there by train. Lucky we're not far from the station. I know the trains run north at night - I've heard them lots of times," Patrick said, pulling a tee shirt over his head.

"Okay, wake up Ian again and tell him we'll be back before dawn, but don't tell him where we're going. Ignorance is bliss when being questioned. I've got some money left, I'm sure it'll be enough for tickets. Meet me outside in five minutes." Miranda and Patrick's whispers grew more secretive as they made their plans.

❧

Miranda and Patrick arrived at Dr. Blume's house just moments after he had come home. Miranda pushed the buzzer.

"Hello? Who is it?" the distortion of Dr. Blume's voice through the intercom was comical.

"Dr. Blume? It's Miranda Pauer and Patrick Barton. We've come to use your computer tonight to show you what we found on the Web?"

"At this hour? You crazy kids! It's after midnight!" Dr. Blume chuckled. "Wait a minute. Pull the door open when I buzz you in. Come up to the second floor apartment 203B."

They did as he told them, and moments later were sitting at his computer, waiting for the connection to clear. "This website is really cool," Patrick said as he typed in the search words. The skeleton came up and vanished.

"That's how this one works. You have to go back a second time before they let you in," Patrick said, deepening his voice to sound more confident. He typed in the search words again, and just as before, the skeleton icon faded slowly into a child's face. The website took them through the same sequence of events, into the rainforest, then into the laboratory, then showing the recovered monkey leaping about his cage.

"This is where the screen went blank last time," Miranda said.

The screensaver remained as the information appeared, with several choices. The first step requested registration with the company.

"Shall we?" Patrick asked. "Whose email account should we use?"

"Use mine," said Dr. Blume. "I never have the time to surf the Net, and if this is even remotely what it says it is, I'll be glad to get the information available on this compound."

"Okay." Patrick typed in the web address. "Second step, get information or order the product?"

"Information first," Dr. Blume instructed as he turned on his printer.

"It's downloading. Give it a couple of minutes at least."

"Now tell me, why do you think this is the substance in your parents' blood?"

"We aren't sure at all. But I do know my grandfather has been going to Brazil for years to get medicine to prevent senility. Sort of coincidental, huh?"

Miranda's face was natural and fresh with her youth. Dr. Blume listened without filtering her words, trying to hear what she meant by what she said.

"My grandfather is a very rich man, and he always gets his way. My dad has been in business with my grandfather since before he divorced my mom, but no one knows how they make all that money. The only thing I can figure is that my grandfather, Landon Pauer, also sells the drugs he takes to stay clear minded. I just have this idea stuck in my head, and I can't shake it. Why my mom and Patrick's dad survived the bombing is anybody's guess. This compound might have a connection. Who gave it to them and why? Maybe we'll never know."

"Complete!" Patrick took three pages from the printer and re-shuffled them to put then in order. "It isn't what I thought it'd be." His voice trailed off with disappointment.

"The first page is nothing but a couple of maps and an encyclo-pedia explanation of the Amazon River. The second page is just an ad claiming this stuff called 'Eternal Happiness' is drawn from the fountain of youth. The third page says to order you have to go to Brazil. Oh, sure. Just like that. Call this phone number for more information on how to meet with the supplier.

"So? Let's call the number," Dr. Blume suggested as he picked up his phone and punched the speakerphone button. "You'll want to hear this, I'm sure." The kids nodded and poked each other with their elbows. He dialed the international number, which connected an answering machine.

"If you are calling about Eternal Happiness, please accept our apologies. This month's supply is sold out. We'll place your name on our waiting list for the next shipment. Since you have registered with us to become one of our clients, we'll provide a complete prospectus on our product for you to download from the attachment. Please hang up, and wait a few moments while we send our information to you. Thank you for calling." Silence. Dial tone.

"Bummer." Patrick said, as Dr. Blume hung up the phone.

"Well, let's see what they send," Miranda said, trying to stay positive.

"How about a Coke while we wait?" Dr. Blume led the two teens into his kitchen. They popped open the cans he took form his fridge and went back to the living room to wait. Minutes seemed more like hours until they heard the computer e-mail reminder beep. Almost instantly, they were reading the single page that came to them:

"You are now member of an exclusive group of forward thinking individuals, who want to live longer and better in their golden years. ETERNAL HAPPINESS is the key to your future. Your doctor may even try to prevent you from considering our product. But you will want to try it anyway. If you are receiving this page, our screening process has cleared you to meet with our representative.

Dr. Blume, you are a wise physician. We see from the requested details you gave on your registration at the beginning of our web site, that you treat geriatric cases very frequently. Your hospital would very likely frown on your use of our product. Our representative will be in your area soon, and will call to make an appointment with you. He will contact you at your hospital, and the representative's name is Mr. Mickey Straader.

We look forward to working with you, since attracting members of the medical profession to our product is our best hope for sharing the cure to old age: ETERNAL HAPPINESS.

Thank you for your interest.

ETERNAL HAPPINESS, Inc."

"That's it? Wait for this Mickey Straader guy to call? What a rip-off!" Patrick shouted. Miranda remained silent, but clenched her fists trying to calm her frustration.

"Listen, it may be nothing, but if this guy calls, I'll get him to meet with me. Okay? It's as simple as that. Come on. I'll take you back to the foster home so you can get some sleep."

The first soft hint of morning sun promised the end to a long night. Miranda and Patrick were silent in the car. Dr. Blume's mind was racing. His skepticism about Eternal Happiness kept him from being too optimistic, but if he did hear from this Mickey Straader person, then he might pursue the potentials of the compound.

"Hey, get some sleep. You both need it," he said as he dropped the kids off. "Thanks for showing me the website."

"You're welcome, Dr. Blume. And, thanks for staying up with us to see what we found." Their faces were sad, though they tried to smile away their disappointment. He had grown to like these two, more than he had ever let himself like any family members of any of his patients.

He yawned, stretched, turned on the radio to a talk station and drove slowly with the windows open trying to stay awake, hoping the cold, late-winter air could refresh him just enough to keep him alert till he arrived home.

PART THREE

19

*A*hi could not move. The cheering of the villagers blared in his silence deafened ears, distorted and frightening. The women laid him on his back in a woven casket filled with flower petals and stroked his limbs with cooling, scented rainwater. He struggled to open his eyes, to see that he was alive, to look for his son's face in the crowd. But he could only flicker his eyelids helplessly, not yet strong enough to accomplish the simple act of opening them to see. The medicine man came toward him, carrying the vase of algala above his head. The villagers shouted louder, and began to sway to the rhythm of their chanting. He held the rim of the vase to Ahi's lips, helping him to open his mouth by pulling his jaw down to its widest extension. Ahi would taste the algala three more times before the ceremony was complete. The liquid filled his gaping mouth, and he concentrated all his efforts to try to swallow. His tongue felt thick and clumsy, but he managed to close his lips and ingest most of the milky elixir.

A rush of heat filled him like the effect from drinking palm tree wine the women made from palm sap. A sudden flush of intoxicating pleasure warmed his being, and he felt a new power enter his paralyzed muscles. All parts of his body began to awaken. His penis grew erect spewing forth a powerful, sexual explosion. The crowd swooned with cries of surprise, ooh-ing and aah-ing in tremulous harmony. Still unable to move his arms and legs or open his eyes, Ahi found himself thrashing his head back and forth in time with the chanting. He lost all control of himself. The contents of his bowels spewed from him, soiling the bed of flowers on which he lay. The shouts from the crowd rumbled and rolled like thunder and died out in the dark shadows beyond the firelight. Then his whole body began to tremble. The uncontrollable thrashing of his head and the involuntary spastic movements of his limbs violently rocked the woven casket. The crowd wailed in high-pitched vibratos achieved by flicking the tongue rapidly from side to side of the open and circular lips.

Two medicine men came forward while the villagers joined the dancers, breaking into smaller circles of five or six and dancing in frenzied unison with the drums. One took Ahi's chin and again opened his mouth. The other held Ahi's head, facing it upward, while the involuntary trembling of his torso continued. But this time Ahi could work the muscles in his jaws. The algala filled him again, this time bringing on a reaction causing him to contract his muscles. His hands clenched. His legs pulled up to his chest. His arms crossed over his feet as they curled up, and his face contorted in a grimacing smile. Every muscle pulled Ahi's body into a constricted fetal ball, making him feel small and insignificant. He wanted to regain possession of his body, to open his eyes, to see his son's face once again. But the algala would not relent. The crowd grew silent, but their dancing grew ever faster.

The pain in his tensed muscles squeezed a cry of agony from him. Ahi could not bear much more. The medicine man approached again and forced Ahi's mouth open enough to pour in more algala. The milkiness changed to a sickening sweetness. Nausea overcame him. His limbs flung outward from his body as he wretched forth all that he had consumed. The excruciating abdominal cramping squeezed Ahi's breath from him. The crowd danced in unison, every dancer's movement a perfect reflection of the next dancer's gestures, and began to sing, each one his own song.

Ahi lay motionless and exhausted in the heap of flowers, fecal matter and vomit. His head was throbbing. He wanted only to sleep. The villagers grew silent. The drums stopped. The fire itself seemed to flicker more slowly. The medicine men came forward for the last time. One picked up Ahi's hands, and pressed them around the vase, holding them in place for him. Another of them lifted Ahi's head and shoulders into a sitting position. The first released his hands, and Ahi held the vase in his own. He opened his eyes. His first sight focused on the face of his son, who had come forward at the beckoning of the medicine man. Amahi placed his hands on his father's hands. Ahi raised the vase to his own lips, Amahi's hands resting reassuringly around the backs of Ahi's cupped fingers. Looking deep into his son's eyes, and seeing that Amahi returned the gaze with love and honor, Ahi drank the last of the algala.

The calm, restorative surge of energy poured from the vase into his being. He felt the strength of his youth return to his arms and legs. He raised the vase above his head and turning toward the fire, threw it straight into the heart of the flames. Ahi sat on his own excrement, but the beauty of that moment could never be explained to another. He had survived death. He had survived the algala. He was reborn, with a strength of heart and mind unknown to any who had not been blessed by Anmala. Ahi stood and descended from the raised platform, the pains of old age forgotten as his legs bore his weight with ease.

The women washed him, pouring warm, orchid scented water over him until he was clean. The white tunic of rebirth was pulled over his naked body. The purple robes of the "Elder of Elders" were placed over his shoulders. Ahi stood proudly before his people, restored in mind, in body and in spirit. The silence broke only when he spoke. "Algala—Anmala—Algala—Anmala..." The villagers joined his chant, sharing his joy, deriving their own sense of rebirth from his, reinvigorated as he was to go on living their quiet lives in their quiet jungle.

20

*L*orraine played the scene over and over in her mind riding in the taxi before it pulled up in front of William's darkened house. She paid the cabby twenty dollars and walked to the front door, pounding on the heavy oak panels with both fists.

"William! Help! Help me!" she shouted, thrusting her fists harder and faster against the door each time.

The lights came on almost immediately in the upstairs window, and then in the living room. She heard him fumbling with the lock to open the door. She stepped back as it swung open. The face that greeted William was wild-eyed and irrational.

"Mother! Mother! Get hold of yourself! What are you doing here? It's two in the morning. What's wrong? What are you doing here?" He pulled her inside and closed the door, more out of concern for waking the neighbors than anything else.

"William! Oh, William, what are we going to do? Landon is dead! Oh, my God, I just can't help myself. It's going to be in all the papers. He's dead, and you and the girls are all the family I have left. I loved him for more than forty years. I couldn't call and tell you on the phone. His body is arriving this morning with one of Harry's people. You've got to help me with all this. I had to come here. I—oh—air!"

Lorraine gasped for breath. She lay back on the couch, grasping at her chest. William ran to the phone and called 911. The automatic answering system put him on hold. He cradled the cordless handset between his ear and his shoulder as he placed the hand crocheted afghan over his mother's trembling body. Lorraine was hyperventilating.

"9-1-1. How may I help you?" The voice on the phone exuded calm.

"Send an ambulance immediately to 4513 Roger Williams Drive. My mother is having a heart attack—I think." William looked at Lorraine as he spoke.

"Yes, sir, within a few minutes, please stay on the line until they arrive."

"Yes, ma'am," William said, obedient to a fault. He retrieved a side chair from the dining room so he could sit next to her, and then patted Lorraine's hand. He hadn't had any reason to converse with the 911 operator, when the wail of the ambulance siren broke the silence of the night, and the flashing of the red and blue lights cut through the private darkness of the exclusive community.

Lorraine continued hyperventilating, so that the paramedics would decide to take her to the hospital for observation. To her surprise, William wasn't convinced she should be moved.

"Listen, Mr. Pauer, I don't think this is truly serious, but with the elderly, everything can become life-threatening in an instant. She'll just be better off there at least for the rest of the night, possibly a day or two. They can give her something mild to help her rest. She's been through a lot of stress, coming here on her own like that."

"No! No drugs! She's just frightened. I'll allow her to be observed, but not drugged."

"All right, just observation, and perhaps some fluids."

The calm in the paramedic's voice persuaded William to let his mother be taken into the ambulance.

"I'll come with you, Mother. I'll stay with you." His voice sounded more like it belonged to a little boy than a grown man.

"Put me near Emily, dear—I'll feel better near family," Lorraine's weak voice seemed so pathetic.

"But Mother, Emily isn't family—any more—Only the girls are."

"Please dear—just for me?" She opened her eyes to look at him. "I need you to help me—feel comfortable—in a place where people go to die. Please?" She closed her eyes with a slight gasp for air.

William spoke with the paramedics, who admitted Lorraine to the Anderson Wing, ostensibly to humor a little old lady. The process took about an hour. But, William stayed with his mother every step to the way. As soon as they were alone, he sat for a while watching her sleep.

"She used to be so beautiful," he said to himself. "She used to smile so warmly and hug just about anyone who seemed to need one. Her face is so old. Her arms and legs are so thin, she seems ready to break."

He remembered how from time to time Lorraine would break a wrist by slipping on the ice, or a couple of toes by dropping something on them. She had always recovered from these little accidents without once complaining. William tried to imagine himself in her place, widowed only hours before, terrified of the future and panicked by her fears, winding up in a hospital tended by strangers who knew nothing of her life.

William let himself cry for the first time since his youth. He didn't care that Landon would never allow him to show emotions of any kind. He no longer cared that to cry meant to be weak. William acknowledged with his tears the multitudes of weak moments in his life, and cried for a long time. He mourned his destroyed paintings, torn to shreds by a raging father who wanted him to go outside and play football instead. He mourned the thousands of times he had given up his pride to keep from angering his parents. He mourned the lost loves, the lost friends, the lost innocence of his youth, wishing he had been strong enough to be the person and to do the things he had truly wanted to be and do. When he could cry no more, he wiped his face with a Kleenex from her bedside table. Then, silently kissing her cheek, he walked to the elevators, pushed the button, stepped inside and was gone.

Lorraine opened her eyes. "What a fool he is," she muttered as she lowered the sidebars on her bed. Then, moving to one of the chairs near the window, she put on the hospital slippers she found on the counter among the other toiletries. She picked up her purse and opened it. She lifted the false bottom, removing a syringe and a vial of fluid. Carefully, she filled the syringe with the liquid and went to the door. The last shift of nurses, just getting off work, gathered at the nurse's station to report the night's activities to the incoming staff. Lorraine turned the opposite way, and without even rustling her gown, walked down the hall. Reading the names at the doorways listing the patients in each room until she arrived at room 135, she stopped for a moment to gather her nerve. Slowly, she opened the door and stepped into the room with out making a sound.

Emily's bed stood nearest the door with the privacy curtain pulled half way around, so that only the foot of the bed was accessible. Dan's bed remained completely surrounded by curtains, except along the interior side facing Emily's bed. The two doctors had their backs to Emily as they adjusted Dan's monitors.

Lorraine startled at seeing the doctors and hid quickly behind the curtain surrounding Emily's bed. It hadn't occurred to her that someone might be in the room. She looked at the arrangement of the beds, curtains and monitors, sizing up the chances of succeeding, all the while trying to keep from being discovered. She held her breath and stilled every muscle, as the two men looked at each other simultaneously, and as if sensing someone in the room, turned to look behind. No one was there. They returned to setting Dan's monitors, giving Lorraine just enough time to escape back to her room unnoticed. She put the syringe in the drawer next to her bed, and slipped under the covers. She closed her eyes, trying to stop shaking so she could pretend to sleep.

"Let's talk this over with some breakfast in the cafeteria. It has been a long night and I've got to do my rounds fairly soon," Dr. Blume said. "We can have the intern come in to observe for the next couple of hours."

"And, I can touch base with my office. I don't want to leave until the children have been here to visit."

"Dr. Blume?" The head nurse's voice came over the intercom.

"Yes? This is Dr. Blume."

"We thought you should know that Mrs. Landon Pauer, Emily Sanders' former mother-in-law, was admitted during the night in a state of hysteria over the death of her husband. He was in Brazil. She's just down the hall in room 1-2-5, if you'd like to stop in to see her."

"Thank you. Why wasn't I notified earlier?"

"You were working, sir. I thought it could wait."

The two doctors walked toward the cafeteria, still engaged in conversation about Emily and Dan.

"The MRI and CAT scans showed nothing physiologically wrong with their brains' completely normal imaging. So, at least there seems to be no damage there. I'm mostly concerned that their problems will be emotional and psychological in nature," Dr. Blume explained. "I just met with Patrick and Miranda last night. They did open up about their hypothesis as you said they would."

"I knew they would. But, I'm concerned about them. Miranda is taking on so much responsibility. I'm worried that she might carry anger and resentments all her life. On top of that, Patrick is living an irrational dream that he is going to solve a very trumped up mystery, when no mystery exists. I keep trying to bring them both to a more realistic appraisal of what's going on right now, but they both stubbornly refuse to accept it." Dr. Eastman said.

"I think they may have something," Dr. Blume said simply. "I sat with Miranda and Patrick as they used my computer to connect to the web. They found a site selling a product called ETERNAL HAPPINESS, which claims to be a fountain of youth. I know it seems far-fetched. But, if you had seen the video that we saw as part of the website, you might at least take a second look at their idea."

"Do I hear Dr. Blume, the pharmaceutical company poster boy, suggesting some off the wall alternative compound sold on the web could be legitimate?" Dr. Eastman's sarcasm fell on deaf ears.

"You have to see what I mean. Then, you might think otherwise," Dr. Blume insisted. "Come into my office. I'll show you," he said, turning down the hall toward his office and beckoning to Dr. Eastman from his doorway. Reluctantly, Dr. Eastman followed him. Dr. Blume signed onto the web, and in a few seconds typed in the keywords the kids had used. The browser came back with the website housing ETERNAL HAPPINESS.

"Watch this—you won't believe it at first," Dr. Blume said, acknowledging the fervent disbelief his friend would maintain in the name of professional ethics.

By the time he'd seen the entire series of images, Dr. Eastman was surprised at his own willingness to consider the possibilities.

"Isn't this too easy to misconstrue? Really, David, think about it. The pharmaceutical companies would have a lock on such a compound, if it really existed. They wouldn't want to miss out on the huge profits it could generate. There would be intense wrangling for market position, papers would have been written to document its effectiveness. People would be all over this thing."

"Maybe so, but I can't blatantly ignore the kids' insistence that Emily and Dan were given a dose of this compound, and it was enough to protect them, if only to keep the kids' trust."

"Sure you can. Besides, how could it protect them from a bombing—"

"—that killed everyone else, and destroyed the whole building they were in. Yet, they were just knocked unconscious? Explain that," Dr. Blume said.

"Well—I can't, but it doesn't necessarily mean they were given this compound, or that the stuff even exists. That's a leap of faith even God and the Apostles themselves couldn't take."

"Maybe so, but I have nothing better to go on. My patients are beginning to show wear and tear. The mystery is taking all of my free time, and invading my sleep. I can't even think clearly about anything else."

Dr. Eastman took a good look at his friend. The dark circles under his eyes, the rumpled doctor's coat, the piles of web site printouts scattered all over his desk and credenza, revealed more to him than his friend's complaints.

"To be honest with you, David, it looks like this is all becoming an obsession. Let's go get that bite of breakfast."

The two doctors stepped into the cafeteria, and continued their discussion as they selected from the hot plate of eggs and sausages, cold plate of fruit and juices, and bagels and doughnuts.

"I can't help thinking there is much more beneath the surface of this situation. My patients are lying here because of something else, some kind of intrigue that they have been drawn into by the bombing," Dr. Blume said in a hushed confidential tone of voice.

"You're not thinking there is some kind of plot, are you?" Dr. Eastman asked.

Dr. Blume just stared at his colleague and smiled.

"David, you've got to pull back from this. The kids think there's some kind of conspiracy. But Emily and Dan don't wheel and deal on the drug scene. How can they possibly be the cause of the bombing?" Dr. Eastman looked at his friend with concern.

"They're not the cause—they're the victims. Someone close to one of them is the cause. The Pauer family has something to do with all this. Miranda told me the other night that her grandfather has been buying drugs in Brazil for years to treat his own senility. I'm really just playing mind games with myself. But, the kids are so intent on the Brazilian connection, until I can prove otherwise, I can't ignore the possibility they're on to something." Dr. Blume just sipped his coffee as he looked dejectedly at his colleague's face. He could see reflected there the worry and the concern he was feeling in his own mind.

"David, you know whatever comes of all this, I'll back you up." Dr. Eastman reached over to place his hand softly on the shoulder of his friend.

"Thanks, I'll hang on to that," Dr. Blume said softly, truly realizing for the first time, that he was going to have to risk his reputation to pursue an unconventional therapy, if only because no conventional options remained open to him.

The two doctors ate the remainder of their breakfasts in silence, thinking to themselves what might be the best course of action to take.

Down the hall, the nurses entered Lorraine's room with her breakfast on a tray. Efficiently moving the bed table over in front of her, they gently shook her to wake her. Lorraine had her plan worked out as she opened her eyes and smiled innocently at the nurse.

"Hi, honey. How's the new day?" she said cheerily. "Help me plump up these pillows so I can eat this gourmet creation."

"Sit forward, Mrs. Pauer. I'll raise the head of the bed." The nurse was equally cheerful. "Need anyone to help you eat?"

"No, of course not. Just turn on the television for me, would you? I don't like the quiet."

"All right. Want a game show or a talk show?"

"Oh, a game show would be just fine, dear. Thank you." Lorraine put on her best sweet little old lady act. She knew she wouldn't be there much longer anyway, so she'd keep the need for attention to a minimum. That way, she might get another chance to do what she had come there to do.

"Oh, by the way, is my son's ex-wife just down the hall? I thought I heard him say something about that last night when he checked me in here."

"Why, yes, she is. I'm sorry she and Mr. Barton aren't responding better to treatment."

"Do you think it would be all right for me to visit them a little later? I understand they won't know I'm there, but since I'm here anyways, I should do the right thing and say hello. My son would like that, I think, and if not him, then my granddaughters certainly would."

"Oh, the children should be coming in fairly soon to visit. Would you like to go in while they are here?"

"No, no, I'd better not. I don't want to upset them. They'd just want to know what happened to Landon. Poor, sweet Landon. He was so far away when he died. I hope William can be at the airport to receive the casket." Lorraine began to cry on cue. Reaching for a Kleenex, she blew her nose and wiped her tears, quickly regaining her composure.

"I'm sorry dear, I didn't mean to cry. It's not as if Landon hadn't lived out his life. I just miss him. I'll have my breakfast now, if you don't mind."

The nurse moved the tray closer for Lorraine to use it comfortably. Starting to leave, she said over her shoulder, "Dr. Blume will come in later this morning to see how you're doing. If there's anything else you need, just push the call button pinned to your pillow."

The nurse smiled absentmindedly at her and disappeared silently into the hall. Lorraine ate a few bites of the bland food, pushed the tray aside, and counted the steps she had planned to take on her fingers, memorizing each one as she gave it a number.

"One, remember the syringe. Two, stay quiet so no one notices you. Three..."

21

*T*he day dawned hot and humid on the landing strip. Mickey
Straader tugged at the reluctant sliding door of his hangar as he had
every day for twenty years. Layers of rust and corrosion flaked off
the door, which had given in to the unrelenting decay of humidity
and neglect. He strode to the back table where the computer waited,
mute witness to the secrets of the night.

"Damn, It's a goldmine!" Mickey muttered happily as he
checked through the fifty or so e-mail messages waiting for him.
"People surf—people stop—want to know what that old skeleton is
all about. Neat!"

On average, he cleared fifteen or twenty phone messages to answer with matching detailed registrations on the website. One of the
registrations came from a Dr. Blume in Chicago. He refilled the paper
tray in the fax machine with the form letter information, and set up
the autodial to send it to those who had left fax numbers. He typed a
personalized e-message to Dr. Blume and sent the e-mail response.

"Whoever said the small businessman couldn't make a killing
on the Worldwide Web?" he marveled, whistling a melody of his own

invention. A fast-talking relic from the fifties, Mickey had adjusted to the onslaught of technology with ease. The rewards had been more than incentive enough.

Rita's decision to keep silent about the event at the landing strip gnawed at her conscience as she drove back to Belém. She didn't like men like Mickey Straader. She felt no concern for his welfare. Harry Smithers was as unsavory a character as she had ever done business with, and she felt no compunction to concern herself with his safety either. She only came to buy the supply of compound and antidote she had ordered and return to Chicago. The unavoidable risks she was taking to get her revenge and subvert Harry and Mickey's smuggling network were worth it. But murder, or even letting a murder take place when she could prevent it, was not a step she had anticipated. In her mind, she'd be as guilty as the murderers, whoever they were. She had seen the setup to the crime. She could not stop Mickey from going to the hangar, but she could prevent his death. Just a phone call to the airport control tower could change everything.

Rita pulled off the road at a dilapidated one-pump gas station. She approached the wizened little man sitting in the only chair on the slanted porch of the tumbledown shack just behind the drive.

"Telefono, por favor?" she asked in an awful attempt at Spanish, owing to her being in a very rural part of the area. The old man pointed in silence to the pay phone at the end of the porch. Rita fumbled with coins. She didn't know the airport number. She rifled through her purse for more change.

"Damn! What the hell do these instructions mean?" she tried in vain to decipher the information on the dirty sign posted next to the phone. She dialed "O" for operator, hoping it would put her through.

A pleasant voice came on the line, "Olá, Hello?"

"Hello?" Rita said, having no more Spanish in her repertoire.

"May I help you?"

"Oh! Yes! You speak English? Yes! Can you connect me to the transport airport outside Belém—the control tower?" Rita spoke clearly to be understood, dropping some coins of she knew not what value into the slots above the dial.

"Here it is," the operator cut off as the phone rang. One ring—two—four—on the sixth ring, a tired man's low voice answered.

"Si?"

"Se habla inglès?" Rita asked in her grossly American mispronunciation.

"Si , yes," the voice answered.

"Don't let Mickey Straader start his plane—there is a bomb—he will die." She hung up.

Marcos only understood Mickey's name, the words 'plane', 'bomb', and 'die'. He dropped the phone just as Mickey sauntered to his plane and climbed into the cockpit. Starting his safety checklist, he radioed the control tower .

"Hey, Marcos! I'm going to taxi out. Adios, amigo!" he chortled as he turned the ignition.

"No Mickey! No go! Not today!" was all Marcos could say into the microphone on the control panel. The impact of the explosion knocked him to the floor. He crawled to the gaping hole that had been a window and looked over the ledge. Mickey's hangar was no more than a crumple of tin and the flaming skeleton of the dismembered plane. Incinerated chunks of the hangar and the wings of the plane lay scattered about. Marcos called the fire department in Belém, but he knew by the time they arrived, there would be only smoldering rubble to snuff out. He sat down on the steps of his tower to wait, shaking from the shock of the explosion, and crying in grief for the loss of his friend.

After the phone call to the airport, Rita regained her composure. Upon arriving at the hotel, she showered, changed into her best and most conservative ensemble, and applied her makeup with the flair of a professional model. Returning her gaze from the mirror was a beautiful blond-haired, blue-eyed sophisticate, perfectly groomed in every detail. Quite a leap from the eccentric bar owner she had once been. Harry would never recognize her. If he did recognize something vaguely familiar about her, she knew it would only be a fleeting moment of that intuitive sense of having met this beautiful woman before in an unremembered somewhere. Safe enough cover for her to pick up her purse filled with the money she needed to buy the compound and its antidote, and smoothly close the door on the night's events.

Detective Cameron's camera whirred softly, watching Rita park her car in the dusty street near La Casa del Norte. She put all thoughts of the night out of her mind. Nothing would diminish her determination to avoid discovery and get what she needed from both Mickey and Harry. She could not be connected to any mishap at the airport. No one had seen her. No one would ever know she was there. She had made the call to cleanse her conscience, and it had worked. She calmed her lingering uneasiness by focusing on her goal. The sun beat down, casting stark shadows on the back door of the restaurant. Rita noticed her hand was steady as she knocked. A moment later, she was sitting at the rundown bar talking with Harry Smithers. The overhead fans turned lazily above the bar, giving off no breeze to stir the humid air. Only the hum of a congregation of flies battling for position on the screen door broke the quiet of the heat.

"It is good to see you, Ms. Dumas," Harry tried to be professional, as he devoured Rita Dumas with his eyes. No woman of her sophistication had ever come to his restaurant, and he was taken off guard by the beauty of her obvious upper class stature. "I hope you find our little town to your liking."

"I am not planning to spend much time here, Mr. Smithers. I have come for one purpose only, and the sooner we take care of that, the sooner I will leave your little town forever. Is Mr. Straader coming to this meeting?" Rita asked.

Clearing his throat uncomfortably, Harry leaned forward on the bar, and looked down at his hands as he tried to explain. "Forgive me, Ms. Dumas, if I seem a bit out of sorts, but Mickey won't be able to meet with us. I had a phone call from the airport a little while ago. There was a mishap out there. According to the control tower overseer, when Mickey climbed into his plane, it blew up upon ignition. There was nothing left but some rubble. The plane and the hangar were completely destroyed. I'm still in shock over losing my friend."

Rita didn't flinch. "Well, then, he won't be here to negotiate any changes to the terms we agreed to on the phone. I have your money with me. One hundred thousand dollars—free and clear. Do you have my compound and antidote?" She stared at him coldly, showing no hint that she knew anything about or even cared about the demise of Mickey Straader.

"Yes, in my safe. I'll get it." Her crisp, hard-edged toughness made Harry regain enough of his composure to hurry into the small office behind the bar. He returned in less than a minute, carrying a small brown paper wrapped package. He handed it to Rita. Opening it hurriedly, and checking to be sure the compound and its antidote were actually in the package, she handed him an envelope containing one hundred new, thousand dollar bills. Harry was feeling the effects of Mickey's death and Rita's beauty. Breathing hard, he counted the money quickly. Sweat beaded up like pearls on his forehead, moistened the armpits and collar of his pale blue shirt. His face broke into a satisfied grin as he turned to take the envelope back to the office. He locked it in the safe, returning to the bar just in time to see Rita pass through the front door and step into the sunlight.

"Strange bitch," he muttered taking particular notice of her chorus girl legs as he watched her get into her car.

Rita's hands were shaking. She could hardly breathe. Trembling, she put the key into the ignition and grabbed the steering wheel firmly to steady her nerves. She glanced over her left shoulder at the restaurant to see two black-clad men go in the front door. Terror overtook her. She fumbled with the door handle, trying to get out of her car to warn Harry. She felt time stop. She struggled to push open the car door, and as she put her feet on the sandy, parched ground, she was caught by the detailed designs of the dust adhering to the tips of her shoes. Every shadow appeared more distinct. Every move flowed in slow motion. She was just flexing her legs to stand when the restaurant exploded, taking her breath away. She fell back into the car as the heat from the fireball reached her. The explosion spewed a dust cloud into the air, and dust into her eyes. She groped for the steeling wheel and felt for the key in the ignition. Wiping the dirt away with the back of the sleeve, she cleared her vision enough to see the road. The ignition kicked the engine to life, and she jammed the transmission into gear. Rocks and pebbles clattered on her car as she spun the car's wheels, accelerating to reach the paved road. Rita's mind was racing faster than the gears in the engine of her car.

"Could the killers know I saw them at the airport? Who will they give the computer disk to? They certainly must have seen me get into my car. Are they after me too? Do they somehow know who I am? Can I get back to the hotel for my things fast enough? Can I elude them if they come after me? Neither Mickey nor Harry knew what hit them. I won't know either. If the killers saw me, they saw the sophisticated businesswoman. I'll go straight to the airport—I'll get on the next plane to Miami. I'll change planes there for Chicago. I'll change my identity again —At least I have the disk from Mickey's computer, the compound and antidote. That's all I came for. I just have to escape these thugs—I

have to expose the network—I have to make sure Emily and Dan get the antidote. I want my revenge, if I live long enough to see it. If I live long enough, it's the least I can do."

She sped along the highway to the airport, driving faster with every thought, afraid of what could happen next. She did not notice Detective Cameron's car following her at a safe distance. She did not go to her hotel. She drove to the airport, left her car at the curb, and slipped into the anonymity of the crowded terminal. She bought a ticket to Miami with only enough time to get out of the clothes she was wearing, do something with her hair, and become someone no one would recognize. In the duty-free shop, she bought a rock group tee shirt, some baggy jeans, sunglasses, a fanny pack, sandals and a satchel. Then, she scurried into the lady's room to change her clothes, ridding herself of the suit, purse and heels in the garbage bin. Removing all her makeup, the colored contact lenses, and letting her hair fall loose. She put on the sunglasses to complete her disguise.

"Not enough," she snapped at the image in the mirror. She went back to the shop and looked for a scissors to buy. In the drugstore section she found a small pair of nail scissors, and nothing bigger. She paid for them and returned to the ladies' room.

"Damn these scissors, if you can call them that," she said, furious at the minute sections of hair she was able to cut off. She hacked at her hair, trying the make it even at the shoulder. When she finished, She swept up the curls of hair from the floor with her hands and a wet paper towel from the dispenser, and paced the bathroom like a caged lioness for another five minutes, before heading straight for the boarding area.

Standing up from the airport lounge chair, Detective Cameron uncrumpled his body to straighten out his aching spine and to watch for Marguerite, whom he figured would be heading north with the body, now that Harry was dead. He waited only a few minutes until she came through the doorway into the departure lobby.

"I dig myself at times like these," he said, crossing the lobby to catch up with her at the check-in counter. She was busy making certain that Landon's casket was accounted for, and signed the papers necessary to have it loaded on the plane. He stood just out of her peripheral line of vision waiting for her to finish with the details. She startled when he spoke.

"Hello again, Ms. Kohl. Remember me? I see you are accompanying Landon Pauer's casket back to the States. I realize this seems strange, but I will help you get him back to the States. If you'd like, I'll accompany you on the plane to Miami and then to Chicago. Mrs. Pauer is expecting Harry Smithers to do this, but Harry is dead too."

Marguerite stared at Detective Cameron with the wide eyes of a frightened child. "Harry? How can that be?" Marguerite spoke softly, but with fear in her voice.

"I can't give you all the facts, but his restaurant blew up a couple of hours ago, and he was in it. I don't think he walked away from the blast."

"I am supposed to meet him here in a few minutes. I will wait for Harry, and then I'll say good-bye to Landon for the last time from this window when the plane takes off." Marguerite walked to the far side of the departure lounge to look at the plane from the large, plate-glass window, ignoring Detective Cameron as he followed her.

They sat in the lounge, Marguerite near the door, Detective Cameron across the room. She worriedly watched every passenger as they arrived, checked in and took a seat to wait. He watched her watching. He spotted Rita, in spite of her disguise. Harry never came. As one attendant announced the boarding, Marguerite approached the counter.

"Excuse me, uh, I need to know if a man named Harry Smithers is on the passenger list," she asked the attendant.

"No, we do not have a Mr. Harry Smithers. Now, please board through that door," the attendant pointed toward to door where she had been sitting.

"Oh, I don't have a ticket. Mr. Smithers is supposed to take the body back." Marguerite tried to ignore Detective Cameron as he approached the attendant at the counter and handed her the return portion of his round trip ticket.

"And, I'll take one ticket to Chicago via Miami in the name of Marguerite Kohl. I presume there are a few empty seats available?"

"Yes, sir, there are—how would you like to pay for this ticket?"

Detective Cameron looked at Marguerite, smiled and handed the attendant his credit card. Once the transaction was complete, he handed Marguerite her ticket.

"I know you want to see this through to its conclusion. Consider this my gesture of faith in family ties," he said.

"I can't accept this!" she said, shoving the ticket at him.

"Yes, you can, and I know you want to. Think about this, Ms. Kohl. Landon's memory would be best served if you accompany him back to the States. It's a right thing to do. Don't worry about Lorraine. You don't even need to see her. Just take him back to Chicago, spend a night in hotel, and come back here. You'll feel better for having done it." He smiled at her, and watched her dissolve in tears.

He helped her board the plane, but sat a couple of rows behind Marguerite, to give her some privacy.

Another few minutes passed, and Rita Dumas was sitting comfortably in her window seat in coach, trying to be Ruthann Mahoney. She began to feel a bit safer, as she watched the passengers file into the cabin. Several businessmen, tourists of all kinds, children, and a little old woman barely able to walk found their seats. The flight attendants began the check of seat belts. Two men entered the cabin. Tall, muscular, unsmiling, wearing black. The men stared intensely at every passenger, as if looking for someone. They were of a different size and build than the two men who had entered Harry's hotel just before it blew up. They were not the same two men Rita had seen at Mickey's hangar. Her heart was pounding. She picked up a magazine and began to leaf through it, trying to seem unaware of them. They looked at her. She held her breath. They went on. She exhaled very softly, and took a deep breath, deciding to stay seated the whole way to Miami, if the plane made it that far.

Detective Cameron watched Rita's avoidance of their glance, deciding by her demeanor that she recognized these men and that she was afraid of them. He thought back to Harry's restaurant just before the explosion. Rita had left the restaurant in a hurry. Two men in black had gone into the restaurant. It exploded. They didn't come out. No one could have survived the blast.

The plane took off. Harry Smithers is dead, and Rita thinks she is next. Detective Cameron knew he couldn't reveal his hunches any more than he already had to Marguerite. The attendants served the first drinks and nuts. His mind played back every image in vivid detail as he began to sort all the events he had witnessed in Brazil. He consumed his dinner and a couple extra glasses of wine in record time. Detective Cameron's susceptibility to wine took effect soon after the meal. He thought how long it had been since he had really slept, allowing the dull hum of the engines to quickly lull him into a light sleep.

The flight was calm. Marguerite welcomed this break from the constant pressure of the last few days. Her thoughts drifted to how she was going to care for Paulo and help him get the education he needed.

"I knew this day would come. I knew all those years that Landon would eventually be gone. I don't care if I get the money he left me. Detective Cameron was right. I do need to return his body to his American family before I can get on with my life," she thought.

SACRED NIGHT

The consequences of Marguerite's choices in life were now all coming together. She had no way to earn a decent living in spite of her boasts to Landon. If she could make amends to Lorraine, then there would be a chance that at least some of the inheritance would come to her and Paulo. She wanted to put an end to the deception. Somehow, she had to meet with Lorraine to explain to her how Landon had been so good to them both.

"Somehow, I have to beg Lorraine for help—for Paulo. Bringing the body back is a gesture of goodwill. It can't hurt—can it? Have to get away from this Detective Cameron. She glanced back at him. He's a problem—Harry is dead. It still doesn't seem possible." Her thoughts swirled through her mind preventing the sleep that could be her only escape from her doubts.

In spite of every attempt to relax, Rita's nerves tensed. She saw the men in black as suicide terrorists, ready to blow up the plane to gain control of the compound for their bosses. She had seen their work three times. It was a simple assumption that if they discovered her on the plane, they'd try again. The other passengers were nodding off to sleep, a sleep that came so easily to them. Why couldn't she just close her eyes and put this world out of her mind? Looking around, she was the only person awake, except for the flight attendants and the two men, sitting at the back of the plane, she thought were the bombers. They were just staring at the people in the plane in front of them. She felt their eyes boring a hole in the back of her seat. She feared the worst, and not without reason.

"Why haven't they made a move yet? Am I just imagining they are bombers? Am I just paranoid? Why not take a nap?"

Resigned to not sleeping, Rita quietly and quickly took her notebook from her fanny pack and spent her time writing down everything she knew about ETERNAL HAPPINESS.

"If anything happens to me, my notes could be useful." Glancing around now and then, she wrote all night long.

SACRED NIGHT

Detective Cameron opened his eyes to the sun as it rose over a horizon blocked by a thick layer of storm clouds. They lay sodden below the wing, like wet shorn wool left to dry where it had fallen from the sheep shearer's hands. The dizzying effect of being thirty-five thousand feet above the earth at dawn with a hangover was not pleasant. The plane banked west, mercifully allowing him to see without the bright yellow glare burning his reddened eyes.

He studied the visible part of the plane from his window port. The flexibility of the plane's wings betrayed their age. The zigzag of rivets outlining every panel of steel seemed barely to hold the patch-work together. Soot darkened the engine's exhaust, revealing the well-worn character of the metal. Hoping it would all hold together long enough to land at Miami, Detective Cameron felt nauseated as the plane leveled its wings. He stood up with difficulty and stead-ied himself on the backs of the seats to walk shakily toward the rear lavatory area. Passing the narrow galley, the aroma of Brazilian coffee reached him.

"A short visit to the john, and I'll put away a pot of Java. That should make all the difference," he muttered as he fumbled with the lever to bolt the bathroom door.

"Occupado / Occupé / Occupied." Detective Cameron stared at the lighted sign as he considered the condition of his stomach. He turned and bent over the toilet where the blue, frothy liquid sloshed with the vibration from the engines, much louder in the confines of the lavatory. Nothing happened. He waited, trying to relieve his nau-sea. The plane banked again and righted itself suddenly, throwing him off balance. He fell toward the back wall of the stall, and his hand hit the flush button with the full force of his weight. The violent suck-ing down of the septic system roared. Detective Cameron wiped his face with some of the tepid water he managed to make trickle from the faucet at the puny sink streaked with soap scum, littering paper

towels and various remnants of other passengers' discomforts. *"Please wipe clean after use."*

"What a lousy world," he snickered as he left the lavatory and stopped at the galley area. "Excuse me, could I get some coffee to take back to my seat? I've had a tough night."

One of the flight attendants looked up from her tedious microwave preparation of the frozen breakfasts, giving Detective Cameron a quick once over.

"Sure," she nodded, "it's not exactly a luxury hotel, is it?" She poured him a large cup of coffee in a real mug, instead of using the usual disposable passenger cups.

"Not exactly," he smiled, swallowing some of the hot, rejuvenating liquid. I'll look forward to breakfast now." As he walked unsteadily back to his seat, the plane settled into a slow decent leaving about forty-five minutes to touchdown. The breakfast was continental and stale, a bit too overdone in the microwave. The orange juice was frozen at the bottom, leaving the liquid weak in flavor. The coffee and the raspberry jam were the only part of the meal Detective Cameron could enjoy. He felt better as the seat belt signs ignited and flashed.

"Excuse me please, this is your co-pilot, Captain Marshall. There is some rough weather at Miami airport," the intercom crackled. "We'll circle for a few minutes to see if it will let up a bit before we land. We've been asked to delay landing because of the stacked up flights. It shouldn't be too long, since we've been given priority landing. Thank you, and if it gets a bit bumpy, please bear with us." The intercom crackled off.

"Shit. Why me?" Detective Cameron lay back in his seat.

Nothing worked him over faster than a turbulent flight. His nerves, not to mention his stomach, would be jangled for hours if the landing was rough. Only fifteen minutes passed from the co-pilot's announcement to the moment they were cleared to land. The plane dipped. Detective Cameron gripped the arm of the seat until his knuckles turned white. The wind caught up under the wings, rocking the plane back and forth as if some celestial child held it in his hand to make it zoom. He tried to look calm, but his firm hold gave him away. Rita closed her eyes and said a word or two of prayer. Marguerite tightened her seat belt and prayed openly.

The flight attendant stumbled her way through the cabin one last time, handing out pillows to each passenger. She then disappeared at the rear of the cabin and belted herself tightly to the bench seat near the rear exit with the other flight attendants, silently reviewing evacuation over water procedures, yet hoping not to use them.

The engines churned as the plane descended through the clouds, heaving the plane from side to side. The pilot tried in vain to keep it level. Visibility was zero. He saw the computer driven gyro-stabilization landing system kick on. Through the breaks in the lower clouds he could see the lights of the airport and the runway stretching out before him. The captain felt a sense of relief as he saw the ground below. He set the landing gears and lowered the flaps. The engines roared as they reduced their output to bring the plane down. Suddenly, the plane dropped, sending every stomach in the aircraft into every throat. The passengers let out a collective shout of surprise.

"Wind sheer!" the captain shouted to the cockpit crew as he struggled to lift the nose. The co-pilot attempted to increase flight speed to keep the plane aloft just long enough to stabilize over the runway. The plane hit the tarmac hard, crushing the right wheel assembly. The overhead bulkhead compartments sprung open with a cacophony of cracking sounds, freeing the stowed contents of briefcases, coats, packages, cameras and paraphernalia onto the heads of the passengers. The children were screaming and crying. One elderly woman was hit hard on the head by a flying box, knocking her unconscious. Several people vomited, others had soiled their seats. The bedlam of shrieks and crying sent terrified shivers through Detective Cameron. He sat bolt upright, stiff and rigid with fear. The engines screamed as the right wing hit the dirt off the runway, swung the plane in a horizontal arc and then broke free with a roar like a thousand hungry caged lions calling for their food. The fuselage slid sideways into the field and miraculously held together until it came to a stop.

The flight crew flew into action. The rear inflatable slide was jammed. Everyone would have to exit through the front of the plane, making time to evacuate incredibly short. The crew knew the fuel tanks were nearly empty, which accounted for the lack of fire. But, they also knew the fumes in the tanks equaled a lethal potential for explosion. One electrical short could blow up the plane.

Detective Cameron would not leave his seat. He still gripped the arms of his chair. He heard the flight attendant give verbal instructions calmly enough to begin evacuation. He saw the passengers filing out of the plane. He was aware that some suffered sprained ankles and wrists as they hit the ground off the slide. He surmised the injured passengers would be evacuated as they were, except the still unconscious old woman. He heard the paramedics working as a team to lift her out and down the slide on a narrow, sled-like gurney. He couldn't move a muscle.

"Excuse me, sir," the flight attendant spoke calmly. "Your luggage may be damaged, but you're fine. Please exit the aircraft."

Detective Cameron turned to look at her, his glazed features animated as he focused on her face. She was smiling.

"I'm not dead?"

"No, sir. Please, let go of the seat and come with me. Please, come this way quickly."

She pried his fingers off the armrest, cajoling him to stand and led him to the slide at the opening of the plane. He saw the length of the slide, and rapidly calculated that he could survive a fall out of the plane. His fear lessened as he felt the soft cushioning of the yellow rubber under his buttocks. He let go, sliding to the bottom with none of the joy a child feels on a playground slide. He watched as some of the passengers were loaded into ambulances and whisked off to area hospitals. The flight attendant led Detective Cameron to a waiting transport bus, staying with him out of fear he might break down. Passengers crammed into the transport, pushing Rita and Marguerite into the back corner as the doors closed. The overloaded transport lumbered toward the terminals, just clearing the runway and turning onto the taxi ramp, when a shock wave hit the bus, rocking it violently as if pushed by a cyclone. Everyone looked back at the plane. In spite of the fire-retardant foam, the fuel tanks had detonated, engulfing the fuselage in a pyrotechnic hellfire.

Rita looked for the killers. Frantically she tried to see them in the crowd. Had they gone up in flames with the plane, but too late to kill the passengers? Why? Were they still on the loose, or had they detonated their bomb without remorse. Or fear of dying? Marguerite broke into tears.

"Poor Landon," Detective Cameron said. The flight attendant looked at him inquisitively.

"Poor landing?" she asked.

"I've seen better," he sighed.

22

*W*illiam Pauer flicked on his television to catch the early afternoon news.

"Our top story today occurred when an Air Inter flight 83 from Belém, Brazil crash landed at Miami's airport early this morning, injuring fifty-five passengers. The captain, speaking with our reporters from his hospital bed, blamed the severe thunderstorms for the wind sheer that caused the plane to crash.

The bandaged, yet still handsome face of the Brazilian Air Inter pilot filled the screen. "It was a miracle that no one died in the explosion. We barely evacuated the passengers and crew from the plane. The airport rescue crews, and the flight crews were fantastic: efficient—cool-headed—on top of the situation right after the crash."

The reporter's glued-on smile and high-pitched voice irritated William as he listened, "...*The captain and several others were burned by the fireball, just as the last emergency vehicles were leaving the scene with the last passengers aboard. One rescue worker was critically injured in the explosion, but passengers suffered mainly minor cuts and bruises. We'll have more on our five o'clock news report.*"

He sat transfixed. A plane crash was not part of the plan. William's phone rang a few moments later.

"You've seen the reports?"

"Yes, what am I to do now?" he answered the voice.

"We got rid of the casket the same way we eliminated Straader and Smithers. Too bad we missed the Dumas woman and that Detective Cameron. Our next team will take care of them. The important thing is to set up the sting at the hospital. The Kohl woman most certainly will be going there as well. Get rid of her, if you want your mother to live out her few remaining years. You know what we can do to persuade you. Be sure everyone is in the hospital this afternoon. Lunch time would be good."

The phone went dead. Even Rita Dumas and Marguerite Kohl were on the hit list. William was trembling with anger. Someone deeper underground had to be making these directives ordering the bombings to wipe out anyone connected with the compound. For the first time, he realized the suicide teams would kill him with all the others. Not even his children were safe. No one would survive. William had no choice but to take control away from the dealers. Either he would stop them, or he would be a dead man.

William had never traveled to Brazil. As his father's stateside distributor, he handled all the accounts, collected all the money, paid the smugglers, laundered the profits and stashed the money in several off shore banks. He did everything his father demanded of him for the business. He deceived his own mother, divorced his wife and abandoned his children all in the name of money. His father's fantasy of power and wealth became William's only truth. One day, his father would be proud, he always thought, but Landon had never given him the satisfaction. He had kept William in line by denying him the approval he craved. Even as a grown man William could be no more than a sniveling little boy in Landon's eyes.

But Landon was dead. William felt the bonds that kept him tied to his past breaking, as he realized his own life was in danger along with the lives of everyone else. His last best chance to do the right thing in life was rushing toward him, like a train speeding through a tunnel, the light growing brighter and larger as it approached, forcing him to choose between his conditioned and corrupted reflexes and the uncomfortable cloak of righteousness. Take action. Intervene or die trying. Save your own soul. William's car careened onto the expressway and sped toward the hospital.

At the same moment, Rita Dumas, Marguerite Kohl and Detective Cameron sat waiting in the departure lounge to board the flight to Chicago. Along with several other passengers, they were willing to go on in spite of the crash. All Rita could think about was getting back to Chicago. She still had the disk and the compound. Since the crash, the two black-clad men had not reappeared, making her even more nervous. Others had to be somewhere, waiting to make a move. Her eyes darted from one person to the next, keeping track of every face in the crowd.

Detective Cameron sat down next to Marguerite. "Hello, again. It's pretty good to be alive, huh?" he tried to be cheerful.

"Yes,I guess. But now I can't return Landon's body," Marguerite said sadly. "I suppose I should just go back to Brazil."

"No, come to Chicago. I am going to need your help to resolve this. I feel certain there will be something good to come of it for you."

"Oh, I don't know—it's so hard to decide," she was more despondent with every passing minute.

"Well, at least give yourself a chance to talk with Mrs. Pauer. You have nothing to lose, and maybe everything to gain for Paulo," he said gently.

Marguerite smiled at him and nodded. "Perhaps, you are right.

I have avoided even thinking about how much the money could help my son, only how it would tarnish me. I could only see it as payment for services rendered. Never, did I see Landon's generosity as the gift that it was."

The boarding process began, and the three of them headed for the gate. Once on board, Detective Cameron took Marguerite's hand to calm her as the plane took off, allowing himself to feel more at ease. Rita sat alone, staring out the window. Tears ran slowly down her cheeks. She could let herself cry at last. No one was watching.

∾∾

Dan looked at Emily sleeping on the grass. The park seemed quiet and deserted. Even though he was uncomfortable on the hard ground, he felt groggy, wanted to sleep again himself. He couldn't move into a different position. His arm was tucked under his head as he lay on his side. Emily was lying on her back, gently snoring, and completely relaxed. Behind her, not more than fifty feet away was a children's play lot. The sand was still tousled and piled up. Footprints and sand castles carelessly scattered in the large sandy pit made him think of summers at the beach he wanted to spend with his kids.

Without prelude four young children came skipping down the walk, two boys and two girls, like the children on the border of the letter. They cheerfully ran toward the sand pit, ready to play. Their laughter was carefree and lighthearted. Dan watched for quite some time at the way they worked together to build a huge castle, complete with parapets and drawbridges. He was pleased to see their teamwork, their cooperation. He wanted to get up and go to them. He still couldn't move. He tried his fingers. No response. He was puzzled and frustrated at not being able to move any part of his anatomy.

The bag lady appeared from nowhere and sat down on the park

bench only a few yards from the children, a dark figure, preoccupied with her bags, did not notice the children. But she was there. He had to find a way to get to the children and keep them away from her. He could only watch as she lifted her head to look ominously at the children. Then turning toward him and Emily, who was still sound asleep, the bag lady rose from the bench. He had to stop her, but he still couldn't move. Two men jogging through the park appeared in the distance. The jogging path wound close to where Dan and Emily were lying. The brim of her hat obscured the bag lady's face, but her words were unmistakable.

"They took everything I had, those egg sucking bastards! Who gives a damn about them all. Drop the goddamn bomb on them all. Let me have some peace. Peace all right. Just a cup of coffee will do."

She raised her hand. The knife blade glinted in the sunlight. Dan couldn't move. Everything in him screamed for help. The joggers approached. Their intrusion intimidated the bag lady. She backed away, turned and walked toward a large tree, taking up a position behind it on another park bench. One of the joggers slowed to a walk and then stopped, not far from Dan and Emily. Bending over, he retied his shoe. The other jogger reached him.

"Say, let's cheat on ourselves and take a little rest over there on the bench. I've pushed myself far enough for now."

"Well, I suppose we could, if only for a few minutes. We've only got a couple more circuits to run," he said looking at his watch. "We're ahead of schedule too. Why not?"

They sat down, splaying out their long legs and arms, letting their heads lean back to catch some of the sunlight. Dan was relieved and no longer felt tired. He had to find a way to move. He had to get their attention. Dan looked over at the children again. Having left the sandbox, they were now playing on the swings and jungle gym. The bag lady still sat on the bench, dozing.

SACRED NIGHT

❧❧

Miranda, Patrick, Ian and Jennifer arrived at the hospital just a few minutes before visiting hours started. As they stepped out of the taxi, they stopped for a moment and really looked at the hospital for the first time since they had been coming to visit.

"Jeez, this place is huge. Just look at it!" Miranda said as she stopped to look at the details of the building. "See? The older part of the hospital is almost indistinguishable from the newer sections in architecture, but the red bricks are different." She pointed out the section where the change of color was most vivid for Jennifer and Ian. "See how the weathered age of the older masonry contrasted subtly with the new bricks? And then there are these majestic oak trees gracing the front of the hospital. The large decorative gardens surrounding them define the wide arched driveways leading to the main entrance."

"You sound like a real estate person," Jennifer said, giggling.

Deciding to play it to the fullest, for the entertainment of her sister, Miranda said, "Great expanses of lawn surround the main building and intricate courtyards inside the hexagonal structure create seasonal floral beauty even in the winter, when the evergreens, holly bushes and bare branches of the fruit trees wait for spring." Sweeping her hand toward the building, she stopped the arc of her gesture at the sight of the new construction of extended parking facilities near the west wing. "Ignore the ugly construction." All of the children paused to take in the view, each seeing the building with very different eyes.

"Babies are being born and old people are dying in there. I don't want Mommy and Dan to die here," Jennifer said sadly.

"I can see into the building with my x-ray vision!" Ian exclaimed. He loved all the hi-tech machinery. "I have all the power of technology in my body! I am the world's most accurate doctor!" He punched his fists at an invisible attacker.

Patrick saw nothing but the darkness, the shadows, and the depression of people losing their lives, their loved ones, their organs and limbs. He had a hard time even stopping with the others.

"Come on!" Patrick protested. "I hate coming here. Let's get it over with. Nothing ever changes. I just want to get it over with and go home." He started walking at a fast pace toward the entrance of the Anderson Wing. The others followed him into the building and through the now familiar labyrinth of hallways leading to their parents' room. They each wrote their names in the visitor's book, and greeted the now familiar nurses at the counter of the nurse's station.

Once inside the room, Jennifer sat next to her mother and picked up the book she's been reading to her at every visit. The boys just sat near their father, watching his face, hoping to see a change. Miranda left them all to look for Dr. Blume, telling the nurses where she was going, and at their suggestion, found him in the cafeteria with Dr. Eastman.

"Hi," Miranda said simply as she sat down. "Anything new with Mom and Mr. Barton?"

"No, except that they're not responding as usual. After all the activity of the last few days, their inactivity concerns me a bit. Even their reflexes have faded. I can't get a knee jerk from either of them."

"What are you going to do?" Miranda knew the answer to her question.

"Wait. There's nothing else we can do." Dr. Blume saw the disappointment in her eyes. "Come on, Miranda," he said gently. "Let's go back to their room, and I'll stay for a while with all of you, if you'd like."

SACRED NIGHT

❧❧

Dan looked at Emily, who had stopped snoring. He had to move. He had to wake her. They had to get out of the park. The joggers stood up to leave. They stretched their muscles a bit and then started off down the path leading away from the play lot. Dan watched till they were out of sight. He worried the bag lady would wake up soon. He looked back at the children again, only to see them leaving the play lot all together. They skipped along the path, coming very close to him. He wanted to call to them. This was the chance he had been waiting for. The words formed in his mind. He could hear his own voice, as if coming from nearby.

"Ian, Patrick. Ian, Patrick. I'm here."

❧❧

The children and Dr. Blume had been sitting in the room waiting for visiting hours to end.

"I'm here," he rasped. They all looked up at the sound of Dan's voice. The sound stopped. Everyone rushed to his bedside. Patrick and Ian stood close to his head, Ian standing on the bottom horizontal support of the bed, wanting to be taller to see his father's face. The girls next to the boys, but toward the foot end of the bed.

"Dad! Dad!" the boys shouted together, grabbing each other's arms and grasping the bed rail to keep from reaching out to shake their father's shoulders. From the other side of the bed, Dr. Blume leaned toward this patient's face.

"Dan. I'm your doctor," Dr. Blume said more softly. "Can you hear me?" Then leaning close to Dan's ear, "Can you hear me?" he repeated.

SACRED NIGHT

∫

Dan looked up at the children as they left the path and stood in a line in front of him. He tried to smile so they wouldn't be afraid.

∫

The smile spread across Dan's face the way the sunlight spreads across a valley at dawn. He opened his eyes, blinking at the light streaming in from the hospital window. As his eyes focused, he first saw Jennifer's astonished expression. He wanted to laugh at her wide eyes and open mouth. No one seemed to know how to react, least of all Dan. He tried to speak.

"Yes, I hear you. Hi." Exhausted by the effort it took to form the words, he closed his eyes again.

"Dad! Dad! Don't go to sleep! Dad! Stay awake!" Ian and Patrick called to him.

"Emily...Em..." Dan muttered and then fell silent.

"Kids, you've got to sit down," Dr. Blume said. He checked the monitors. He picked up Dan's hand and rubbed it. Dan squeezed weakly back. "This is good, this is good," Dr. Blume said.

∫

Dan could move his hand. He reached over to Emily to wake her. He pushed her several times. The children were still standing in front of him. Emily made no sound or movement. He pushed her again, a little harder this time. She reached up to push his hand away, muttering, "Let me sleep."

Emily stirred, "L...m...sl...p," burst from her lips.

"Mom!" Miranda exclaimed. Dr. Blume turned to look at Emily.

"Did you hear that? My Mommy spoke! Did you hear that?" Jennifer said, with the uncontained excitement only a hopeful child could express.

"I sure did, Jennifer. But try to understand. They may come in and out for several days." He checked Emily's monitors, which showed much more activity than Dan's had shown. But they both slipped into the coma again, leaving their children encouraged and disappointed at the same time.

Dan watched Emily go back to sleep. He looked at the children as they walked down the path. He wanted them to stay. He reached out to them, but they went away. Dan closed his eyes, exhausted. He remembered the scrap of paper he had put in his pocket. The fourth corner of the letter, whose borders had been so cheerful with the images of laughing, playing children, was darkened by the image of a ghostly, raging banshee, like it belonged on Halloween stationery, not on a page with happy children. The bag lady looked over at him, smiling, and then followed the children with her hollow eyes.

23

*A*hi sat in his stilt house glad to see the high water begin to recede. The six months since his rebirth were bountiful for his people. The tambaki and pirrah ku flourished more this year than ever in recent memory. The villagers sold many fish at market and filled storehouses to overflowing with dried fish. The fruit trees bore bumper crops and provided baskets of dried fruit for the coming dry season. The waters receded more than twenty inches a day. Chickens were scratching the earth to hunt for crumbs and insects, where only a month before fish swam in schools between the submerged tree trunks. The forest floor was again dry, bringing parrots, kaseeks, and birds of all kinds down from the canopy where they had been held captive in the treetops during the high water. They could again feed on the vast insect population also reclaiming the earth as home. Beaches reappeared along the riverbanks, enriched by the sand and silt washed down from the Andes during the floods. The replanting of manioc and yam gardens promised the granaries would soon be full.

Ahi smiled as he thought of all these things and remembered how the cycles of his own life fit so neatly into the cycles of the river's life. Shortly after Ahi's Sacred Night, Amahi had taken his first wife, and she was already swelling with their first child. To become a grandfather completed yet another dimension of Ahi's renewed life. He would tell the tales of the otherworld to the next generation beyond his own and beyond his son's, ensuring the traditions would continue as they always had.

The sound of motors on the river fractured Ahi's reverie. He looked toward the sound, to see a flat-bottomed houseboat turning from midstream toward the landing. For many years, men from beyond the horizon, white men with goods to trade, had come to Ahi's village. One of them spoke the language of the Tokablaki tribe and went by the name Mickeyahi. But Ahi did not see him among those on the houseboat.

Perhaps these men were coming to take the sacred mud from the bottom of the reservoir, just as Mickeyahi liked to do. At first, he had taken only a few gourds full of the muck. But each year he returned, he had asked to take more. The medicine men were willing to impart their knowledge of the algala to Mickeyahi alone. They trusted no one else with the secrets of the ancestor's methods of purifying and distilling algala from the silt. But recently, Mickeyahi had been sending others, who used his name to gain access to the reservoir.

Ahi was sure there would be more than enough to share. The medicine men wanted to move inland, to the deeper reservoirs that lay much further upstream, hidden away from these people who kept wanting more of the algala. But Ahi argued that the river would not stop the white man from coming. It had no natural barriers, no whitewater rapids, no water falls to prevent them from traveling the full length of the Amazon. He reasoned with the medicine men that the sacred algala was safe. In his mind, he could see no way to ever mine the huge quantities of the life-restoring mud from all the reservoirs along the river.

SACRED NIGHT

The head medicine man resisted Ahi's generosity. He would not provide the sacred information to anyone from beyond the horizon again. Ahi tried to reason with him, but he could not convince any of the medicine men to change the decision against sharing the secrets of the algala.

Ahi watched the men moor their houseboat at the beach and walk up the hill toward his house, the first house of the village. No one could pass by his porch without his consent. Amahi and some of his friends joined Ahi on the verandah. They noticed these men dressed in black garments in spite of the humid heat of the Amazon River. They were much bigger than Mickeyahi and his men. The looks on their faces conveyed anger. Ahi stood up, leaving his purple robe draped over the chair where he had been sitting.

In a heartbeat, the men raised the metal sticks in their hands and without speaking, sprayed Ahi's porch with fire beads. All of those standing with Ahi and Amahi fell bleeding their life's blood onto the floor. He heard the sharp sounds, like tree branches breaking, stopped almost as quickly as they had begun. He frowned at the pool of blood that was already seeping away through the weathered cracks of the floorboards, leaving a dull red stain in its wake.

Ahi rolled to his side, struggling to reach Amahi, who lay on his back bleeding from his stomach and his neck. Amahi's eyes stared unseeing toward the sky. Ahi pulled himself toward him, though his own blood poured more profusely from his wounds.

He called to him, "Amahi, Amahi, Amahi." The villagers came running to see what had caused the barking the sounds. Shouting to Ahi and Amahi, they gathered to the side of the porch. The gunmen waited until they all had come. The wailing of the women and the shouts of the men rose in plaintive unison at the sight of Ahi lying in a pool of blood.

"Algala—Anmala—Algala—Anmala..." the chant began.

Only the sound of gunfire returned the wail, which then fell silent. Ahi saw the killers turn away without emotion, board the houseboat and head back downstream.

Waiting until they were gone to move again, Ahi was alone. His strength was returning. The pain was subsiding. He crawled toward the mound of bodies, tangled together, eyes staring wide in shock. None moving. He knew no one had survived the fire sticks. His eyes searched the faces for his daughter-in-law. She lay half buried under the bodies of her family. Her belly was blown open by the force of the fire beads, and the baby she carried lay dead in her womb. Ahi wept without restraint. His son, his grandchild, his village—all were dead.

Why was he spared? His wounds stopped bleeding. His pain was so slight, that he no longer noticed it. He walked to the banks of the Amazon and knelt down on the sand. He began to chant, "Anmala—Anmala—Anmala," as if begging the river goddess to come to him. Then Ahi rolled himself into the water to cool his anguish. The current caught him, pulling him away from the edge of the river. Ahi lay limp. He let himself be taken. In a matter of minutes, he lay face up, floating downstream, gratefully carried away from the carnage that stood witness to the greed and jealousies of modern men. They had come to take it all, all the algala, all the goodness it brought. Ahi could now see that the medicine men had been right, but he could change nothing to bring his tribe's way of life back. He could not regain the protective isolation he had given away so easily. He could not undo all that had been done. His despair overcame him. His heart ached with every beat. The silence of the forest hung like a pawl on the stifling air. His lungs labored to draw in each breath. His tears burned with the vision of pure heartbreak.

"Anmala—Anmala—Anmala—" he chanted, allowing the slow current to carry him where it willed him to go. He rolled over to look into cool, lazy water of the river to see if she had heard him. The light filtered in blurred rays through the silt-laden water. In the diffused light, Ahi could see fish swimming in lazy circles and weeds growing on the murky bottom.

He turned his head to breathe, and when he looked down again, Anmala's glowing green hair billowed on the undercurrent. She was beautiful, as white and serene as on the sacred night of his crossing over. She swam upward toward him, smiling. She had come to take him to her otherworld, and Ahi was willing to go, sooner than he might have had his world not changed. But, he was willing to go now, to end his agony of guilt and loss. Taking his last breath, he lowered his face into the water, and reached for her hands. She grasped him, pulling him into the darkness below.

24

Lorraine awoke from a short nap. She got up, reached into the drawer and took the syringe. She stepped silently into the hall and walked toward Emily and Dan's room. Just as she had hoped, none of the nurses thought anything of seeing her walking slowly in the hallway. She knew she had missed the chance she had to be alone with them, and decided to go entirely the other direction.

"Hello, kids!" Lorraine said loudly as she entered the room. "Oh, doctor, I hope I haven't disturbed anything. Is it all right for me to visit with my grandchildren for a few minutes?"

"You must be Mrs. Pauer," Dr. Blume said. "I apologize for not coming in to see you yet, but as you can see, we've been a bit busy."

"They woke up!" Jennifer burst out. "Oh, Grandma, there's a chance they'll be okay!"

"Isn't that wonderful?" Lorraine said a little too happily. "Let's all go to the visitor's lounge for a few minutes. I'm feeling perky and just fine. Are these the boys I read about in the paper—Patrick and Ian?"

"Yes, Grandma," Miranda said. "Could they come with us too?" she looked over at them and gave them a gesture with her eyes to say 'yes' to the idea.

"We'd like that a lot," Patrick piped up, having caught Miranda's hint. Ian looked at him funny, but went along with it.

"All right, then," Lorraine spoke as if to three-year-old children. "You go there, I'll be along in a minute. I'd just like to talk with the doctor for a moment."

The children dutifully did as they were told, while Lorraine approached Dr. Blume.

"I hope everything goes well. Emily was my daughter-in-law for many years. She's the mother of my granddaughters. But, of course, you know that. Anyway, may I just see her alone for a moment? I understand she won't know I'm here, but I'd like to say a word or two to make myself feel better." Lorraine's eyes sparkled as she looked up at the doctor.

Dr. Blume's pulse increased and his face flushed, as he considered her request. Ignoring his body's response, he said, "Well, I suppose so, but please make it a quick visit, just a couple of minutes. We have to watch these monitors very closely."

ॐ

Emily was still sleeping, even more soundly, it seemed to Dan. The children went over to the swings, laughing as they played. The bag lady stood up. His mind saw the drawing. She picked up her bags and placed them on the bench. She bent over the collection, arranged them, one inside the other, with careful movements, making sure each crease was lined up with the next. When she had finished, she stood up straight, turned very slowly, and looked at Dan, her eyes searing into his. Still groggy, numbness had replaced his inability to move. His arms flopped onto the ground like the broken wings of a bird. He still had no control of his muscles, though his instincts begged him to get up. He was too weak.

The bag lady began to move toward them, in slow motion, saying nothing. Her eyes peered at them, menacing and dangerous. She moved her coat. Dan caught a glimpse of the shiny blade in her hand. He froze as fear seeped into his body. He pushed the fear away and struggled to move his legs. He wanted to protect Emily.

The bag lady drew closer. Dan watched her approach, growing taller. She reached out and slashed Emily's arm. Before Dan could respond, she slashed his arm. Dan tried to struggle, but the cut on his arm bled profusely, and he weakened almost instantly.

❧

Lorraine took the syringe injecting some of the liquid into Emily's upper arm. She turned and quickly emptied the remainder into Dan's upper arm.

❧

Rita was the first passenger off the plane. She rushed to the cab stand alone. She could only think of getting to the hospital. The specter of the black-clad men pushed her forward. She had to get the disk of Mickey's clients into the hands of the right people, whoever they were, and bring the antidote to the doctors tending Emily and Dan.

She still couldn't understand why William Pauer had phoned her the night of the bombing to warn her. But thanks to him, she had known the blast was coming. She had known the compound could protect them from the blast. She had no logical reason for slipping the compound only to Emily and Dan, except for not having enough time or enough pills. She had only had time to escape out the back door and run a couple of blocks before she heard the explosion. The lingering guilt had been tempered only by the fact that she had been the intended target in the bombing, and she had escaped. She hoped the killers still believed she had been killed in that blast, so she'd have a chance to get the compound and antidote to the doctors. At this point, she figured Emily and Dan would be the living proof of the compound's powers and the antidote's effectiveness.

The taxi ride seemed to take an eternity. As she paid the driver, Rita looked up and down the streets beside the hospital for the black-clad men. No one appeared to be blatantly out of place. Rita entered the hospital and rushed to the information desk.

"I'd like to find Emily Sanders or Dan Barton, please."

"Are you a family member?" the volunteer asked.

"Yes, I'm Emily's cousin, from Denver," Rita lied. "I hope I can see her. I realize it may be upsetting, but, she and I have been close since we were children."

"Go to the Anderson Wing, and talk with the nurse on duty on the third floor. She'll direct you to the right room," the attendant said before turning back to the television on the credenza behind her.

Lorraine stepped out of Emily and Dan's room and spoke to Dr. Blume briefly.

"Thank you, doctor. I'll go see the children now."

Turning quickly, Lorraine made her way directly to the lounge where the children were waiting for her.

Rita slipped silently through the labyrinth of hallways and back stairwells, trying to stay out of sight. Her heart pounded both from the exertion and from the fear of the danger approaching. She reached the second landing. Running faster to the third floor landing, Rita could barely control her nerves as she opened the door into the hallway. She looked in both directions and saw the nurse's station to her right and about halfway down the long hall. Gathered herself together, she walked as calmly as she could to the reception area.

"Yes?" One of the clerks looked up, and noticed the beads of perspiration on Rita's face. "May I help you?"

"Yes —uh—they told me to ask someone at the nurse's station for the room number of my cousin, Emily Sanders. I have come a long way to see her and they told me I could." She sounded almost like a child trying to explain why she had done something wrong, but the clerk responded curtly.

"Oh, that's room number 1-3-5. Follow this hallway to the end and turn right. You'll find her room at the end of that corridor, on the left."

Rita nodded as she listened and peered down the longest hallway she had ever seen. Hospitals terrified her. Ever since she had watched her father die slowly of Alzheimer's, hospitals had meant only death to her. Through every door she passed, saw his bony, wasted body, and the pallor of the skin drawn tight across his face, the fear in his eyes and the fading of his thoughts, as he had struggled to speak to her. The very sight of an orderly in the hall recalled the loss of dignity and the rough handling he had suffered at the hands of careless caretakers. She walked faster, trying to escape the memories of the despair in old age. She was nearly running as she turned the corner to the right.

"Room 1-2-6, Room 1-2-8, Room 1-3-0, all even numbers." Looking to the other side of the hallway she mumbled aloud, "Room 1-3-1, Room 1-3-3."

Now she would be able to release the burden of the package she was carrying. She would be the messenger, even if it meant she could be nothing more than that. Rita heard only her own heart pounding in rhythm with the cardiac monitors as she paused to catch her breath and enter room 1-3-5, quietly. Dr. Blume was standing at the foot of Dan's bed.

"Doctor? Are you in charge of caring for Emily and Dan?"

Dr. Blume turned to look at her. "I am. Who are you?"

"That's a very long story. Some people know me as Rita Dumas. My name is actually Ruthann Mahoney. I was the owner of Rita's Bar when it was bombed. I am not dead. I am alive. But, I have very important things to give you," she said and handed him the package containing two bottles of pills she had bought from Harry Smithers.

"I have brought these from Brazil, directly from the suppliers. The antidote will save Dan and Emily, and the compound will bring an end to the suffering of the elderly stricken with senile dementia or Alzheimer's. I am afraid there are killers coming to eliminate your patients. Let me give these bottles of the compound, its antidote and this computer disk to you for safekeeping. Please, lock them in a vault somewhere. The disk lists the network of smugglers, drug dealers and underworld connections developed by Landon Pauer, William Pauer, Harry Smithers and Mickey Straader. The medical technicians will discover the biological components from the pure compound. The secret dosage information along with the outline for a potential cure for Alzheimer's is contained on the disk. "

"Are you telling me this is the compound I saw on the website? This is the substance Mickey Straader was selling on the Web?"

"Yes, and everything I know about what has happened is written in this notebook. All the statistical information you need is on the computer disk. I have to leave. The children are in danger. Mrs. Pauer is in danger. I am in danger myself. I am sure the killers, who eliminated Mickey, Harry, and Landon, are after me and anyone even remotely connected to the smuggling operation. Get the children out of the hospital right away. Don't let anyone in to see Emily and Dan. Not anyone. I will try to stop the killers. Remember, the antidote pills will save Emily and Dan. And, Doctor? Thank you."

Before Dr. Blume could answer, Rita turned and ran toward the exit stairway.

As if timed to the moment, Lorraine's injection took effect. The monitors went wild. Everything was in motion. The heart rates were dropping fast. The body temperatures were dropping. Dan and Emily were having trouble breathing. Dr. Blume called for help. The room instantly filled with interns, Dr. Eastman, and several nurses, all working feverishly to save the two helpless patients.

The labels on the bottles Rita had given glared up at him. *"COMPOUND of ETERNAL HAPPINESS." "Antidote to E.H."*

"Poster child for the pharmaceutical companies." Dr. Eastman's words swirled in his mind. How could he trust this woman, appearing from nowhere? How could be believe her? "I just know my grandfather's compound has something to do with this." Miranda's words rang in his ears. The bottles. Miranda had seen the bottles.

"Nurse!" he tapped one of the nurses on her shoulder. "Nurse! Get the children from the lounge." He'd lose his license, if he was wrong and even though he could be prosecuted for malpractice if was right, they would die without doubt if he didn't try at all. The monitors screamed in his ears. He looked at the two nearly lifeless bodies. He looked at all the nurses and doctors struggling to save them.

Miranda rushed into the room. "Are these bottles like the ones you saw in the medicine cabinet?"

"Yes, they are," she said, looking very carefully at the labels.

He opened the bottle of pills, dissolving two tablets in some sterile water. He filled two syringes with equal amounts of the liquid. So risky. So illegal. So dangerous.

"Step aside," he shouted, wild-eyed like a man who had transformed into Dr. Hyde. "We're going to try this. It's our last chance."

As he spoke, the medical team stepped away from the beds, falling silent and watching in wide-eyed surprise. He was counting on the fact that no one would have the courage to contradict him. He was relying on having saved so many patients by trying the unorthodox, that this time no one would think it odd if he wanted to try something out of the ordinary. And no one did question it, not even Dr. Eastman, who knew his colleague's doubts and the price his friend might have to pay, who knew that even the best, the most creative doctor in the hospital, Chief of Neurology in less than five years, known for the unconventional, even experimental, would face questions for his ethics or his purpose if he failed, as Dr. Blume injected the contents of the syringes into each of his patients.

25

*T*he bag lady walked threateningly toward the children. Dan stood up, all weakness gone from his body, and ran toward her, grabbing her by the arm. She struggled to free herself, and without much difficulty pulled her arm from Dan's grip. She turned and ran down the path toward the lagoon. Emily sat up just in time to see the struggle.

"Emily! Wait here! I'll stop her!" Dan shouted, running after the evaporating shadow of the bag lady.

"Wait! Dan! Wait! Don't follow her!" Emily screamed. He didn't hear her or he ignored her. Emily was torn with indecision. She wanted to run after Dan, and she wanted to stay with the children. She looked at them playing on the swings, so innocently, so happily. She realized there was no imminent danger as long as the bag lady was gone. Emily turned to follow Dan, running as if she had infinite energy to burn.

The bag lady shuffled along the path with surprising ease. She stopped and turned, looming larger than life from the top of a small rise in the pathway. She held out her arms, allowing her enormous coat to billow outward, raising her hands above her head, and throwing back her head to scream a scream that drowned out all other sound, filling the air as if it came from another world. Every ounce of courage Dan could summon held him motionless in front of her. The wind rose from nowhere, thrashing the low vegetation and trees against the gray-green sky. Emily stopped short behind Dan, her mouth and eyes wide in disbelief. The wind tore at the old woman's tattered clothes transforming her into a creature unlike any they had ever seen. The banshee rose up, black and eyes burning red from her face, first dwarfing the bushes and then the trees, until the blackness of her robes engulfed the sky. The cosmic blackness erupted in fire. Dan grabbed Emily, pulling her to the ground and throwing himself upon her to protect her.

"The children!" she shouted, barely audible in the roar of the elements unleashed by the supernatural fire storm. "We have to save the children!"

Using all their strength to stand, they stumbled back the way they had come. The fire from the sky fell around them, as unrelenting as the wind was unforgiving. Emily and Dan struggled to regain the route toward the playground swings where they had last seen the four children playing.

&oetext;

Rita turned the corner on the landing of the exit and heard running footsteps, heavily pounding upward. The sound of boots was unmistakable. She could hardly breathe as two men dressed in black reached her landing only seconds later. One of the killers pulled the trigger on his assault weapon. Shots exploded from behind her. Two bullets from the killer's gun seared like meteors into Rita's abdomen. She fell, rolling down the stairs, landing at the bottom. She looked up to see William Pauer standing with a gun in his hand. He returned her gaze feeling both fear and compassion. Walking over to the gunmen, he lowered his gun at their lifeless bodies, shouting at the top of his lungs, "This is for my dog!"

He fired into the chest of the first dead gunman. "This is for my father!" he cried, beginning to tremble as he fired two rounds into the second gunman.

"This is for me!" he wept openly as he sprayed the bodies with the remaining ammunition in the clip.

He never spoke to Rita. He simply mouthed the words "goodbye" to her, turned and ran. She looked at the two gunmen laying motionless in their own blood and passed out. Only moments later, hospital staffers converged on the stairwell. Rita was still alive, though barely. They rushed her to the emergency room. With his one moment of courage, with one round of ammunition, William gave Rita the revenge she had wanted. It was now up to the doctors to save her so she could live to enjoy it.

"Doctor Blume!" shouted the head nurse. "There's been a gunfight! Three people were shot in stairwell 3-H, a woman and two men. The woman is on the way to surgery with gun shot wounds to the abdomen. The two men are dead."

He barely slowed down as the nurse spoke. "Keep me informed, but I have something to tend to," he headed directly to the lounge. Miranda had not returned to the lounge and the children were sitting together talking with Lorraine. She looked up at Dr. Blume.

"Is something wrong, doctor? We heard all kinds of commotion. I made the children stay here, though. Is there anything I can do?"

"Yes, tell me what you did while you were visiting Emily and Dan."

Lorraine looked startled and guilty. She pursed her lips and stared at him with a hate-filled look that burned into his soul. She broke her gaze as she stood up, looking at the children and then back to Dr. Blume.

"No one is going to profit from this but me. I am not going to let anyone get away with this. If it takes everything I have and every day I have left to live, I am going to get Landon's estate and the business he had going from Brazil." She grabbed Jennifer by the hand, jerking her from her seat. "I am the one who paid for it with sorrow, loneliness and isolation," she said, taking Jennifer's terrified face in her hands, slowly squeezing her cheeks together. "I am the one who looked the other way, as my husband lived a double life. I played the sweet, loving wife, when in reality I hated everything about my husband." She released Jennifer's face, and turned her around and pulling her back into her arms, wrapping them around the child like she wanted to engulf her. "I was the good little woman, while he had lovers, money, and power. I am not going to let anything stop me now." Jennifer was struggling, squirming like a fish in a net, trying to get away from her grandmother's clutches.

"Grandma!" Miranda shouted, rushing into the room and grabbing her sister away from Lorraine. The boys, momentarily immobilized by their fear of this crazed woman, moved toward Miranda and Jennifer, putting their arms around the girls to protect them.

"I am going to win this battle. I am going to have all the power. It's all set up. I am not going to let you or anyone else get in my way!" Lorraine was screaming, the rasp of her voice filled the room like the sound of a saw hacking through metal.

Lorraine strode toward the door. Dr. Blume grabbed her arm and held her firmly as she tried to push past him.

"I'm afraid not, Mrs. Pauer," he said gently. "You are going to tell the authorities everything you know. The compound doesn't belong to you. It didn't belong to Landon. It belongs to the world, just like penicillin or the Salk vaccine. This is not a substance you can control. You cannot own it. It must be developed and used for the greater good."

"No! It is mine! It is mine!" Lorraine twisted her arm to pull away, but Dr. Blume held her in his grip.

❧

Dan and Emily rounded a curve in the path to see the children crouching under the only protection they could find, the octagonal merry-go-round. It was swirling above them, though they had wisely pulled themselves together around the center post, clasping hands and drawing up their legs as tightly as they could. For no apparent reason, the sky brightened, and the wind died away. Emily and Dan ran toward the children, who were crying at the sight of someone coming to help them.

❧

Suddenly, the monitors stopped screaming. A minute or two later, Dan and Emily opened their eyes, almost simultaneously.

"Dan? Emily?" The nurse spoke softly. "Can you see me?"

"Yes, ma'am, I can," Dan said easily. "Could you tell me where I am?"

"Dan?" Emily asked timidly. "Did we save the children?"

"I don't know for sure. We were trying to reach them . . . and then we were here," he said simply, as if that were the most natural thing he could have said.

"You're both in the hospital. We'll explain it all to you later. Just rest now while I go find Dr. Blume," the nurse said.

Dan looked over at Emily. "Hey! You've got your wrinkles back," he laughed.

"And your hair is gray," she giggled.

Dan smiled, and reached across the space between their beds. She took his hand.

26

Marguerite and Detective Cameron walked into arrival lounge at the gate, and worked their way through the crowd. The lounge televisions were turned to the news channel reporting live from the scene of a shooting in the city's most prestigious hospital.

"Two men were killed, one woman critically injured in a shooting in the stairwell of Rush St. Luke's this afternoon. The Chief of Neurology, Dr. David Blume, told us earlier that—"

"Dr. Blume? He's the doctor tending to Emily and Dan. Let's go, Marguerite. You're going to meet Chicago from its backside," Detective Cameron said, grabbing her hand and running as fast as his overweight body would allow to the cab stand outside.

Every traffic tie-up imaginable had kept their taxi from getting into the city quickly. A three-car pileup on the Kennedy Expressway stalled traffic all the way back to the junction. Once they had cleared Hubbard's Cave, more than an hour and a half after they had landed, their taxi made good time to the hospital. They made their way as quickly as possible to the Anderson Wing, only to find the third floor blocked off by a police order which limited access to law enforcement personnel and medical staff only.

"You don't seem to understand what I'm telling you," an agitated Detective Cameron explained. "We're connected to this situation, and I must see Dr. Blume immediately! The information we can provide is essential. Let us pass!"

He pushed past the guardsman as he held out his badge. Marguerite's anxiety increased with all the commotion and the frightening prospect of meeting Lorraine face-to-face. She had known this day would come, but she had never imagined the circumstances that surrounded her at the moment. The policemen and women stationed up and down the hallways, the watchful demeanor of the medical staff and the general heightened level of activity made her nervous. Why hadn't she just gone back to Belém and left well enough alone? Why had she listened to Detective Cameron and so willingly come all this way, and for what? Was what she was doing right for Paulo in the long run? She couldn't find her own answer for any of her questions. She suddenly felt overwhelmed by fatigue.

"Detective Cameron? Can you wait a minute? I have to sit down, I'm feeling weak."

Marguerite sank into a chair just outside Emily and Dan's room. "I'll be all right in a minute or two. Could I have some water?"

Detective Cameron tapped a nurse on the shoulder and asked "Could you watch over Ms. Kohl here for a minute while I find Dr. Blume?"

The nurse nodded, "He's in the visitor's lounge down the hall."

Detective Cameron broke into a clumsy jog, running toward the lounge.

"Dr. Blume—Mrs. Pauer," he nodded in acknowledgment, "I have someone for you to meet. She's sitting outside."

"Just a minute, Detective, I think we'd do well to fill you in on the most recent developments here. Do you know of a Rita Dumas?" Dr. Blume asked.

"Yes, she was the owner of Rita's Bar, and she was killed in the blast that leveled the building. Why?"

"Well, she wasn't killed in the blast. She was shot just a short time ago on the third floor landing of this hospital."

"Who shot her?"

"A couple of unidentified men."

"Wearing black clothing?" Detective Cameron asked.

"Yes, what difference does that make?"

"Oh, not much, unless running into teams of suicidal killers, all wearing black, all over Brazil has anything to do with anything," Detective Cameron said, with no attempt to hide his sarcasm.

"She brought a computer disk loaded with vital information on ETERNAL HAPPINESS clients, and the compound itself, along with its antidote. She told me that in this notebook is everything she knew about ETERNAL HAPPINESS and the network of smugglers, drug dealers and underworld connections Landon Pauer, William Pauer, Harry Smithers and Mickey Straader had developed. It names names. It gives phone numbers and addresses. The computer disk holds the entire ETERNAL HAPPINESS database, and the secret dosage information for the compound. There is enough information here to shut down the illegal operation at its source. And according to her, this computer disk outlines the potential cure for Alzheimer's." Dr. Blume paused for a moment to let Detective Cameron respond.

"And, William Pauer? Where is he?" Detective Cameron was mentally adding up the scorecard of players, trying to account for everyone.

"I don't know—the Dumas woman said she saw him in the stair well—just before she—"

"And Lorraine Pauer?"

"The officers are holding her for questioning."

SACRED NIGHT

"Tell them to cuff Mrs. Pauer and keep her in custody," Detective Cameron said as he turned to run. "Call the airport and tell security to shut down the International Terminal. I'm going after William. And call for some back up!" he shouted over his shoulder.

People in the hallway stepped out of his way as he lumbered toward the exit stairway. Even in his overweight, out of shape condition, the stairs would be faster than the elevator. As he burst from the hospital, breathing hard, he hailed one of the squad cars blocking the hospital drive, grabbing the door handle and shouting at the officer, "Get me to O'Hare Airport—International Terminal—police business—forget there is any traffic! Get me there NOW!"

The rookie cop reacted instantly, with lights and sirens, driving at high speed, weaving insanely between the outgoing traffic. Taking the express lanes he sped toward the airport, slamming the squad from side to side as he passed vehicles on the right and then on the left, never letting up on the accelerator. Seventy, eighty, ninety miles an hour, the officer pushed his old squad to top speed on the straightaways, and screeched to a halt in front of the terminal in less than fifteen minutes.

"Wait here!" Detective Cameron barked at the officer as he ran toward the gates. He rushed into the departure lobby, hesitating in front of the departure monitors just long enough to see the flashing gate number for the only flight to Brazil. In final boarding process, the plane was leaving in less than five minutes. No one had closed the terminal.

Detective Cameron shoved his way past the baggage security station, flashing his badge as he ran. The years of unhealthy habits and lack of sleep wore hard on his middle-aged body, increasing the strain of exertion. He felt his heart pounding, his breath laboring, his legs aching from running in dress shoes. He felt unable to go further as he approached Gate M-3, where the American Airlines flight to

Brazil was loading passengers. He ran into the departure lounge area and sagged over the counter as he gasped for breath.

"Please—stop the boarding process," he showed the attendant his badge between gulps for air, "Police matter—we have to find . . . passenger you have going out on this flight."

William Pauer slipped behind the nearest column, trying to hide just long enough to decide in which direction to run, and then took off down the hallway, darting into the first open doorway he could find. Airport security converged on the area

A small child pointed toward the doorway where William stood motionless behind the door. "Mommy! Look! That man is playing hide and seek! See? Over there!" The child's high-pitched voice cut like a laser through the hubbub of the startled passengers. William Pauer sneered at the toddler as he ran from his hiding place to escape. But there was nowhere to run. Airport security swarmed around him, subduing his half-hearted struggle to squirm out of the grasp of the agents who shoved him against the column and pinned him there.

Detective Cameron made his way unsteadily through the crowd toward William. "Cuff this man, read him his rights and take him downtown," he said, pushing his face close to William's. "You'll pay for this for a very long time," he gasped, slumping to the floor, exhausted.

ॐॐॐ

Dr. Blume's pager beeped. He picked up the phone in the lounge, where he had been talking with Marguerite Kohl, and called the number to hear a crackling connection from the ambulance transporting Detective Cameron.

"Dr. Blume? Paramedic Johnson. I have a Detective Cameron here. He insists on talking with you. We're bringing him into emergency - he collapsed from exertion at the airport."

"We've got William Pauer in police custody at the airport... get this thing off my face!" Detective Cameron growled, yanking off the oxygen mask. "We caught him just before he tried to board a plane headed for Brazil. He'll be booked on charges of international drug trafficking, illegal use of drugs with the intent to commit murder, and felony conspiracy to commit fraud on the Internet and by mail. If you wouldn't mind, you can turn Mrs. Pauer over to the authorities for me."

"We already did. Patrolman Rodriguez has everything under control here. In her purse we found the syringe she used to inject Emily and Dan with a lethal dose of the compound, along with a second computer disk labeled ETERNAL HAPPINESS. I think we have the mastermind of the killing spree in custody. But, now I need to get back to Emily and Dan, who are completely out of danger. I'll check in on you when you get here." Dr. Blume hung up the phone.

Dr. Blume stood up to leave the room, as Patrolman Rodriguez escorted Lorraine into the hallway. The children followed Dr. Blume to Emily and Dan's room.

"I'm sorry, ma'am. We have to do this. Mrs. Pauer, you have the right to remain silent. You have the right to an attorney. If you refuse to remain silent, everything you say can and will be held against you in a court of law."

Patrolman Rodriguez read Lorraine Pauer her rights as he ushered her out of the hospital, and into the waiting squad car. Lorraine struggled all the way to the car.

"You won't get away with this! My attorneys will prevail! Who the hell are you to talk to me that way! Don't you ever talk to me that way again! You're all wrong! Listen to me. Shut the hell up! I don't live here. I'm not the one who did it! You are! You are! Get out of my way! They took everything I had, those egg sucking bastards! You're wrong! I'm right! Let me have some peace. Peace all right. Just a cup of coffee will do."

Jennifer was the first of the children to run into Emily and Dan's room.

"Mommy! Mommy! Are you really awake?" Jennifer was sobbing as she patted her mother's arm in disbelief.

"Yes, darling, I'm really awake. I feel wonderful. I've never been so relaxed in my life," Emily smiled at her and reached out toward Miranda as she came into the room.

"Hey, Dad!" Ian and Patrick were jostling each other to get the closest to Dan's bed. "Are you feeling okay? Where were you?"

"Hey, there! Sure I'm feeling okay. Are you feeling okay?" Dan pulled both boys onto his bed, tousled their hair and then hugged them both with the playful bear hugs fathers give their sons.

"Mom?" Miranda looked at her mother. "Are you really back for good?"

"Sure am, honey. I love you so much. Wait till you hear the stories I—we have to tell you." Emily looked over at Dan and his sons, feeling she'd known them and loved them all her life.

27

Four months later —

The headlines of the evening editions of the Chicago Tribune and the Chicago Sun Times shouted the same thing from every newsstand in the metropolitan area: "GUILTY!" For four months the trial of William and Lorraine Pauer drew international attention to the courtroom of Judge Ellory Macintyre, and now it was over.

The articles detailed the long trail of drug deals and smuggler payoffs leading from Landon Pauer's estate to Harry's café in Brazil and back to Chicago. Dan and Emily Barton were sitting in the kitchen, having a quiet Saturday morning breakfast. Emily set a pot of steaming coffee on the table in front of Dan.

"It says here," Dan began to read aloud. " 'William Pauer and his mother, Lorraine, were tried together for their roles in illegally supplying untested, impure and unapproved drugs, and were convicted on three felony counts for international terrorism, illegal use of drugs with intent to commit murder and felony conspiracy to sell illegal drugs on the Internet and by mail. William confessed to killing two of the many gunmen hired by his mother, but the judge did not reduce his sentence.' "

"Poor William, he never gets a break," Emily said, pouring the coffee.

"He doesn't deserve one either," Dan said, and then continued reading, as he picked up his cup.

"There was enough evidence for the jury to find Lorraine guilty of ordering the bombing of Rita's Bar, of Mickey Straader's plane, Harry Smithers' restaurant the overdose of her husband, Landon Pauer, and the gunning down of the Tokablaki villagers. She masterminded the extermination plot against Emily Sanders and Dan Barton, survivors of the bombing of Rita's Bar, Rita Dumas the owner, Marguerite Kohl, longtime mistress of Landon Pauer, and her son, Paulo, to secure her fortune and control of the ETERNAL HAPPINESS business."

"She really was an angry woman under all that sweetness," Emily said. "I'm glad I never suspected that when I was still married to William."

Dan took a sip from his cup, and swallowed the hot liquid burning in his mouth, gasping for breath and taking a gulp from his orange juice to put out the fire. He continued to read, clearing his throat a couple of times for effect.

"William was convicted as an accessory to her crimes, with very little clemency for his attempts to stop the slaughter. They were both sentenced to life in prison, Lorraine Pauer with no parole, and William Pauer with a possibility of parole after fifteen years. Mr. Pauer will immediately begin serving time at Stateville Penitentiary, a maximum security facility in Joliet, and Mrs. Pauer will serve her time at Dwight Correctional in Dwight, Illinois.' I suppose this means we won't really ever be free of this."

"I'm just glad it's over. Listen honey, we can't spend the rest of our lives with this hanging over our heads. We were the victims. Whatever they say in the papers, whatever was revealed at the trial, and whatever really happened makes no difference. We have four children to think of and a goal to achieve," Emily said calmly, "the development of a synthetic version of the compound that saved us."

"Well, at least we have the start up capital for our Longevity Institute: thanks to Marguerite."

"Yeah, her ten million dollars will help. Thank God Dr. Blume is Director of the Institute. Did you get his voice mail?" Emily asked, with a playful tone in her voice.

"No," Dan said, drawing the word out teasing his wife into confessing. "Have you been listening in on my messages again?"

"Yes. I couldn't help it. He called while you were in the shower this morning, and I just happened to hear it."

"What did he say?" Dan's inflection rose in a teasing way as he playfully twisted her hand to get the 'truth' out of her.

"Well, the team of specialists who will manufacture the synthetic algala compound think it will provide a radical improvement in safety, delivery and dosage control of ALGALIFE. They can make it guarantee longer life of higher quality for a minimum of ten years," she said, pausing to take a long breath, "Aaannnnd, they can also see a derivative, ALGAPRO, being developed at the same time to slow physical degeneration and to reverse the effects of stroke. Not bad, for a day's work, huh?" Emily freed her hand from Dan's loving grasp, sat down, and started to eat her eggs.

"Nope, not bad." He spread some homemade raspberry jam in a thick slather across his nearly burnt toast. "You know, we should ask Ruthann Mahoney to be the primary international spokesperson for the Institute. Dr. Blume and Dr. Eastman both have said they think she's a natural," Dan said, garbling the words through the sweet mass in his mouth. "And actually," he swallowed and rinsed his mouth with more of the orange juice, "you should share that job with her. But, let's just enjoy the quiet before the kids wake up," Dan put his palms together in a prayerful pose, pretending to beg her for silence. Just at that moment, Patrick and Ian burst into the kitchen running at full tilt, laughing, each grabbing a piece of toast from the plate at the center of the table.

"We're gonna play basketball with Mark, Billy and Jack," Patrick said, bouncing the Wilson regulation basketball twice on the kitchen floor.

"Outside!" Emily ordered, standing for emphasis as she pointed at the door and laughed in unison with the two boys' noise and commotion.

"See ya" later alligator!" Ian shouted, shoving open the screen door and disappearing into the yard, Patrick close on his heels.

Emily sat down, picked up the paper and tried to read. She put it down only a minute later. "Listen, why not make a whole new beginning? We can set up the Institute anywhere we choose, as long as Dr. Blume and the others are willing to relocate."

"If they will relocate, then we can go wherever we choose. But for now, let's just stay here and read the morning paper. The rest will take care of itself."

꙰

The medicine men had not followed the others to Ahi's house the day of the massacre. When they saw the boat coming, they gathered up the baskets and pottery containing the sacred secrets of algala and led their own wives and families into the forest, escaping unnoticed. Many miles upstream, they settled near a more secluded reservoir site near the spot where they had found Ahi's lifeless body, washed up on the riverbank. In accordance with tribal teachings, they believed that Anmala, the river goddess, had carried Ahi's body against the current of the river to show them where to establish a new village for

SACRED NIGHT

the Tokablaki tribe. There they live, hidden deep in the forests of the Amazon, undisturbed by modern man.

ABOUT THE AUTHOR

Valerie Connelly lives with her husband, Michael, in the northern Midwest. She divides her time between writing, publishing, speaking, painting landscapes and waterscapes, composing and traveling to visit grown children.

An educator and international traveller since her days as a Peace Corps volunteer in Togo, West Africa in 1969, she made her living teaching French literature, language, and culture in the United States and in France, as well as teaching English as a Second Language in West Africa, Iran and the United States.

Ms. Connelly founded Nightengale Press in 2003, and by 2009 had published eighty titles for authors in the USA, Australia, Canada, Dubai, Cyprus, and with her husband formed Nightengale Media LLC, which launched WEB4W.com and YourBookTube.com early in 2009 to meet the internet needs of authors.

She has hosted a weekly internet radio program, *Calling All Authors* on Global Talk Radio since 2005. Listen to the archives at www.globaltalkradio.com/shows/callingallauthors

Her mystery thrillers, SACRED NIGHT and SIDETRACKS, CALLING ALL AUTHORS, How to Publish with Your Eyes Wide Open, an information-packed guide for authors, and ARTHUR, THE CHRISTMAS ELF, a holiday adventure tale with a craft section for children of all ages are all available at:
www.nightengalepress.com
all online bookstores,
and upon request in bricks and mortar stores.